DEATH
FORETOLD

Catrin Surovell Mysteries
Book Two

Angela Ranson

SAPERE
BOOKS

DEATH
FORETOLD

Published by Sapere Books.

24 Trafalgar Road, Ilkley, LS29 8HH

saperebooks.com

Copyright © Angela Ranson, 2024

ISBN: 978-0-85495-239-7

In memory of my beloved grandmothers:
Nellie Ranson (1912–2002),
a strong, brave lady with a lovely smile;
and Nellie Symes (1920–2012),
a funny, wise and beautiful soul.
You are missed.

ACKNOWLEDGEMENTS

My friends and family are always listening to me brainstorm ideas, mourn complications, and celebrate the successful maneuvering of a plot twist. My mother Ruby, my sister Sarah, and my friends Sally, Nia and Louise are particularly good partners in crime, and I want them all to know how grateful I am.

I'm also grateful to Amy Durant and the team at Sapere Books for their insightful editing and suggestions. I've learned a lot from them in the past few months, and I'm already looking forward to the next one!

Finally, I want to thank everyone who has given me reviews or gotten in touch with me to offer their encouragement and congratulations. I have been so pleased with the feedback; it is the culmination of a dozen dreams to know that people are reading and enjoying my stories. Heartfelt thanks to every one of you, especially my youngest and most fervent supporters, Colin and Rachel, and my most avid and encouraging reader, Isaac.

CAST OF CHARACTERS

Queen Elizabeth I, daughter of King Henry VIII and heir to her sister Queen Mary

Ladies of the Bedchamber, companions to the queen:
Catrin Surovell, the queen's 'talisman'
Lucretia ('Lucy') Howard, her closest friend
Mary Sidney, sister to Lord Robert Dudley
Kat Ashley, the queen's former governess and current friend
Blanche Parry, personal attendant of the queen
Katherine Grey, granddaughter of the queen's aunt
Mary Grey, her sister

At the Queen's Court
Robert Dudley, the queen's favourite courtier
William Cecil, Secretary of State
Sir William Paulet, Marquess of Winchester
John Paulet, Lord St John, his son
Matthew Dyer, heir to Viscount Cotherston
Joan Howard, Lady Lincoln, Lucy's mother
Pierrick de Bourbon, Comte de Soissons, a new courtier
Griffin Petre, Lord Heatherleigh, a recently returned courtier
Jolye, Lady Ingolde, a guest in the queen's court

At Ersfield
Lord and Lady Ersfield, an earl and countess who live near London
Mathilda Ersfield, their daughter, a maid of honour at the queen's court

Niada, a wise woman and healer
Margery Roos, a former ward of the court
John, Baron Wicke, her son

In London
Finn, a waif
Owain Kyffin, precentor at St Paul's Cathedral
Master and Mistress Starlyn, pub owners
Thomas Starlyn, their son
Maurice Webb, a priest
Zophia, a wise woman and healer

PROLOGUE

February 1561

Beside the London Stone, which stands sternly upright on Candlewick Street wrapped in bars of iron, hangs the body of a young man with a rope around his neck. His toes brush the ground as he sways gently in the wind.

A barge slides upstream through the dark waters of the River Thames. White-draped figures hunch on its deck, glowing in the moonlight. Its destination is the Tower, where the dark shadows of men wait unmoving until the barge is tied up at the wharf. Then they leap into action, lifting the figures without a sound and carrying them swiftly through a hidden archway near the Traitors' Gate.

On the hearth-stone of the fireplace, in the banquet hall of Greenwich Palace, there rests a tiny coffin. Inside is the figure of a woman, formed from wax. Her features are distorted but easy to recognize, and she is clothed as if for court. Thorns pierce her heart and stomach, blood-red and sharp as any blade.

In a manor house outside London, words of warning are offered by a lady swathed in robes of grey, and soon the whole city will hear her. A young girl remembers every word, and carries them with her to the royal court.

This is where it all began.

CHAPTER ONE

May, 1561

After four months of fulfilling her duties as countess at Ashbourne Manor, it was a pleasure for Lady Catrin Surovell to rejoin the royal court at Greenwich Palace. Even as she rode into the stable yard she could feel the intense vibrancy of it, hear the humming life of the hundreds of people who surrounded Queen Elizabeth, enjoy the sight of people buzzing by, each with their own tasks, talents and troubles.

That day, it was even busier than usual. Men carrying long scrolls of paper strode about shouting orders. Servants bustled past bearing bundles of streamers and flags. Stable-boys brushed their glossy charges and walked them about, carefully checking for any signs of trouble in their legs or hooves. Carpenters dragged carts full of lumber toward the tiltyard, where a dozen lean-tos had been erected and shopkeepers were busy setting up their wares.

Catrin found the commotion quite comforting. Ned, her steward and escort, definitely did not. "What chaos," he muttered. "Are you sure you do not need me to stay with you, my lady?"

"I will be quite content, good Ned," she said. "The manor needs you more than I."

He shook his head. "It still seems wrong, my lady. Your status with the queen allows you to have servants with you in your own rooms, but you choose to stay with the others in the ladies' chamber and leave all your servants in Ashbourne. How will you live without us in such mayhem, my lady? It must be so upsetting for you."

She hid a smile. Ned had always thought her more delicate than she was, even when she was a child under the evil thumb of the old Earl of Ashbourne. "I will manage, good Ned. And this mayhem will not last — all this activity is merely because a tournament begins tomorrow."

"A tournament?" He looked around in immediate interest. "Will there be a joust?"

"There will. The last letter I received said that there will also be combat on foot, combat on horseback, wrestling, running the ring, naval battles … it will last at least a fortnight. You can stay to watch if you like."

"Thank you, my lady, but I don't think so," Ned said. "I have arranged lodging for tonight, and then I must return."

"Very well. If you change your mind, let me know," Catrin said, and jumped down from her horse. Ariadne whinnied, and Catrin paused to stroke her nose.

"Yes, my lady," Ned said. A young man scurried by, carrying a bundle of broadswords, and fresh interest lightened the man's weatherbeaten face. "Ah, look at that — he must be taking them to the armoury to be tested."

A stableboy ran out to take Ariadne's reins in time to hear him. "Yes, he is, but he may have to wait. The armoury is very busy making the lances for the joust," he said, and actually started hopping about with excitement. "I hope I will be able to see it."

"Duty first, lad," Ned advised. "Do you know where the ladies of the bedchamber lodge?"

"Yes; in the building by the water. The ladies are on the same floor as the queen, next to the chamber for the maids of honour," the boy said, and sent Catrin a shy glance. "One of the pages will help your man make sure all your things go there straight away, my lady."

"Thank you. Can I leave you to sort out the horses and packs, Ned?"

"Certainly, my lady."

"And please do find me before you leave so that I know all is well."

Ned jumped down from his horse and bowed. "Yes, my lady."

"Thank you." Catrin gave Ariadne a final stroke and walked out of the stable-yard into the outer court. Lodging-houses lined one side, and the imposing brick facade of the outer wing of the palace lined the other. At the bottom of the courtyard was a water-wall, high enough to hold back any floods, with a door hanging half-open that gave her a glimpse of the River Thames. There was a chapel on the left, with the royal closet above it and the Great Hall next to it. From what she remembered of Greenwich, if she went in through the chapel, it would lead her through to the royal lodgings. If she went in through the hall, she would end up in an enclosed inner court and have to take a much more convoluted route to find her room.

"My lady! Great lady, I beg thee, listen! Please!"

Catrin started at the sudden shout. It was a woman speaking, small and thin, with wild dark eyes. She ran up to Catrin on bare feet and dropped to her knees. "Please! I see that you are a great lady of the court — a good, God-fearing lady, and I pray for mercy. Please listen to —"

"Tush, goodwife." A large lady with a generous bosom bustled up and blocked the thin woman from Catrin's view. "Lady Ashbourne has just returned from a long journey; do not bother her."

"I am not bothered, Lady Lincoln," Catrin said mildly.

"Oh, tush, of course you are," Lady Lincoln said, and took some coins from her purse. "Take these, goodwife, and begone."

The woman's thin fingers closed around the coins. "I thank thee, good lady, but it meets not my need. I ask only —"

"That is all the aid we shall give today. Take it and be grateful," Lady Lincoln said impatiently. "And begone, before I call the guard."

At this, the woman leapt to her feet and darted away like a rabbit that spies the fox.

Catrin watched her go. "You could have let her finish speaking, my lady."

"Why? It would have been much sound and little meaning," Lady Lincoln said, and a broad smile spread across her round face. "It is good to see you, Lady Ashbourne."

"And you as well. Are you here to visit Lucy?"

"Aye, I have news of great import. And I have travelled a long way to share it with that daughter of mine, but I have not yet been able to find her."

Knowing Lucy, she was probably hiding. That was how she usually dealt with a parental visit. "Once I am settled, I will try to find her."

"Thank you, my lady. Until then, I will keep looking." Lady Lincoln gave a gusty sigh. "We do the impossible for those we love, don't we?"

An image rose in Catrin's mind of the day she had left home for a position at court. Her mother had stood straight and tall at the door of Ashbourne Manor, a smile on her face but heartbreak in her eyes, bearing the impossible for Catrin's sake. And a few weeks later, she had disappeared. Catrin had spent years looking for her, only to finally learn that a man she had considered a friend had murdered her.

Ruthlessly, Catrin locked the memory away, focusing instead on the elegant buildings that towered around them and the dozens of people dashing around, determined to create something beautiful for their queen. "Yes, we do."

Catrin had a new silk kirtle and gown in a deep shade of blue that matched her eyes. Once she had washed herself clean of the dust and grime of travel, she put it on, tied up her jet-black hair under a new French hood lined with small glittering sapphires and exchanged riding-boots for soft court shoes. "There," she said with satisfaction. "I believe I am presentable now, am I not?"

The chamberer who had helped her change smiled a shy smile. "Lady Catrin, you are more than presentable. You have the sort of beauty minstrels write songs about."

"What a charming notion! Alas that it cannot be true."

"Why can't it be true?"

"Because I have never heard such a song," Catrin said. "But it's still a lovely thought; thank you."

The chamberer blushed, bobbed a curtsy and left, carrying the used washing-water with her.

Catrin left the palace for the gardens, where most of the courtiers were enjoying the warmth of the sun while it lasted. Groups of ladies in light silks paced along the gravel paths between green hedges and beds of roses. Noblemen moved between the groups, elegant in velvet breeches and satin doublets with brass buttons that gleamed in the sun. Feathers fluttered in the men's hats, lace fluttered over ladies' wrists, and the murmur of conversation was continually enhanced by light laughter. It smelled of summer, of fresh grass crushed underfoot, of the last lingering apple blossoms in the orchard.

Lucy was nowhere to be seen, but Catrin did spy Robert Dudley about to go through the central archway of the wing traditionally used for the queen's household. Since Queen Elizabeth used the king's lodgings, it was usually deserted and locked up. That day, however, it was full of guests eagerly awaiting the tournament. Squires were polishing shields, archers were making fresh arrows, servants were polishing their masters' boots and sweeping dust from silken cloaks.

Lord Robert stopped when he saw Catrin, and swept off his hat in a courtly bow. "How lovely to see that you have returned, Lady Catrin," he said. "The queen has missed you terribly."

Catrin sunk into a curtsy. "I have missed her as well," she said. "But it looks like you are just returning to the palace, so I imagine you have been missed all the more. Have you been away long?"

"Just a few hours." He wiped his forehead before he put his hat back on. "The queen sent me to search out the truth regarding rumours that some cattle-barns had been adorned with holy candles."

"Was it true?"

"It was."

"Interesting. That sounds like the old superstitions are rising again."

"Perhaps they are." He drew his hand down over his beard. "And if so, I suspect my next task will be to find a way to stop them."

"And I have no doubt but that you will manage it," Catrin said. "Have you seen Lady Lucy in your travels?"

"Aye." He pointed further out in the gardens. "She was walking with her mother near the guardhouse when I arrived."

"Thank you, my lord." She curtsied again and followed the path he had pointed out, leaving the blossom-scented orchard behind for the colourful beds of flowers and greenery in the great garden. There were nooks scattered everywhere, formed by arching branches or hollows in the brick walls, all containing giggling girls or amorous couples.

It was not until she reached the new knot garden near the edge of the palace grounds that Catrin saw Lucy walking with her mother amongst the formal structured paths. Lady Lincoln seemed agitated; she was throwing her arms about in evident anger and frustration, and in response Lucy was wringing her hands. Catrin's first instinct was to go and defend her friend, but Lady Lincoln had said she had news of great import. That suggested that Lucy had to hear it, no matter how upsetting it was.

Catrin hung back until a red-faced Lady Lincoln strode away from her daughter, then hurried into the garden. The scent of lemon balm and chamomile rose up around her, but they did not have their usual soothing effect. Lucy was weeping as if her heart would break.

"Lucy, dearling, what is the trouble?"

"Oh, Catrin. You've come home — I'm so glad." Lucy raised both hands in a mute appeal. "I have great need of you in a time like this."

"A time like what?" Catrin said it lightly, hiding her concern. "Has your great love, Sir William Cecil, beaten you at chess?"

At the sound of the name, Lucy's tears came faster still. "There will be no more games of chess. Nor will you and I spend evenings laughing together by the fire, and mornings walking with the queen through the gardens." She sank down onto a nearby bench, her white gown billowing around her. "It's all about to end, Catrin, and I can't bear it."

Catrin sat down beside her. "Why do you think it will end? Have you displeased the queen?"

"No, not at all. She is pleased with me ... pleased enough to grant permission for me to marry." Lucy buried her face in Catrin's neck and sobbed. "And my mother has found me a husband."

Catrin didn't quite know what to say to that. She wrapped her arms around her friend and rocked her gently, thinking hard. "Who is he?"

"A Frenchman," Lucy said bitterly. "Pierrick de Bourbon, Comte de Soissons."

Catrin's heart dropped into her stomach. "So you will have to go to France?"

"I hope not." Lucy sniffed, wiping her tears away with the back of her hand. "His father is dead, so he lives with his mother and her brother — Baron Audley — here in England."

"Is he at court?"

"He arrives today." Lucy burrowed closer, which knocked her hood askew. She pulled it off with one impatient tug. "I don't want to leave court, Catrin. I don't want to follow a stranger to a place I've never been."

"I can certainly understand that."

"I don't want to meet him. I don't want to have anything to do with him."

"Then don't," Catrin said. "Refuse him."

"I cannot. My mother and father would be humiliated, and I cannot hurt them that way. They have been negotiating with his family for months."

"If that is the case, why didn't they tell you?"

"They didn't want to distress me any more than I want to distress them." Lucy fished a handkerchief from her sleeve and wiped away her tears. "I know I must go through with it. My father has no male heirs: when he dies, I will inherit much of his fortune from shipping but neither the title nor the estate. I will have no status among the peerage unless I marry."

"Status means nothing if you are unhappy." Catrin smoothed her friend's tumbled blonde curls. "I will meet this French count, and if I think him uncouth or cruel or in any way inferior to you, my dearest, we will reject him. I will spirit you off to Ashbourne, and there my men and I will defend you from his every advance."

Lucy giggled. "And I'm sure you will be victorious."

"Of course we will." Catrin spread her hands wide. "He's *French*."

It was not long before Catrin was called to attend upon the queen. She and Lucy responded immediately, and found the privy chamber full of older courtiers. On such a warm sunny day, only those who held positions of power and needed to speak to the queen about business remained inside. Thus, it was no surprise that Sir William Cecil was there. He seemed very concerned about something, and did not notice when Lucy sent him a single longing look before she fixed her gaze firmly on the floor.

Catrin understood his concern when she saw the queen. She and Lord Robert were nestled together in the curve of a window. They were as tense as lute strings, and speaking in low tones. It spoke clearly of inappropriate intimacy.

Catrin drew closer, hoping they would see her and separate, but they were too absorbed in their conversation to notice.

"Perhaps I should go to the continent and find a war to fight," Lord Robert muttered. "I am making no progress here."

"No, I cannot allow it," the queen returned fiercely, and dropped her voice to a whisper. "You are essential to me, sweet Robin."

"But I feel useless. I have no status except as your Master of the Horse, and there is no sign that that will ever change. Our marriage is —"

"Tush — we cannot speak of that here." The queen turned away abruptly and noticed Catrin at last. "Lady Catrin, our talisman!" she said, referring to her pet name for Catrin. "We bid you welcome."

"Thank you, Your Majesty," Catrin said, and knelt before her feeling like she had finally arrived home. "It is good to be in your presence again."

"You may not say that once Lady Mary has given you tasks to complete. There is much to do before the tournament begins tomorrow," the queen said merrily, and took a seat at her writing desk. "Ah, Lady Lucy. We have not seen you all day; have you been busy preparing the banners?"

Lucy's eyes flicked wide in sudden terror. To Catrin, it was obvious that Lady Lincoln's arrival had made her forget all about them. "I — oh, woe — ah — they —"

"She was waiting for me," Catrin interjected smoothly. "I am going to help finish them."

"How kind," the queen said wryly, and Catrin knew she was not fooled. "How was Ashbourne?"

"All is well there, Your Majesty. I have made some much-needed changes that I believe you would like to see. You are welcome to come visit while you are on progress this summer."

"A very kind invitation; we will consider it," the queen said. "Now both of you come forward; I must speak to you in confidence."

They did as the queen asked, and settled down on their knees at her feet. "We are at your service, Your Majesty," Catrin said.

"For this I need your discretion, Catrin, not your service," the queen murmured. "The task is for Lucy, and Lucy alone."

Catrin glanced at Lucy, whose eyes were big and round. "Shall I withdraw, Your Majesty?"

"No; you may as well hear what I have to say now, for I know you will hunt it out eventually." There was amusement rather than rebuke in her words, which was a relief. "But both of you should know: this is a very great secret."

Lucy shifted anxiously. "I understand, Your Majesty. I won't tell anyone."

"Very good." The queen looked around the room, and bitterness turned down the corners of her mouth. "Mary and Katherine Grey are acting strangely once again, and I suspect they plot against me. But they are clever; they know my spies and say nothing when they perceive that they are being watched. So I turn to you. Find out their secret, Lady Lucy, and learn how far they have spread their poison."

Lucy's jaw dropped; it took a moment before she could speak. "But Your Majesty — surely Catrin would be better —"

The queen waved a dismissive hand. "They would suspect Catrin," she said, and rested her fingers under Lucy's chin with a faint smile. "But no one could suspect sweet little Lucy. I am sure you will be able to earn their confidence."

Lucy gulped. "I-I will do my best, Your Majesty."

CHAPTER TWO

To celebrate the start of the tournament, the queen had invited a small group of her favourites to dine with her that evening. Catrin and Lucy found themselves waiting in the privy dining chamber with a most illustrious group of people, while the queen started the evening in the next room, participating in the everyday ritual of choosing her dishes.

Catrin knew most of the people the queen had invited: there was the archbishop, several royal councillors, Sir William Cecil, Lord Robert of course, and the elderly statesman Sir William Paulet, Marquess of Winchester. However, there was also a man in full clerical dress sitting at Catrin's left whom she did not recognise.

"Good evening, your reverence," she said. "I am Lady Catrin, Countess of Ashbourne, and I don't believe I have had the honour of meeting you."

"I am Owain Kyffin, the precentor at St Paul's Cathedral," he said, and she recognised the lilt of a Welsh accent in his voice. His cheekbones stood out over a scrawny beard, and even his lips were thin. "I have heard much of you, Lady Catrin, so I am pleased to make your acquaintance."

"As am I," Catrin said. "What brings you to court this evening?"

"The queen and I are planning a venture together, and today we met to speak about it."

"What is it?" Lucy asked. "Does it have to do with your work as a precentor?"

"Not in the least. As precentor, I am responsible for the liturgy and music at the cathedral," he said. "This venture will see the Bible translated into Welsh."

"It is a fine venture, too," Lord Winchester said. "I think it will do much to strengthen the true faith in Wales."

"I agree, my lord. It will be worthwhile, but difficult," Sir William Cecil added. "The church has gone through so many changes in the last twenty years; people are finding it more and more difficult to settle their beliefs."

"Fear not, my friend," Owain Kyffin said. "I know that the religious settlement you helped create will prove the genesis of a beautiful, stable faith. We will see our Church of England wax strong in the next few years; of that I have no doubt."

The queen came in then, followed by a trail of ladies carrying platters of food. And, strangely, a page boy carrying a chair. "My lord Winchester, I seem to have found something you lost many months ago."

The aged marquess rose to his feet and bowed creakily. "I do not recall losing anything, Your Majesty, but still I thank you."

"You will have further cause to thank me in a moment," she said, and stepped aside so that a man with the same hooked nose as the marquess could enter the room behind her.

Lord Winchester's face lit up and twenty years fell away in an instant. "My son!" he cried, and held out his arms. "You're right, Your Majesty, I lost him to his governorship on the Isle of Wight many months ago."

The queen smiled. "And now I have returned him."

"Thank you," Lord Winchester said, and drew his son into a tight embrace. "It is good to see you, my boy."

The man's black eyes glittered with tears. "And you as well, Father."

"Join us, Lord St John," the queen said briskly, and the page placed the chair next to the marquess. Both men sat down, and with a final satisfied smile the queen turned to the precentor. "I see that you have met my talisman, Lady Catrin," she said, and wagged her finger at him in a teasing rebuke. "And you doubted that I could provide you with a table-companion who shares your homeland."

"I did, Your Majesty, and I humbly apologise," Owain Kyffin said with a smile. "Lady Catrin is a fine example of the beauty and grace one can find in Wales."

"Truly? Even though I have been away from Wales for so long?" Catrin flashed him a smile. "You are very kind, your reverence."

"It cannot be so long; the queen has reigned less than three years."

Catrin leaned out of the way as one of the ladies set a dish of baked fish on the table in front of her. "Alas, I left Wales when I was eight. My mother married an Englishman after my father died."

"One does what one must," Owain Kyffin said with a twinkle in his eye that made Lucy laugh. "Do you miss Wales?"

"Oh, yes indeed," Catrin said, and paused as more dishes were set in place. Mussels in a creamy sauce, chicken in white wine, sliced beef surrounded by small round onions. "I still dream of the garden in my childhood home, and in the winter I always think of my father telling me the old folk-tales before a roaring fire."

"Which folk-tales were these?" the queen asked, and granted permission with a nod for one of the ladies to fill her plate. "Do tell me, Lady Catrin; I love hearing old stories."

The twinkle strengthened in Owain Kyffin's eyes. "I would be happy to oblige, Your Majesty, if that is acceptable to Lady

Catrin." Catrin nodded, enjoying the man's enthusiasm. "Then I will tell you one of my favourites. Hundreds of years ago, a king by the name of Vortigern decided to build a castle on the hill of Dinas Emrys. He wanted it to be a great fortress, where his people would be safe from the Saxon hordes. And to that end, he sent out royal masons and skilled carpenters to build the castle. They were thwarted at every turn. Every day their walls would fall without warning; every night their tools would vanish. The great Vortigern sought the counsel of the sorcerers and magicians, who said that only the blood from a child born of a human mother and a father from another world could cleanse the site."

Lucy paused in the middle of transferring some pieces of capon to her plate. "They killed a *child* to build their castle?"

Owain Kyffin chuckled. "No, no. They found the child, a boy you would probably know best by the name of Merlin. He determined that blood was not necessary; rather, the trouble was caused by two dragons who lived under the hill. The wise king believed the child, and sent his labourers to dig deep under the mountain. There, just as Merlin had predicted, they found an underground lake and two dragons lying on its shores asleep."

Catrin smiled to herself, for she could hear her father's voice. "One white, one red."

"Yes," Owain Kyffin said. "The damage was caused by the two dragons fighting; while their conflict lasted, there could be no fortress. So the king's men woke the dragons and urged them to fight. The battle was long and arduous; fire roared from the dragons' mouths and blazed through the cavern; the king's men quavered with fear but stood their ground, forcing the battle to continue to the bitter end. And finally, with the whole mountain smoking in the wreckage, the white dragon fled. The red dragon returned to its lair, satisfied that he would at last be at peace. And the king was free to build his fortress and defend his people."

"And now the conquering red dragon stands on the royal badge of the English monarch," Catrin murmured.

"Indeed. Where it belongs," Owain Kyffin said, and patted Catrin's shoulder. "Your father taught you well."

Catrin's heart ached. "Aye, he did."

The meal over, they all withdrew. The marquess and his son went out to walk, and the archbishop and precentor went back to the city. Lucy and Sir William Cecil departed for a chess game, while Lord Robert and the queen began a game of cards with two of the councillors. Catrin played a game of cards with a handsome young courtier and strongly suspected that he allowed her to win. Perhaps that was why he seemed so surprised when she gently rejected his offer of a stroll through the gardens. Instead, she went searching for Pierrick de Bourbon, the Comte de Soissons. It was time to see if he was worthy of her dearest friend.

He was not in the privy chamber, where all the snatches of conversation she heard revolved around the question of who the queen should marry. He was not in the presence chamber, where the maids of honour were dancing with young men to loud, vivacious music. He was, however, hovering in the shadows of the great staircase outside the presence chamber. The lanterns on the walls cast tongues of flickering light into a dim corner, and she recognized him by the gold-stitched fleur-de-lis on his crimson doublet. He was with a young courtier with hair so blond it looked silver, and they seemed to be having a very intense discussion.

"*Merci*. I have all I need, thank you," Lord Pierrick whispered stiffly.

"But at what cost?" the courtier asked. "Have you thought of what you risk?"

"I risk nothing."

"But if you return —"

"*Non*," Lord Pierrick said, and his voice rose enough to echo faintly off the walls. "I will not be part of anything dishonourable. Good day to you, sir, and *adieu*."

The courtier gave a shake of his head and slouched away. Lord Pierrick muttered something under his breath and walked with a heavy tread toward the presence chamber. Catrin retreated just enough so that he would not think she had heard, but not so far that he could avoid seeing her. And when he did, and gave a courtly bow, she smiled back. "Well met, *Monsieur le comte*."

"Well met indeed, my lady Catrin." He gave a charming smile that made his green eyes sparkle. "I have heard much about you, so I hoped to make your acquaintance this evening."

"I am flattered, my lord." Catrin turned back to the presence chamber. "Let us grow acquainted through a dance."

Two hours later, Catrin and Lucy left the presence chamber and went down the great staircase. It was late, and the corridor was clear, so it was a safe place for Catrin to reveal her findings. "Lord Pierrick seems a goodly gentleman, dearling. God-fearing, honourable. He dances well, and seems intelligent."

Lucy let out a long breath of relief. "How did he treat the servants?"

"Fairly and courteously."

"That bodes well, then. Sir William always treats his servants well, and he is a man of great integrity and honour." Lucy bit her lip. "I suppose I shall have to meet him tomorrow … Lord Pierrick, I mean, not Sir William."

"It would be wise." Catrin paused. "Is the date for your nuptials set?"

"Not yet. My mother is allowing that decision, at least, to be mine."

"Then we will not rush," Catrin said. "After all, the count is going to be participating in the tournament; we may learn much when we see how he handles victory and defeat."

"Yes, we — what is that?" Lucy tensed. "I see something in the banquet hall."

Catrin peered into the room, which was nearly dark. All she could see was a huddled mass reflecting the dying orange glow of the fire. It had many heads, and all of them seemed to be whispering. "'Tis the maids of honour. *All* of the maids of honour, I wager."

Lucy huffed out a breath. "The Mistress of the Maids told them to retire ages ago — why are they still up?"

"Methinks they're doing what all girls do when the firelight burns low; telling tales of ghosts and goblins."

"So they're terrifying themselves for no reason, and they will all have terrible dreams and keep everyone up all night," Lucy said. "We have to stop them."

Catrin followed as Lucy approached the group. They were just in time to catch the tail end of what one of the girls was saying. "…you, Mistress Mathilda? You just returned from Ersfield Manor; do you have any tales of dark deeds to tell?"

A tiny girl with a cap of smooth black hair looked shyly from one girl to the other. "I do, actually. We had a witch at the manor this week." The horrified gasp from the other girls encouraged her, and she sat up straighter. "She comes often, wearing a grey veil and long robes with many pockets. Her hands are gnarled and scarred, and she drags one foot on the ground."

"Why does she come?" one of the girls whispered.

"To tend the sick, both human and animal," Mistress Mathilda said breathlessly, then leaned into the circle. "And to tell prophecies — prophecies about people that *always* come true."

"Did she prophesy this time?"

Mistress Mathilda waited until every eye was on her and pulled a solemn face. "Yes she did."

Several girls squealed in fright, but one pushed out of the circle. "I don't believe it."

"It's true!" Mathilda said. "I remember exactly what she said."

"Tell us, then," the girl challenged.

Mistress Mathilda took a deep breath, closed her eyes and held out her hands like claws. When she spoke, it was in a deep and distorted version of her own voice:

"For the green lady to live
There must be a sacrifice
A new altar, a new virgin.
Fell the ancient pillar
Let the lions roar and the fires burn
Halt the death that crosses the waters
And the falcon will rise once more."

Catrin shivered; she couldn't help it. The words seemed eerily familiar, as if she could hear the voice that spoke them. But at the same time they seemed unnatural … far outside the world she knew. Far outside any world she wished to know.

The girls were similarly disturbed; the youngest of them was crying and most of the others seemed to be struck dumb. "Who is the green lady?" the sceptic asked, but her voice had lost its confident edge.

"I don't know," Mistress Mathilda said. "But she's obviously going to sacrifice someone."

"Who? When?"

"I don't know that either," Mistress Mathilda said. "But it's going to happen. And it could happen to *anyone*."

"I don't *want* to be sacrificed!" the youngest girl wailed, and triggered tears in several more of the girls. The sound of weeping rose to the rafters, and for Lucy, that was the last straw.

"This is foolishness — silly, superstitious foolishness. Enough is enough," she said, and marched up to the group. "All of you, get to your beds at once."

She was not much bigger than them, it had to be said, but the fire in her eyes and the authority in her voice had the maids scrambling.

Catrin watched in amusement as they scattered, creating a chorus of pitter-patters on the mats of rushes. "Perhaps the queen should make *you* Mistress of the Maids."

Lucy groaned at the thought. "If she did, I would welcome exile in France."

As soon as Catrin climbed into her bed, she could feel her eyelids growing heavy. She drifted to that strange place between — neither awake nor asleep, neither at home in Ashbourne nor at court with her chosen family. She found herself alone, riding a horse she did not know, on a well-worn path with fields all around her. A crossroads lay ahead, and a misshapen form huddled in the middle. A great desire to turn aside rose within her, but the horse would not respond to her. It kept plodding relentlessly forward until they were level with the form.

Immediately withered arms arched upward and Catrin saw white hair yellowed with grease and a face so hideous she had to turn her own away. "You are *Gwrach-y-Rhibyn*," she whispered. "The Hag of the Mist."

Batlike wings unfolded, revealing a ragged tunic and legs so pale they looked like those of a corpse. "Will you not look at me, Catrin of Aberavon?" the hag croaked. "Are you afraid to see your future?"

"A distant future," Catrin said coolly. "The *Gwrach-y-Rhibyn* foretells of death, and I have no intention of dying before my time."

"Death takes many forms," the woman said, and clicked her black teeth. "You will soon see, Catrin of Aberavon, whether love remains after beauty is taken away."

Catrin tried to make the horse move onward, her heart beating fast. "You have no power over me, old woman."

"Power? You question my power?" A great wind arose, whipping the hag's robes into long ribbons, like banners on a battlefield. They wrapped around Catrin, black and stinking, and she let out a shriek that disappeared into the hag's own howl. She fought with all her might, pushing herself off the horse. And then, suddenly, she was falling — falling — the hag's screeches following her down...

Catrin woke up while still fighting herself free of the blankets that had somehow wrapped tight around her. She jumped up and away from the bed, and felt the night's chill on her bare feet with relief. Safe. She was safe.

"Catrin?" Lucy asked drowsily. "Are you ill?"

"No." She forced herself back into bed, her heart pounding. "Fret not, dearling. All is well. It is just those silly superstitious maids infecting my dreams."

CHAPTER THREE

The next morning dawned fine and bright, the perfect weather to open the tournament. Catrin and Lucy took their places in the great mass of people following the queen, and together they processed out to the tiltyard, presenting a grand spectacle of gold and silver embroidery and brightly coloured gowns. The queen herself was resplendent in a gown of deep red silk, embedded with rubies on her neckline and sleeves, with a stiff lace collar framing her face. Her hair was piled high on top of her head and woven with diamonds and pearls, and ropes of pearls spilled over her chest and down to her waist. She positively glittered in the sun.

She waved at the people watching them pass — servants and peasants dressed in dull shades of orange, rust-red and brown, merchants in sober doublets of black and grey, men and women of the peerage standing proud and haughty in their blue, yellow, scarlet and green. They all cheered for her, shouting her name, and joyfully followed the procession into the tiltyard.

There was room for all of them there. Old King Henry, the queen's father, had built two eight-sided brick observation towers linked by a two-storey viewing gallery for members of the court, so that he and his friends would not miss anything. On the other side, there was a field for the poor to stand in and rough stacked benches for those willing to spend a pence or two.

Catrin and Lucy, along with the other ladies of the bedchamber, followed the queen into the first of the towers while most of the court continued on to the gallery and the second tower. Only Sir William Cecil and Lord Winchester remained with them, for Lord Robert intended to participate. The very thought of a sword-battle or a joust made his eyes sparkle with a joyful determination that always worried the queen. Catrin could understand that. The queen's father had been knocked from his horse in this very tiltyard, and rumour had it that he was never the same after that.

The queen settled into a cushioned chair in front of the large diamond-paned windows, and Lady Mary Sidney placed a cup of watered-down wine on a table at her elbow. The rest of the ladies settled onto cushions on the floor around her, and such was the design of the tower that they could all see the tiltyard easily. It was strictly rectangular, made of layered plaster and gravel and topped with sand. A wooden barrier — the tilt — cut it cleanly in the middle.

The spectators gathered on the far side in the field, held back from the action by a waist-high fence. It was covered in the shields of the men who intended to joust, and Lucy could identify most of them. Catrin only half-listened to her descriptions, however, until one of the shields made her friend chuckle.

"There's a snail on that coat of arms," Lucy whispered. "See? The azure one. I've never seen that before. Who wants to be represented by a snail?"

Catrin stroked thoughtful fingers down her cheek. "A good question, that," she said, and turned toward the queen. "Your Majesty, may I ask whether a snail is likely to win a joust?"

The question made the queen blink in surprise and peer toward the shields. Then her hearty laugh shook the room. "There is a strong chance of it today," she said. "That is the shield of Griffin Petre, Viscount Heatherleigh. He is recently returned from business in Calais."

"The snail represents patience and reward," Sir William Cecil said. "And the lamb, below it, is a sign of his Christian faith."

"Making him a worthy champion for our games today," the queen said. "And his riding-companion for the procession should surely interest you, Lady Lucy. It is the Lord Pierrick."

Lucy winced. "Thank you, Your Majesty. I will look for his shield on the lists."

"It is golden, with a crimson lion and two fleur-de-lis," Sir William Cecil said absently, his gaze focused on the tilt. "Ah, the trumpet calls. And so it begins."

Everyone leaned forward, waiting with bated breath. A tongue of fire suddenly shot through the gate, and a red dragon lumbered into view. It was wooden, of course, and attached to the side of a cart, but cleverly designed so it hid the horses which drew it and looked almost real. The queen chuckled. "No white dragon today — he has fled in terror from our English knights."

"Indeed," Catrin murmured, as the dragon passed. "We shall have to remember to tell the precentor."

"There is my father," Lucy said, as a squire carrying a shield with two yellow stars and six black crosslets came into the yard. Behind him rode the Earl of Lincoln, on a grey stallion with trappings of silver. "Followed by ... I don't know. Who is that?"

"The shield is argent with a maunch sable — that is the Earl of Huntingdon. His squire wears the bull's head," Sir William said. "And there is the Earl of Oxford, with his quartered shield of red and gold."

Another cart followed them, liberally decorated with Tudor roses of white and red. A lady dressed as Hope sat on a gold-painted chair in the middle waving bravely. Above her, on a small platform, stood a boy dressed as Cupid. He swung his bow up toward the queen, and the room became very cold all of a sudden. It always did, when mention was made of love or marriage.

Catrin gave a great gasp of mock shock. "He aims for Lord Winchester. Beware, ladies — no one will be able to resist him!"

A chorus of laughter relieved the tension and the aged Lord Winchester took the jest in good humour. Cupid passed by without causing any further harm, and several more knights followed in his wake. The tiltyard gradually filled with colour and movement — waving banners, shields that rose and fell with the pace of the squires, the flick of the horses' tails and the shaking of their manes, the armoured arms of the knights which rose to salute their queen.

"There is Lord Heatherleigh," the queen said, nodding toward a man on a white horse with azure trappings as he came through the arch. The horse kept nuzzling the squire's head, dislodging his cap, but Lord Heatherleigh didn't seem to notice. He was very concerned with keeping his vivid green cloak hanging properly over his shoulders.

Beside him rode a lanky figure carrying a lance striped in crimson and gold. He wore armour that shone like silver, with the face-shield up so that they could see the laughing face of the knight within. "And that is Lord Pierrick," Catrin murmured.

Lucy peered down at him, a range of emotions chasing themselves across her face. Interest, repulsion, fear, awe, curiosity, pride, uncertainty. Poor Lucy was facing a gauntlet far more difficult than the knights would, Catrin thought with a twinge of sorrow, and no one could help her through it.

Except, perhaps, the man who had caused it.

Lord Robert escorted the queen from the tiltyard after the procession, an arrangement which did not please much of the court. Catrin could hear the muttered protests as they entered the palace, and wondered if the queen knew just how unpopular her favourite had become. She certainly did not seem to, for she was beaming with happiness and pride as they arrived in the long gallery that faced the river.

The first tournament event was a mock naval battle, so chairs had been placed by the windows overlooking the Thames. The queen settled in, and soon after two ships sailed into view. In truth, they were two barges, but they had been decorated with wooden facades that made them look like the greatest warships ever built. They even had real brass portholes, masts and rigging, and each carried so many sailors that Catrin wondered how they stayed afloat.

Several people cried out in shock when the first cannon fired, but the queen clapped her hands in delight. The second ship sent a volley of arrows in return, and people crowded closer to see.

Catrin decided to withdraw. Such things did not really interest her, so it seemed best to allow others a better view.

She wandered along the length of the gallery as clouds of smoke arose and the boom of guns and whoosh of arrows grew louder and more frequent. All around her, ladies of the bedchamber were scattered about in circles, chatting. Men gathered in pairs to talk in low voices about serious things. Couples withdrew to quiet corners. Page boys circulated with trays filled with tankards of ale and wine. The maids of honour darted about like the young girls they were, chasing God knows what and giggling madly. Lucy was watching them, her face creased in mild disapproval.

"Lady Catrin!"

Catrin turned toward the voice. It was Lady Lincoln, and she seemed rather intensely excited. "Good afternoon, my lady," Catrin said. "Fare you well?"

"I am greatly troubled," Lady Lincoln said, and indicated her companion. "This lady was just telling me about the new prophecy. Have you heard it?"

"I have. There is nothing in it, my lady; it was just a story told by a young girl who thinks that the local wise woman is a witch."

"*Everyone* is talking about it," the other woman said, and grasped Catrin's arm in a grip that was far too tight. "I spoke to one of the chaplains about it; he thinks it might foretell the date of the apocalypse."

Catrin hid a smile. "The end of the world? I doubt it."

"But what if it does?" Lady Lincoln asked. "I heard one of the clerks say that such messages are given to help us survive when trouble comes. We can't just ignore it."

"Nor can we attribute too much significance to it," Catrin said. "Prophecies are like a nose of wax; they can be turned in any direction you like."

"True," Lady Lincoln admitted reluctantly, and then brightened. "But still — perhaps we should tell Lord Winchester about it; a man of his wisdom would know how to interpret it."

Her companion agreed to that plan with enthusiasm. The two of them started to hurry away, only to freeze when a scream tore through the air, so loud and shrill that every eye turned toward the sound.

It was the littlest maid of honour, the one who had sobbed in terror at Mistress Mathilda's prophecy. She stood in the centre of the room, her doe-like brown eyes fixed on the doorway where an elderly woman was entering the room, dressed all in Tudor green. She was using a cane to help her walk, and it struck the floor in a slow, relentless rhythm. *Clunk, thud, whomp. Clunk, thud, whomp.*

"She's here — the green lady is here!" the little girl sobbed. "Please — please, lady. Don't sacrifice me! I don't want to be sacrificed!"

The queen turned in her chair, her face pink with irritation. "What disturbance is this? Lady Catrin, do take care of it."

"Yes, Your Majesty," Catrin said, but she wasn't entirely sure how to obey. Stop the crying girl, or remove the source of her distress? She met Lucy's troubled gaze, and her friend nodded in instant understanding and went over to the girl, enfolding her in her arms. That left Catrin free to go to the lady in green. "Good afternoon. Would you mind following me?"

The lady frowned. "No; I wish to thank the queen for allowing me room at court."

"The queen is currently engaged," Catrin said. "But soon she will go to the middle court to watch the wrestling; if we go there now you will be in an excellent position to talk to her."

That convinced the lady; she followed Catrin out of the room with goodwill. "I am Jolye, Lady Ingolde," she said. "My husband, God rest him, was Viscount Ingolde."

"I am Catrin, Lady Ashbourne," Catrin said, and steered the woman in the right direction with a subtle gesture of her hand. "What brings you to court?"

"The queen invited me, for she has sent my last family member to the continent and left me all alone in his house."

"I see," Catrin said, although she did not. "Do you not have your own household?"

"At my age? Certainly not." Pride puffed out her chest. "I am related to Sir Thomas Chaloner, so I usually live with him.

But he is gone now; it is he whom the queen has sent to the continent. So I have come here."

"What a timely arrangement," Catrin murmured. "And I must say, that is a lovely gown."

"Thank you. I had it made just for court." She straightened the lace at her cuffs. "I expected it to draw attention, but certainly not of that kind. Why would that child make such a fuss?"

"Do not worry; the maids were frightening each other with ghost stories last night, and one featured a lady in green."

Lady Ingolde's watery eyes narrowed. "I wager it was the daughter of Lord and Lady Ersfield who started it," she said. "Mathilda, I think her name is."

Catrin was surprised into stopping. "It is, and it was," she said. "How did you know?"

"That child is overwrought, and no wonder. There are strange things going on at Ersfield Manor."

"Such as?"

"Things which a *lady* doesn't talk about." Lady Ingolde lifted her chin. "You should talk to that girl instead. Find out why she's telling stories at all."

"I will speak with her," Catrin promised.

"Telling ghost stories. Hmmph." Lady Ingolde picked up her skirts and swept out through the nearest door. "No good will come of that. Mark my words."

Lucy was on duty to serve the queen for the evening meal, and she knew that it was no coincidence that Katherine Grey was placed next to her. The queen obviously still wanted Lucy to find out what plots the girl was involved in, and she was providing an opportunity.

It was also obvious why the queen was suspicious; Lady Katherine was pale and shaky, and avoided prolonged contact with anyone. But that made Lucy's task all the harder. How could she broach the subject? How could she get at the truth?

A fanfare of trumpets announced the arrival of the gentlemen ushers with the queen's food. Lady Katherine jumped at the sound, and her eyes darted nervously about, so Lucy decided to start by offering comfort. "Don't be nervous," she said. "It is not difficult to serve the queen in this way."

Katherine gave her a strange look. "I know that. I have done this duty before."

"Oh, very good. Then you know." Lucy offered a smile. "The queen makes it easy; she is very clear about what she expects, is she not?"

Katherine started to look a little sickly. "Very clear."

"I made a mistake once, but she forgave me."

A sheen of sweat stood out on the girl's forehead. "It is impossible to avoid mistakes."

That was promising. "Oh? Like what?"

Katherine folded her lips tight together and sent a hunted glance toward her sister Mary, who stood at the other end of the room. Mary Grey immediately hurried toward them, hampered somewhat by her diminutive size and the pronounced hump on her back. "I'll take this duty, Katherine," she said firmly. "You go lie down."

Katherine scurried away at once, and Mary took her place by Lucy's side. She was far more clever than her elder sister, and had already survived more than one dangerous brush with treason, so she was well versed in saying nothing. Lucy started to feel like her task was a lost cause, but she tried again. "I hope I didn't upset your sister. Is she ill?"

"She has a toothache." Mary turned sharp dark eyes on Lucy and she felt the gaze like a blow. "It would be best to leave her alone."

The music was calling her, and as much as Catrin's feet itched to dance she knew she had a duty to perform first. So she left the evening revels behind and went in search of Mistress Mathilda. Fortunately, the task was neither long nor difficult; she found the girl standing in the privy chamber next to the tables of food, gobbling sugared strawberries.

She bobbed a curtsy when she saw Catrin and swallowed her last bite. "Lady Catrin. How can I help you?"

"You and I are going for a walk," Catrin said, and ushered the girl to the nearest door. "And you are going to tell me why the whole court is suddenly terrified about a new prophecy that sounds much like one I heard *you* recite just yesterday."

Mathilda's small oval face turned nearly as red as the berries. "I — I heard it when I was last at my father's house. *And it's coming true.*"

"Nonsense. How could it be coming true?"

"The first bit of it says: 'for the green lady to live, there must be a sacrifice'. And *the very next day* a green lady arrived at court!"

"A lady dressed in green is not the same as a green lady," Catrin pointed out. "And now poor Lady Ingolde is being besieged with questions about a prophecy she had never heard before."

The girl's chin set stubbornly. "Just because she hasn't heard it doesn't mean it isn't coming true. *I* heard it straight from the wise woman herself."

Catrin opened the door that led to the outer court and prayed for patience. "And who is the wise woman?"

The girl emerged into the dusk of a summer's night and looked around as if delighted by every cobblestone. "She answers only to Niada."

"That is a strange name."

"She is a strange person. She lives in the village near our manor." The girl kicked a pile of discarded chestnut shells, and they scattered in every direction. "And she is never wrong."

"Why was she telling prophecies in the first place?"

"I don't know. She was there when Mother told me it was time to return to court, and all of a sudden she —" The girl's face suddenly went white and she grabbed Catrin's hand in a grip so hard it hurt. "He's back."

"Who —?" Catrin didn't need to finish the question. She could see a figure walking ... no, more like drifting ... across the far edge of the courtyard. It wore a robe so white it glowed, and a necklace with a round disc pendant. There was a white rope around its neck which swung grotesquely behind it, and it held its head at an angle that suggested its neck was broken. Its eyes were but two black holes, and when it turned its face towards them Catrin suddenly felt chilled to the bone. "What is that?"

A moan was her only answer. Mistress Mathilda's eyes rolled up into her head and her knees buckled. Catrin caught her just before her head hit the cobblestones, and watched helplessly as the pale figure floated out of sight.

"Wake up, child," she said, and wished Lucy was there. She was much better at showing sympathy and concern. "Mistress Mathilda, wake up."

The girl moaned again and lifted her head with difficulty. "He's come for me," she mumbled, and tears swelled up from the corners of her eyes. "He said he would, and he has."

The strain on her arms was considerable; Catrin had to shift the child's weight if she was to remain upright. "Who? What are you talking about?"

"Thomas. Thomas Starlyn." The girl turned in Catrin's arms, burying her face in Catrin's chest. Her dark hair tumbled over her shoulders like water. "He was my friend. I met him at my father's manor months ago."

"Did he work there?"

"No, his father owns a pub in London." Her voice dropped so low as to be nearly inaudible. "Well … he used to own a pub. I think he sold it after Thomas … did what he did."

"And what did he do?"

"Hanged himself," she whispered. "At London Stone, so everyone saw. Everyone knew what he'd done."

It was a shock. Catrin had to take a minute to absorb it. "Why would he do such a thing?"

Fresh tears trickled down Mathilda's cheeks. "I don't know. I truly don't. The last few weeks before he died he did not come to the manor as often as he once had. He stopped wearing the wax pendant he was so proud of, and he seemed strange — he kept saying that there was so much more in the world than I could understand."

"That's true of all of us," Catrin said dryly. "Did he ever explain himself?"

"No, he would not. He just said I would follow him one day." Her breath caught on a sob. "That's how I knew … when I first saw him yesterday … he was coming for me. I must follow him into death."

"There is no 'must' about it," Catrin said briskly. "Young men, living or dead, are not the ones who decide when someone dies."

"But what if —"

"I will not entertain 'what if's," Catrin said sternly. "You are young and strong and will soon recover from this whole experience. Understood?"

"Yes, my lady," the girl said meekly.

"Very good." Catrin set the girl on her feet and gave her a gentle push. "Now go back to the maids' chamber and get some rest."

Mistress Mathilda cast a haunted glance toward the dark archway where the figure had disappeared. "What are you going to do?"

"Chase a ghost."

The girl drew in a frightened breath and took tight hold of Catrin's hand. "Oh, please, my lady — don't. Not alone — not in the dark. I beg you! Please!"

"Very well, very well," Catrin said hastily, for the girl was rapidly losing control. "It can wait until morning."

CHAPTER FOUR

Catrin kept her word, but the sun had barely risen when she returned to the outer court. She went directly to the far edge and examined the brick wall that divided the outer court from the stable yards, then walked along it, searching the ground. The crowd who had come to watch the tournament procession had certainly left their mark, but there was nothing unusual among the debris.

She retraced her steps, widening the search. There had to be something — something to show how that pale figure had drifted along the ground rather than walking. She did not believe that it could truly be a ghost, but it had moved in a distinctly unearthly way, so there had to be an explanation. Wires, perhaps? Some sort of harness?

She found it a few feet from the wall. A pair of wheel tracks, less than a pace apart. They were dug deep into the packed earth, as if whatever had made them was carrying a heavy weight. From that she could guess that the figure had been standing on a very low wheeled platform, greased so that it didn't rattle or hesitate on its track and ruin the illusion.

Clever indeed, but why would anyone go to such trouble to frighten a young girl?

She raised her head, listening. A horse was approaching at a fair clip, which was odd. It was early for anyone to be out; she was almost the only person in the palace who was stirring. Seconds later the horse itself emerged into view, with a young boy in cathedral livery on its back. He reined in when he saw her, and the horse cantered to a stop at her feet. "Good morrow, my lady," he said breathlessly. "I have an important message for the queen, from her humble servant, the precentor."

"I can take it," Catrin said, and the boy handed over a small folded piece of parchment before wheeling his horse around and urging it back to a gallop.

"Something important, Lady Catrin?"

Catrin jumped at the sudden voice. "Lord St John," she said. "I didn't see you come out of the palace."

Lord St John emerged from under the archway that led to the gardens. "I have been out walking for a long time now; indeed, I watched the dawn break in the garden," he said. "People start working there early, do they not?"

Catrin tucked the parchment into the purse at her belt. "I'm afraid I don't know."

"I think they must; I saw one of them in the far corner of the knot garden before it was fully light. He wore a strangely stiff hat."

"Perhaps there was some sort of damage they wanted to fix before the queen went out walking this morning," Catrin said. "And speaking of the queen … I must return to her. Good day, my lord."

He bowed low. "Farewell, my lady."

Lucy yawned as she entered the privy chamber. She was one of the last ladies to arrive; some had already started their daily tasks even though no one had yet broken their nightly fast. Katherine and Mary Grey, however, stood apart from them all, and their whispers had an air of intensity that immediately intrigued her. She dared to draw closer, trying to step as lightly as Catrin did.

"No, it could not have been *prevented*," Katherine said scornfully. Mary put a restraining hand on her shoulder and hissed out a warning, but Katherine brushed it away. "I will listen no longer," she said, and promptly walked out the door.

Lucy dared not follow immediately, for Mary Grey's face looked like a thundercloud and that always meant she was about to take out her anger on the first person she noticed. Fortunately, a little maid chose that moment to drop one of the tankards she was setting out, and Mary Grey pounced on her. In the ensuing tearful quarrel, Lucy was able to slip away.

She saw Katherine right away, leaving the presence chamber. Her shoulders were bowed and she seemed distracted, but she moved with purpose out of the palace and around the Great Hall, into the outer court. She seemed to be aiming for the archway that led to the orchard, but Lucy had no chance to find out. As she passed the gate to the tiltyard, a hand took hold of her arm and forced her to stop.

"Lady Lucy." The voice was deep, pleasant, but had an edge of exasperation. "*Enfin*, I have found you."

"How dare you? Let me go!" She pulled her arm free, but still she was blocked. A man had placed himself directly in front of her, hiding Katherine Grey from view.

"I am Pierrick de Bourbon, Comte de Soissons," he said stiffly. "That is how I dare."

Oh. It was her betrothed, not a random stranger. But still, his timing was deeply out of joint. "I cannot talk now, *Monsieur le comte*. Please do excuse me."

"Why must you go?" He flashed a smile that would have been charming were she in such a mood to find it so. "I have come far to meet you, Lady Lucy. I would like to spend time with you."

"I am on an errand for the queen," she said impatiently, and stepped around him when he still blocked her path. But it was too late; Katherine Grey had vanished. "Oh, woe. You have cost me my chance. Could you not have let me go when first I asked?"

He frowned. "I apologise if my eagerness to meet my fiancée has proven ... inconvenient."

"It is more than inconvenient," she retorted. "What you have done may cause great harm."

His jaw set firm, and the charming smile vanished. "I have apologised once, my lady: I will not do so again. Good day to you."

"Good day," she said, and left him standing there.

Several events were due to start at the same time that morning, but Catrin knew which one the queen would attend: the first round of the joust. It was a certainty, simply because Lord Robert was one of the combatants.

The queen was in her cushioned chair in the viewing gallery when Catrin arrived, her hands clenched on the arms and her eyes locked on Lord Robert. He sat on a massive black stallion, holding a lance painted in dark blue, canary yellow and glowing ruby. At the other end of the tilt, a man wearing a tawny cloak was carrying a lance with alternating stripes of straw-yellow and deep black.

The flag lifted. The men went still. The horses pawed impatiently at the ground. Then the flag dropped with a flutter of green and the horses leapt forward. Two lances lowered, straightened, pointed inexorably at ironclad chests. The queen caught her breath and had no time to let it go before there was a mighty crash and splinters flew in all directions.

Both lances shattered, and both men reeled backward from the force of the blows. Their squires leapt out to catch and calm the horses, leading them back to the starting-points. And once there, Lord Robert pulled himself upright and handed the shattered remnants of the lance to one of his men. It was a simple ordinary gesture that said as clearly as words that he was hale and hearty.

"Oh, that he would stay safe by my side," the queen whispered. "I cannot endure seeing him in such danger."

"Let me distract you," Catrin said, and drew the message from her purse. "This arrived for you early this morning by special messenger."

The queen sighed, but slid her thumb smoothly under the seal and broke it open. "From the precentor," she murmured, and her eyes flicked over the words. "He reports that he heard people talking about a nocturnal vigil which is due to take place tonight."

"A prayer vigil, Your Majesty?"

"No, it is a ritual where they attempt to foresee the future by conducting rituals at the shrine of a saint. In this case, St Edward's shrine in Westminster Abbey." She passed a hand over her forehead. "Once again superstition rears its ugly head and threatens my new church."

Catrin's spine tingled. "It seems to be becoming more prevalent, Your Majesty. Do you have any idea why?"

"God alone knows," the queen said, both humour and frustration mingling in her voice. "Take this message to Lord Robert. Tell him I charge him to ensure the vigil does not take place."

It was an attempt to take him out of the joust and they both knew it, but Catrin took the letter without saying so. "Yes, Your Majesty."

That evening, Catrin had just finished dancing the galliard with the Earl of Bedford when she saw Sir William Cecil leaving the card-table. She took her leave of the earl, who was still catching his breath, and hurried over to intercept Sir William before he could leave. "Good my lord, may I have a word?"

Sir William looked down at her in mingled curiosity and caution, which confirmed her opinion of him as a very wise man. "Of course, my lady."

She drew him aside into a quiet corner which boasted a window that looked out over the inner court. It was dark outside, but the crescent moon cast a cool glow over the silvery-green grass and the pebbled paths. "Have you heard any rumours of a ghost at Greenwich Palace?"

To her surprise, he laughed. "A ghost, here? Hampton Court and the Tower must have grown too crowded with spectres if one has moved out here to the country. Why do you ask?"

"I saw something yesterday and wondered if I was the first."

He drew his hand down over his beard. "I did not think you believed in ghosts, my lady."

"It rather depends on the ghost, but I certainly don't believe in this one," Catrin said. "It seemed designed specifically to frighten Mistress Mathilda — a manifestation of someone she knew."

He gazed thoughtfully out the window. "A young boy who hanged himself?"

"Exactly," Catrin said, surprised. "Has someone else mentioned it?"

"No." He pointed out to the court, just as a pale figure emerged from the archway and began to drift toward the palace. "I see it."

Catrin stiffened. "We must try to capture it. I will go —"

"No need." Sir William signalled with his hand and a guard at the corner of the room left with all speed. "Now tell me, why do you think this false apparition is targeting Mistress Mathilda? She seems harmless enough."

"She is just a child; barely thirteen. But she has been telling tales of a prophecy," Catrin said. "I do not know why it would lead someone to try to frighten her into silence, but it seems the only explanation."

Sir William rubbed his hands together in slow, deliberate movements. "This girl is the daughter of Lord and Lady Ersfield, is she not?"

"Yes." Catrin eyed him with new suspicion. "Have you too heard of strange events at their manor house?"

"I fear we have. Smuggled goods. Unlicensed preachers. Veiled women arriving at all hours. Clandestine meetings, involving people of every rank."

That answered one question. "At least such meetings explain how the son of a London publican could forge a friendship with an earl's daughter."

"Aye; it is a start." He gazed out the window, where guards ran in every direction, carrying torches and waving swords. "Perhaps I should speak to Mistress Mathilda."

"I think she would be frightened by someone of your status, my lord," Catrin said. "I will speak to her again tomorrow."

"Very well, my lady."

The activity outside the window gradually petered out, and they watched until a heavy footstep behind them made them turn. It was the guard Sir William had signalled, and he was breathing heavily. "My lord."

"What have you found?" Sir William asked.

"We saw it, but could not catch it." He held out something long and thick, bleached white. "It left this behind."

"A rope." Sir William took it, turned it over in his hands. "'Tis but an ordinary rope."

Catrin stroked a finger over the rope's rough fibers. "Yes, my lord, but its ordinary nature tells us something extraordinary."

"How so?"

"It suggests that the creature was an ordinary man," Catrin said thoughtfully. "Not an apparition."

A few hours later, Catrin had just drifted off to sleep when the sound of her whispered name brought her back to full wakefulness. There was something urgent in it — urgent and afraid. And it was the queen's voice.

She rose swiftly from her pallet on the floor of the royal bedroom, blinking her vision clear. There was little light, but she could see the slim figure of the queen in a white nightgown, standing next to a woman wrapped in a dressing-gown so dark that it was hard to see anything beyond the pale ruffled collar that circled her neck. For a moment she looked like a disembodied head, floating in midair, but then she spoke and Catrin recognized Lord Robert's sister, Lady Mary Sidney. "You must go with Lord Robert," she said. "He is waiting for you."

Catrin reached for her petticoat at once, but had to ask. "Lord Robert?"

"The guards found something, and reported it to him." That was all Lady Mary would say, but her fingers were icy cold as she helped Catrin dress. She escorted Catrin out through the presence chamber to the grand staircase, where Lord Robert himself stood still and silent. He lit the lantern he carried when he saw them coming, nodded his thanks to Lady Mary, and led the way down the stairs and out of the palace.

It was so quiet outside that Catrin could hear the snap of Lord Robert's cloak when the wind caught it. They moved together across the inner court, with its short-cropped grass and gravel paths, and into the shadows of the archway that led to the orchards. There were doors on either side, behind which floated muffled voices and snatches of song.

"The queen's guests are not yet a-bed, it seems," Catrin whispered.

"They are not asleep, but neither are they fully awake," Lord Robert said grimly. "I sent my man to enquire if they had seen anything, and they are all too deeply into their cups to remember their own names."

Catrin stifled a chuckle and followed him out into the orchard. They were not alone; several small circles of lantern-light were bobbing in the direction of the knot garden. They all seemed to stop in the same place, for Catrin could see the light gradually converge in the distance. By the time they arrived, it was shining bright on one of the red brick observation towers to their left and the hedges that bordered the palace grounds directly in front of them.

In that little corner stood a crude altar. It had been woven of dark red branches that bristled with thorns, and a slight figure laid on top of it. Her hands were folded on her chest, and her eyes gazed sightlessly up at the stars.

"It's Mistress Mathilda," Catrin whispered, and rested gentle fingers on the livid red marks on the girl's neck. "Oh, the poor child. She's been strangled."

One of the other men shifted restlessly on his feet. "For the green lady to live, there must be a sacrifice," he murmured. "A new altar, a new virgin."

Another man nodded, sweat standing out on his forehead. "The prophecy foretold this."

A general murmur of uneasy agreement made Catrin glance up at Lord Robert. His sorrowful dark eyes met hers for a moment, and then he sighed. "A prophecy does not have hands. It cannot kill," he said. "If you cannot see that, then God help us all."

CHAPTER FIVE

Catrin sometimes wondered if light fled before the advance of Death, for the night always seemed darker after a soul left its body. Perhaps the soul itself took the light, to guide it on its journey.

The fanciful thought held back the horror of what she had seen as she hurried back to the palace and climbed the back stairs to the royal lodgings on the third floor. It was remarkably quiet; she passed a page boy lying in a window-well and an elderly courtier hunched before the fire in the banquet hall, but both were fast asleep and making no sound.

The doors to the maids' chamber and the ladies' chamber were both shut, and there was no sound or movement bar a stray leaf that drifted in lazy circles on the floor. It was swept away in a gust of air when the Mistress of the Maids strode in from the direction of the gallery, muttering in fury.

"My lady," Catrin said, and lifted her candle to cast light on the woman's lined face. "I must speak with you."

The Mistress scowled. "Can it wait until the morn, Lady Catrin? I am having trouble with my young charges tonight."

"I am sorry, but no. It is about Mistress Mathilda."

Enormous relief spread across her cheeks. "You have found her? Thank God and all the saints. I have been looking for hours."

"When did she leave the maids' chamber?"

"Alas — she never left, for she never came. Lady Katherine Grey saw her leave the queen's privy chamber after supper with a young man who had silver hair, and that was the last any of us saw her." The Mistress sniffed back tears. "Such a silly girl she is — if she has run off to elope I will never be able to look her mother in the eye."

"Do you know the young man?"

"No, he has not been at court very long, and he is not well-connected. But I heard Mistress Mathilda call him 'Thomas'."

Catrin's shoulders stiffened. "Forgive me for asking, but this is important. Did she call the young man Thomas, or was she talking about someone named Thomas?"

"A fair question, that. The young man mentioned the name too, so I suppose 'tis more likely they were talking *about* a Thomas." Suddenly her scowl returned and she set one hand on her hip. "Now, would you please tell me where that wayward girl has gone? She deserves the tongue-lashing of her life."

Catrin winced. "I'm afraid I have bad tidings, my lady. Mistress Mathilda was found dead in the garden this night."

The woman's mouth dropped open, and tears gathered in her eyes. Afraid that a wail was imminent, Catrin raised both hands.

"Please, do not cry out; we do not want to frighten or upset everyone."

The woman nodded mutely but the tears spilled over, just as faint footsteps on the stairs preceded the arrival of Lord Robert. He too held a candle. It cast shadows into the hollows beneath his cheekbones and darkened the smudges beneath his eyes. Catrin relayed what the Mistress had told her in a whisper, and he listened gravely.

"We can assume that they left the palace," he said. "The door to the archway by the tiltyard was found hanging open, and the guards swear they closed and locked it at dusk."

"So she went into the garden by her own will," Catrin murmured, and the Mistress' sobs redoubled. "Foolish child."

"Caught in the throes of love, perhaps," Lord Robert said dryly.

"I doubt love had anything to do with it," Catrin said. "My lord, may I suggest that we speak to Lord St John? He saw something in that corner of the garden yesterday morning and may be able to explain some of this."

"Perhaps he could, but he is not here right now," Lord Robert said. "The queen gave him permission to leave just after yesterday's midmorning meal."

"Then it's not likely he killed Mistress Mathilda," Catrin murmured. "And that makes me all the more certain that this all has to do with Thomas Starlyn — and the person who pretended to be his ghost."

"That may be so, but we must now search for the young man who left with Mistress Mathilda," Lord Robert said grimly. "Finding the ghost is a task for another day."

Catrin stayed out searching with Lord Robert and his men until the queen recalled the two of them to the palace. They left the men with orders to examine every hillock in Greenwich Park for any sign of the silver-haired courtier and returned to the royal lodgings, where they were immediately sent to the private room off the gallery that the queen called her cabinet.

Shortly thereafter the queen came in, fully dressed in a black brocade gown. She wore no jewellery and her hair was covered with a hood, which spoke clearly of her mood. Catrin and Lord Robert knelt down, and she crossed to a chair and sat.

"Tell me all."

"A young girl has been foully murdered, Your Majesty," Lord Robert said. "We examined the body, then sent it to the cold-room below the kitchens, so the coroner may examine it this afternoon."

The queen leaned back in her chair. "Is the dead girl truly the daughter of Lord and Lady Ersfield?"

"I fear so, alas." Lord Robert paused. "She was posed on an altar fresh made."

The queen's lips tightened. "So the superstitious fools that surround us will give new weight to that prophecy. What did it say again?"

Catrin had heard so many people reciting it that she didn't have to make any effort to remember. "For the green lady to live there must be a sacrifice. A new altar, a new virgin."

"Meaning that many will suspect the lady who wore green on the day the tournament opened," the queen said. "What is her name?"

Catrin supplied that answer as well. "Jolye, Lady Ingolde. She is the widow of the Viscount Ingolde."

"Ah, yes. She approached me during the wrestling to thank me for including her at court. Does she have any connection to Lord and Lady Ersfield, or to Mathilda herself?"

"That is not yet clear," Catrin said, and dared to look up and meet the queen's gaze. "But I will find out, if it would please you, Your Majesty. With your permission, I will find any and all connections that would lead to the capture of the man who murdered that girl."

"I rather thought you would," the queen said dryly. "Uncovering the source of that evil last autumn has given you a taste for the hunt, I wager."

Lord Robert gave a slight shudder, and Catrin felt for him. The evil the queen so lightly mentioned had led to the death of his wife, and the villain who had killed her had suffered nothing but exile for his crimes.

"The hunt, Your Majesty? One could put it that way, yes."

"Then I grant you permission." The queen clapped her hands, and the cabinet door swung cautiously open. A man stepped in who looked strangely lean, as if God had taken him by the ears and the ankles and stretched him. Even his face seemed too long and thin, and there were hollows under his cheekbones emphasized by his long forked beard.

He knelt before the queen. "Your Majesty."

"Lady Catrin, this is Griffin Petre, Viscount Heatherleigh. You saw him in the tournament procession," the queen said. "I have a task for you, Lord Heatherleigh."

Lord Heatherleigh bowed his head. "I live to serve you, Your Majesty."

"Mistress Mathilda, the daughter of Lord Ersfield, is dead. I have given Lady Catrin the task of finding her murderer. You will help her."

"Help her?"

The words seemed to be surprised out of him, and when the queen went very still it was obvious he had displeased her. "Do you have difficulty accepting the guidance of a woman, my lord?"

"No, no, of course not." Lord Heatherleigh glanced beyond Catrin to the man kneeling beside her. "I expected that Lord Robert would be the better choice, that is all."

"I dare not risk the scandal of being involved in another murder," Lord Robert said dryly.

"And I have need of Lord Robert," the queen said coolly. "Fear not, my good man, you are in good hands with Lady Catrin. I have no doubt that she will succeed in her task."

"Of course, Your Majesty," Lord Heatherleigh said, but Catrin could tell that he was not convinced. She could see the doubt in his eyes.

No matter. She would soon prove him wrong.

Before Lucy even reached the privy chamber, she knew something had happened. The courtiers in the presence chamber were oddly quiet, and the petitioners who hoped daily to present their cases to the queen were sitting idle in the corner, looking dejected. The guards at the door of the privy chamber were sober-faced and stoic, and when one of them opened the door for her, Lucy was immediately hit by the sound of wailing and weeping. She went in and found the maids of honour gathered in one corner, huddling up to the Mistress of the Maids like chicks surrounding a mother hen. All of them were in tears.

Catrin was speaking to Lady Mary Sidney near the bedchamber door. She had deep shadows under her eyes, which suggested that she hadn't slept, and she was wearing her riding clothes. Lucy hurried up to her. "What has happened? Are you well?"

Catrin took Lucy's hands in hers. "Dearling, I have sad news," she said. "Mistress Mathilda was murdered last night."

"Murdered! But why — who —"

"That is what I must find out," Catrin said. "I am going to Ersfield Manor to tell her family and see what can be discovered about her death."

"Would you like me to come with you?"

Catrin shook her head. "Lord Heatherleigh is accompanying me, and we will be riding at speed, which I know you do not like to do," she said. "Besides, you will have other duties. The queen has decided that the tournament will continue."

"Then I must prepare the prizes for the events this afternoon." Lucy bit her lip. "It seems ... wrong, somehow, to play at sport when a girl is dead."

"No, it is necessary. It will distract people and give us time to find the killer." Catrin straightened her hat and offered a smile. "I will return as soon as I can."

"Very well." Lucy wrapped her friend up in a fierce hug. "Be safe."

CHAPTER SIX

It was a short journey to Ersfield, a mere ten miles. It passed quickly for Catrin, whose horse Ariadne was fresh and eager to run. The only difficulty was occasionally slowing down to allow Lord Heatherleigh to catch up.

Ersfield Manor was a three-storey building of pale brick shaped like the letter 'J', with an ancient octagonal guard tower at the short end. She and Lord Heatherleigh approached via the long wing, circled around past the tower, and presently found themselves in a tidy inner courtyard. The grass was ruthlessly trimmed, the paths covered in small white stones to keep the mud at bay, and two rows of glass windows shone bright in the afternoon sun.

They reined in, coming slowly to a stop near a group gathered in the middle of the courtyard. Lord Ersfield, with two very large men hulking behind him, stood next to a bent shrouded figure who was delicately balancing a sieve in claw-like hands. On top of the sieve stood a pair of shears, and two women — kitchen servants, based on the state of their aprons — each had a single forefinger on the top of the shears. Before them stood a boy and two young maids, all three fidgeting as if desperate to be anywhere but there. The crowd around them seemed just as uneasy, the men tugging at their caps and the women wringing their hands. And one of the women had to be Lady Ersfield herself. She wore the finest gown and the stiffest hood, and her fingers were heavy with gold and jewels.

"St Peter and St Paul," the shrouded figure cried out, and Lady Ersfield jumped. "There is a thief in our midst. Is it Bess, the maid?"

Bess whimpered and the crowd went silent, every eye riveted on those shears. Nothing happened. The shrouded figure spoke again in a clear ringing voice. "St Peter and St Paul, hear the plea of an old woman and tell me. Is the thief Wat, the stable-boy?"

Suddenly the shears turned and the two women balancing them cried out in shock and horror. Wat burst into tears. Lord Ersfield gave a curt nod to his men and one slouched off toward the stables. The other took the sobbing boy by the arm, as if to keep him from fleeing.

The crowd stayed still, but many a gaze dropped to the ground. Lady Ersfield noticed Catrin and her escort and came scurrying over. "Lady Ashbourne! What an honour — we did not know you were coming."

Catrin unhooked her knee from the pommel of her side-saddle and jumped down instead of waiting for help, which seemed to shock Lord Heatherleigh. "You must be Lady Ersfield," she said, and clasped the woman's hands in both of hers. "I am sorry to come upon you unannounced."

"It is no trouble, no trouble. I am so sorry that no one has yet come to take charge of your horses. We — ah —" She glanced back at the crowd behind her, hands quivering helplessly. "We are having some difficulty."

"So I see." The shrouded woman, Catrin noticed, had not moved. She still held the sieve steadily before her, and somehow the shears still stood upright upon it. "Is that Niada?"

"Yes. The village wise-woman." Lady Ersfield's hands quivered again and dropped down to her sides, like two white doves falling to earth. "A silver cross went missing from the chapel this morning — one that has been handed down through the family for generations. Ersfield could not get anyone to confess who had taken it. I knew Niada could find out what happened; she has remarkable powers."

Catrin declined to comment. The hulking figure of the servant loomed back into view, and in his hands gleamed the unmistakable shine of silver. Wat's wails redoubled, and a great sigh wafted up from the crowd. Lord Ersfield dismissed them all with a wave of his hand, and as the servants dispersed he dropped some coins into Niada's sieve. She bowed low, and the sieve disappeared into the folds of her robes. Then she turned toward the gate, and the sun lit up her face. Catrin was instantly captured by the woman's remarkable eyes — a glowing clear blue, pale against her weathered, pitted skin. Her hair was iron grey, but a streak of white flowed backward from her right temple, where a puckered purple scar stretched downward over her cheek.

Catrin found herself wanting to reach out to the woman, and shook herself free of the sensation with difficulty. Forcing herself back to the task at hand, she turned to Lady Ersfield. "Shall we go inside?"

Lady Ersfield ran to her bedchamber wailing like a banshee, and her maidservants followed her to provide what comfort they could. Lord Ersfield stumbled outside, reeling as if he was drunk, and Lord Heatherleigh followed him. This left Catrin alone in the chamber, unsure that to do. She could offer no solace to either of Mathilda's parents, but it felt wrong to simply sit and do nothing.

Perhaps it would be best if she went to Niada's cottage, and left the grieving couple alone for a little while. She could offer further condolences later, before returning to the palace.

Catrin rose and followed the path Lord Heatherleigh had taken, and found the two men wandering along the pebbled paths of the inner courtyard. Their backs were to Catrin, and they were so engrossed in their conversation that they did not seem to hear her approach.

"It is a great blow, Ersfield," Lord Heatherleigh murmured. "I am very sorry."

Lord Ersfield let his head fall back. "Mathilda … my baby … dead."

"And tormented by a false ghost," Heatherleigh added. "Do you know of anyone who would want to —?"

"No," Ersfield said harshly. "No one knew of her friendship with Starlyn, but … our people, here at the manor."

"And none of them are missing?"

Sudden anger hardened the man's voice. "If they are, I will learn of it."

"And if you do, prithee send me a message," Heatherleigh said. "I'm sure it will prove useful as we delve into what has happened."

Ersfield looked up at him. "You are going to find the man who did this?"

"Aye. With Lady Catrin — as per the queen's orders."

"I want to help."

Heatherleigh sucked air through his teeth. "No. Look to your own house, Ersfield. You have enough to deal with here, and people must be continually informed of … any developments."

His jaw set. "In times like these, I care not about developments."

"You will, once the initial shock wears off. And by the time it has, the man who did this will be in shackles." Heatherleigh stopped and put his hands on the man's shoulders. "This I swear to you."

"Thank you, but … my br—" Lord Ersfield saw Catrin then, and swallowed the rest of his words. "My lady."

Lord Heatherleigh lifted his chin. "Do you need something, Lady Catrin?"

"Not really," Catrin said lightly, but she caught the flash of fear in his eyes. What did he think she had overheard? "I come merely to tell you that I am going to visit the wise woman."

"I will accompany you," Lord Heatherleigh said coolly. "We will return anon, good my lord."

"Anon," Lord Ersfield said, and obviously did not care. He looked bowed and broken as he walked away, and the weight of his grief kept Catrin and Lord Heatherleigh silent until they had left the manor far behind.

They skirted the edge of the village, walking along a path that followed a bubbling stream through the forest. The leaves were a vivid emerald, with silver tints from the poplars. A dark verdant carpet spread out beneath their feet, muffling their footsteps so the only sound was the chirping swallows.

Catrin was happy to say nothing for the whole journey, and simply absorb the sweet scents and sounds of the forest. Lord Heatherleigh, it seemed, was not. "Lady Catrin, may I ask you something?"

He seemed anxious, and she wondered if he was about to explain what he and Lord Ersfield had been talking about. It was obvious that they were well acquainted, but he hadn't mentioned that before. "Certainly."

"It may seem an odd question, in the circumstances, but..." He paused to contemplate a rounded stone poised at the edge of the stream. "Do you intend to marry?"

"Not today," Catrin said, and thought it best to change the subject. "Ah — that is a lovely summer breeze, is it not?"

He would not be dissuaded. "It is rare for a maiden not to marry. Especially one with your ... attributes."

"Oh?" She gazed at him limpidly. "What attributes do you mean?"

Asking the obvious question threw him into confusion, as it often did with men who were trying to flirt. He stumbled and stammered a bit, and finally gave up. "Yes, the breeze is lovely. And there is fine hunting around here, I'm told."

"I'm sure there is," Catrin murmured, and turned onto the lane that one of the servants had told them would lead to Niada's cottage. A moment later the cottage itself came into view, tucked away in a little hollow. It was small, but looked tidy and well-cared for. A white cat was hunting for mice in the thatch on the roof as they approached, and it hunched down and stared at them.

"Two angels came from the West. The one brought fire, the other brought frost." The voice came ringing out of the cottage, pure and clear like glass. "Out fire! In frost! In the name of the Father, Son and Holy Ghost."

There was a low keening cry, and then a woman appeared in the doorway with a child in her arms. "Thank you, Niada, thank you," she said, and kissed the child. "You'll be fine, sweeting. Niada has made it all better."

The child buried his face in the woman's shoulder as she scurried around the side of the cottage and into the woods beyond. Niada appeared in the doorway, her veil pulled forward far enough to hide the scar on her cheek. "Good morrow, Lord Heatherleigh." Her gaze shifted to Catrin. "Lady Catrin, I presume."

Catrin found herself captured once again by the allure of those vivid eyes. "Yes."

"Did Lord Ersfield send word we were coming?" Lord Heatherleigh asked.

"There was no need; the fairies told me," she said. "Come in, come in. We shall have a drink first brewed by the ancient Egyptians."

"No thank you." Lord Heatherleigh pointed to the spot where the woman and child had entered the forest. "What was that all about?"

"The child scalded himself," Niada said. "He'll recover now."

"You think your incantation will save him?" Lord Heatherleigh scoffed.

"In truth, I have more faith in the ointment that accompanied it."

"Foolishness." Lord Heatherleigh frowned. "I should send the vicar here to ensure you are not working with the devil."

"He will find me innocent of such evil, I am sure, for it is not yet a week since my herbs cured his horse," Niada said dryly. "And he is a good man — a man of the proper faith, not a decaying remnant of our popish past. Now, what do you want of me?"

"We want you to tell us where you heard that prophecy," Lord Heatherleigh said. "The one about the green lady."

She smiled at him, but her eyes were flat and wary. "The fairies told me that, too."

Lord Heatherleigh folded his arms. "Do these fairies have names?"

"I am sure they must." She sighed. "But they have not yet trusted me with them."

"And how do you know that they're fairies?" Lord Heatherleigh asked. "Can you bring them out to talk to us?"

"No … they do not come when called," she said solemnly. "I see them only when they have wisdom to impart."

"I wish they spoke more plainly," Catrin said. "We might have been able to save Mathilda's life."

Niada's gaze softened. "That poor child… I am truly sorry," she said. "If I had known, I certainly would have warned Lord Ersfield."

"You can warn us now," Lord Heatherleigh said.

"But I know of no danger or trouble."

"You know about the prophecy. Tell us what it means."

"'Tis not my role to interpret, only to speak," Niada said, and drew her hands into her sleeves. "It is wise men such as you who must find out what — or who — the fairies are warning us against."

"This is pointless." Lord Heatherleigh turned away from her with an oath. "Come, Lady Catrin. We would learn more if we asked questions of the trees."

"Perhaps." Niada's eyes sparkled with mischief, but her tone remained serious. "The oak is wise, but the beeches are too young as yet to know anything much."

Catrin hid a smile. "And the willow will say whatever you wish to hear."

"Aye, it will bend every which way," Niada said with a chuckle.

"Tell me, what of the hawthorn?" Catrin asked, and Lord Heatherleigh sent her a sharp glance. "What can it tell us?"

The humour in her eyes winked out. "In this month of May, hawthorn is used for the wreath of the Green Man, the herald — and some say the god — of spring. It symbolizes the cycle of death and rebirth, and so it was the symbol of fertility for the souls of this isle before the Christians came." She lowered her voice and fixed that bright blue gaze on Lord Heatherleigh. "They say never to bring its blossoms into the house; keeping hawthorn inside will be followed by illness and death."

So the hawthorn altar on which Mistress Mathilda was posed was meant to symbolize death and rebirth. A new cycle — a new spring. And perhaps, a new god, in the form of the Green Man. "Thank you, Niada."

"You are welcome, my lady," she said, and then suddenly folded her arms. "Lord Heatherleigh, do leave us a moment. I wish to speak with Lady Catrin."

Lord Heatherleigh scowled and walked away, and Niada waited until the sound of his boots crunching on the dry dirt road had faded somewhat before she retrieved a small vial full of a yellowish powder from her cottage. "Take this, my lady. I know how dangerous the court can be."

Catrin read the label and felt herself blush. "I assure you, I have no need of it."

"Not for its usual purpose, I know. But in this case … it will help reveal the truth." Niada lifted her eyes to the sky, gazing at something only she could see. "I am sure of it."

CHAPTER SEVEN

Catrin and Lord Heatherleigh left the manor and rode fast enough that the wind made conversation impossible. Catrin was not at all bothered by that, for there was much to think about. Mistress Mathilda had been killed in a way that was simple and expedient; it would have taken no skill and little effort to choke the life from a girl so young and small. But the posing of her body was dramatic and deliberate. The branches had been carefully formed to make it obvious what it represented; the killer had even woven a cross above it, as if to leave them in no doubt that it was an altar.

But why use a Christian symbol on a scene ripe with pagan meaning? Perhaps the choice of hawthorn was not significant; the killer could have chosen it merely because it was available. There was certainly no connection between it and Ersfield Manor; hawthorn did not feature in their coat-of-arms and there were no hawthorn trees on the estate. She hadn't even seen any in the forest surrounding Niada's cottage.

Unless the pagan connection was meant to be a hint as to the strange events at Ersfield Manor. Could Lord and Lady Ersfield be secretly practicing the rituals of pagan religion? The thought nearly made her choke with laughter … rotund little Lord Ersfield, with his wide moustache and flabby lips, did not fit the image of the Green Man. And a hawthorn wreath would not make him so.

Then there was Thomas Starlyn. He was connected to the manor, just as Mistress Mathilda was. Both of them had died far, far too young. And someone had tried to convince Mistress Mathilda that Thomas Starlyn had come for her.

Why? To stop her from fighting her murderer? It seemed foolishly elaborate, but then so did an altar of hawthorn branches.

They reached the entrance to the palace, with the long brick wall on the left. The sun was low, so their shadows looked huge against the wall as they rode toward the stables.

"I believe our next step should be to learn more about Thomas Starlyn," Catrin said. "Mistress Mathilda was greatly concerned about him, and fearful he would come back to haunt her. Someone took advantage of that, and it may have been our murderer."

Lord Heatherleigh grunted. "More likely the 'ghost' was another of the maids, playing a trick," he said. "I doubt that Starlyn will lead anywhere."

Catrin reined in and let Ariadne walk into the stable yard. "And what do you suggest instead?"

"That we discuss it with the queen and Lord Robert in the morning. They can tell us how to proceed."

"You do that, then." Catrin unhooked her knee from the pommel and let herself drop. "While I go to London."

Catrin had expected the queen to be watching the youths practicing their jousting skills by running the ring, but instead she found her tucked in a corner of the privy chamber with Sir William Paulet, the Marquess of Winchester. The marquess was murmuring to her, his elderly face creased with concern, and Catrin was reminded of a father rebuking a daughter. The queen's face reflected a child's stubborn distress, until she saw Catrin.

"Why, my talisman has returned," the queen said, in a merry tone that did not match the strain around her eyes. "Do excuse me, Lord Winchester, we must prepare for the evening."

And with that she swept Catrin up and retreated to her bedchamber, where she immediately covered her face with her hands and gave a sigh that was nearly a groan.

Catrin shut the door. "Are you well, Your Majesty?"

"I am angry," she said simply, and started to pace. "The marquess is the latest of my courtiers to urge me to marry and start issuing children — or, at the very least, name an heir. He made it sound like I am proving a disappointment to him, my privy councillors and my entire realm."

"That, at least, is not true," Catrin said. "I was riding in the countryside just today, and I did not hear a single soul say they were disappointed in their queen."

The queen sent her a wry glance. "That may show their wisdom rather than their opinion," she said. "Expressing such a sentiment could easily become a charge of treason."

"Why, so it could." Catrin tucked her hair carefully back into place under her hood. "Shall I say so to the marquess?"

The queen laughed at the thought. "Rebuke a man born during my grandfather's time? I dare not."

"He is still vulnerable to the executioner's axe — and even to the threat of it."

"I am not so sure — he is of such an age that I sometimes wonder if anything can kill him." The queen walked the length of the room again in long angry strides. "Nay, I must just forget what he has said, just as I forget so many similar rebukes offered merely because I am a woman. But it does make it hard to face the evening."

"Perhaps you could remain here for this evening."

"Nay; he would know then that his words upset me. Better to appear as I always do, with queenly dignity. And thus I must rally." She dropped into a pile of cushions by the unlit fire. "Did you learn anything in Ersfield?"

Catrin thought of the conversation between Lord Ersfield and Lord Heatherleigh. "I am not sure yet. But we did meet the wise woman, Niada."

"Was she the witch young Mathilda described?"

"No, she was not a witch." Catrin shivered. "But she had extraordinary eyes — they draw you in and make you believe every word she says ... no matter how strange those words are."

"Do you think she has anything to do with Mistress Mathilda's death?"

"Not at all; she seemed genuinely grieved to hear of it."

"Then we shall leave her to her potions and prophecies," the queen said. "I need some music to calm me. Do sing something, my talisman. Give me an old folk tune from Wales."

"Yes, Your Majesty," Catrin murmured, and took a moment to bring the old words to mind. Ancient words, sung for centuries to soothe and lament and amuse. "*Dacw 'nghariad i lawr yn y berllan, Tw rym di ro rym di radl didl dal... O na bawn i yno fy hunan...*"

It was a song of hopeless love, of a man watching the woman he most desired live her life without him. If the queen had understood it, it may have grieved her. But instead the melody relieved her anger ... brought her peace ... gave her strength. Much like the man she could not claim as her own.

The ladies' chamber was dark, and silent but for the raspy snores emanating from the Chief Lady. Catrin lay on her back in her bed with Lucy at her side. Lucy's chest was rising and falling in the slow steady rhythm of one who is fast asleep, and Catrin didn't want to disturb her. So she lay as still as she could and stared out the window, watching the faint lights in the village slowly wink out, one by one.

Then Lucy suddenly sat up and stretched her arms high above her head. "There is no point in pretending," she whispered. "Sleep eludes us both."

"So it seems." Catrin rolled onto her side to face her. "Let us talk instead."

"Very well. What shall we talk about?"

"Whatever has formed those worry-lines on your forehead."

Lucy buried her face in her pillow. "It is that task the queen gave me. I have gotten no further — indeed, I may have made things worse."

"Why do you think that?"

Lucy told her about the awkward conversations, the lost opportunities, the barrier that was Lady Mary Grey. "Hmm. That is unfortunate." Catrin stared up at the ceiling, hoping for inspiration. "I fear you may have already warned your quarry."

"I fear the same thing," Lucy said gloomily. "I am not meant for a life of intrigue, Catrin. Why can we not simply live at court and serve the queen? Why do people feel the need to make trouble?"

"'Tis the siren-call of power and influence," Catrin said, and gazed out the window for a moment. "May I make a suggestion?"

"Oh, yes. Please do."

"Ask your French count to help you."

Lucy made a face. "I don't want to talk to him."

"But he is the perfect person to help with this task. He is handsome."

"So?"

Catrin lowered her voice. "Your quarry falls easily for handsome men. He could win her confidence easily, I think."

"Or — and even better — he will fall in love with her and our betrothal would be dissolved."

Catrin's lip quirked in a half-smile. "Either way, you have made progress."

Lucy hugged herself with delight. "It's perfect. Thank you, Catrin."

"You are very welcome, dearling," Catrin said, and then sat bolt upright. "What is that?"

Lucy sat up and tilted her head to listen, just as a skitter of footsteps passed the door. "There are people out there."

"The maids of honour, I wager, causing a different kind of trouble," Catrin said, and rose up out of bed. "Come, we must stop them before they wake the queen."

Lucy got up reluctantly and followed Catrin out of the room. A mass of grey moved ahead of them, the individuals within it undistinguishable until they arrived into the gallery. There, the rows of windows gave greater light and a view of the Thames. They could see not only the maids, but the boats bobbing about in the waves below them. Most of them were anchored close to shore, but a few water-ferries moved slowly along, lit by yellow lantern-light, passing by groups of men drinking from brown bottles as they dangled fishing lines in the water.

It was perhaps because of the contents of those bottles that some of the men were suddenly inspired to sing. Off-key strains of 'O Mistress Mine' were wafting through the air when Catrin spoke. "What are you all doing out of your chamber at this time of night?"

The girls jumped at the sound of her voice and crowded closer together, but the sceptical girl Catrin had noticed before just laughed derisively. "They wanted to see the ghost ship."

Lucy bit her lip. "The what?"

"There's a ghost ship. Lady Katherine told us about it," the littlest girl whispered. "She said it's flat and long, and it glows."

"And if we see it before midnight, it means that someone else is going to die," another girl said. That made several of the girls squeal with fear, the sound cutting through the air like arrows.

"Tush!" Lucy hissed. "You'll wake the queen!"

The girls covered their mouths and vowed in muffled voices not to do it again, a vow they forgot as soon as another girl flattened her hands on the window. "There it is!"

They all turned as one, and Catrin's heart caught in her throat. There was indeed a flat boat sailing up the river. White shapes hunched on its deck, glowing with an eerie light. The small water-ferries moved out of its way, and its passage made the fishermen stop singing.

"It's just a barge," Catrin said, but her voice wasn't quite steady. "It's probably on its way to collect goods from the city."

"But I can't see anyone moving it," the littlest maid whispered.

Nor could Catrin, for all that she strained her eyes to find any sign of rowers. It made her distinctly uneasy, and it seemed Lucy was reacting the same way. She had to clear her throat before she could speak. "Regardless, you have seen it now, as you wished," she said. "So off to bed with you, or you'll be no use to the queen tomorrow."

"Aye, to bed," Catrin agreed, and helped Lucy shoo the maids back into their chamber. Then they returned to their own, and silently got back into bed. Both pulled the blankets up high around their cheeks.

But it was no easier to get to sleep. The unasked question burned in their hearts until Lucy finally gave it voice. "You don't think it was really a ghost ship, do you?"

Catrin closed her eyes tight. "No. No, of course not."

CHAPTER EIGHT

Catrin stood in front of the London Stone, thinking of her father. He had fervently believed that the ancient Trojans had carried that stone from their fallen city of Troy and set it up as a new altar to their god Diana, before they moved their settlement to Wales itself. Catrin remembered him speaking of the Stone with reverence and a deep longing to see it himself. She had always wondered if he had realized that dream before he was imprisoned in the Tower. The two sites lay close together ... so close.

A stray tear surprised her and she wiped it away, glad that Lord Heatherleigh was not there to see it. He had declared this a useless undertaking and left her at the end of Candlewick Street, and she suspected that he had expected her to give up the idea and follow him.

She had done nothing of the kind, of course.

Instead, she had checked that her *stiletto* knife was still sheathed in its usual place beneath her left sleeve and woven her way amongst the carts and horses until she came to St Swithin's church. Across from its northern door stood the pale yellow Stone, about a yard high, fastened with iron bars. Wooden noticeboards had been erected behind it, held in place by tall pillars on either side. Dozens of advertisements were fixed to them, offering everything from fresh cuts of meat to bondservants. Sometimes crude drawings accompanied the hand-copied words: a sword, the face of a missing woman, a doublet with its arms stretched wide.

Between the noticeboards and the brick wall of the building behind them, a boy was sitting cross-legged in a nest of rags.

He looked up at Catrin with enormous blue eyes in which were mingled both charm and wariness. "Good morrow, my lady," he said. "Have ye a penny to give to a poor boy?"

"I do." Catrin took out several pennies and pressed them into the boy's hand. "Do you live here?"

"Nearby, my lady, with my mother." The pennies vanished into one of the boy's many pockets. "I've never seen you here before."

"I have never come before," Catrin said, and looked up at the wooden walls above them. There was a raw scrape on the near edge that wrapped around the top of the pillar. "I hear a man died there recently."

A shadow crossed the boy's freckled face. "Thomas. Thomas Starlyn. I saw him, but he didn't see me."

Catrin went onto her tiptoes to see the scrape better and realized that there was something next to it, carved into the wood. It looked vaguely like an animal — a sheep, perhaps? "Was anyone with him?"

"'Twas just him and his rope." The boy shivered. "He hanged himself."

So there was no doubt it had been suicide. But what had driven him to do such a thing? And why here? Catrin offered more pennies. "Did he say anything before he did it?"

"Oh, yes. He never stopped talking ... muttering, really." The boy's hand darted out and the pennies disappeared from her hand. "He said 'poor child' over and over. And 'how could he'. I don't know what he was talking about, though."

"Nor do I," Catrin said thoughtfully. "Do you know if Thomas had any family?"

"A family he had, indeed. Mother, father and two sisters. They live not two streets away." Indignation turned his cheeks

82

faintly pink. "He should have thought of them afore he did it. They be sorrowed now, and ashamed, and all because of him."

"Where can I find them?"

He glanced up at the sun. "This time of day, they'll be in Paul's Walk."

Catrin rose to her feet. "Thank you for your help."

A surprisingly sweet smile spread over his face. "Whenever you have need, my lady, I am but your humble servant."

"Then I thank you for that as well," Catrin said, and moved off into the crowd.

St Paul's Cathedral was not far from the Stone; she soon caught the scent of paper, glue and ink from the printers' booths that lined the streets just outside it. And not long after that she emerged into the centre of the book trade. Manuscripts of every kind surrounded her — bound, unbound, tied up in scrolls, printed, handwritten. Some were lying open so that their woodcut illustrations could be clearly seen, and some were rich with coloured inks and gold-tipped illustrations. Catrin was fond of books, and it was difficult not to stop at every booth. Only her determination to find the Starlyns kept her from lingering.

She slipped into the nave of St Paul's Cathedral and was soon enveloped in a crowd. It was called Paul's Walk simply because that is what people did: gentry, lords, courtiers, and men of all professions walked from end to end gathering news, conducting business, gossiping shamelessly. Boys ran about between them all, passing messages, chasing chickens, picking pockets. Everywhere there were tables, selling pamphlets, fabric, roasted nuts, apples, meat cooked on sticks, and drinks of every kind.

Catrin had to ask several people about the Starlyns before she was finally directed to a small table near the end of the nave. A big bucket of wine sat there, with a dozen wooden cups lined up beside it. No one was buying; indeed, it seemed that people were pretending that the table was not there. Even the other sellers had angled their tables subtly away from it.

Catrin walked up to the table and the man sitting behind it jumped to his feet. "Yes, my lady?"

Catrin offered pennies. "May I have a cup?"

"Aye, indeed." He used a wooden ladle to draw some rich red wine from the bucket. "Only the finest vintage for you."

"Thank you." She sipped and found that it was indeed good wine — not the finest vintage by any means, but good. " Have you had this table long?"

The man ducked his chin. "No, my lady, we just started. After we lost the pub by the Stone."

We? It was only then that Catrin noticed a woman behind him, hovering over a bucket of water with a cloth in hand. "Oh — good morrow, goodwife."

She put on a weary smile. "Good morrow, mistress. Come ye to Paul's Walk often?"

"No," Catrin said, and set down her empty cup. "And today I have come for a specific reason. I need to ask you about your son Thomas. Your name is Starlyn, is it not?"

"Aye," the man said heavily. "But we'd rather not talk about Thomas, if it's all the same to you."

"I'm sorry to upset you, but it's important," Catrin said. "I have some questions that need to be answered."

Mistress Starlyn picked up Catrin's cup and let it fall into the water. "People usually don't want to talk about my poor boy, and somehow that's all I want to do. So I'll answer, even if my husband won't."

"Did he know a girl by the name of Mathilda? Daughter of Lord Ersfield."

"He did. Thick as thieves, they were, but I never understood why," Mistress Starlyn said.

"By rights, they should never have met," Master Starlyn grumbled, and flicked the tiny bell that was tied around his wrist with a leather cord. It rang so faintly that the sound was almost drowned by the noise around them.

Mistress Starlyn nodded. "Especially since I don't think she was part of it."

Interesting. "Part of what?"

"Magic," Master Starlyn said, and lowered himself back into his chair. "It was all Thomas could talk about. Turning metal into gold. Predicting the future. Conjuring spirits."

"We feared it was the devil's work." Mistress Starlyn pulled the cup out of the bucket and watched water droplets gather at its base. "We forbade him from mentioning it in the house, but that seemed to spur him on. And then ... then he started to seem afraid. Sorrowful. And one day..."

"He rose up looking like he had the sweating-sickness," Master Starlyn said. "We asked if he was well and he said, 'no one talks of penance any more, but that is what I must do. I must cleanse myself of what I have done.' We pressed him to explain himself, but he would not. He left the house soon after. That night ... the guard came to our door."

Catrin's heart ached for them. "Do you know why he chose to die at London Stone?"

"No," Master Starlyn said. "Doing it there was as senseless as the rest of it."

"You know, they would not let us have his body," Mistress Starlyn said, and a tear dropped into the bucket of water, sending out ripples that broke against the sides. "People who die as he did are not buried in consecrated ground."

"I am so sorry," Catrin said, and pressed a half-sovereign into Master Starlyn's hand. "Thank you for telling me."

"Aye, mistress," Master Starlyn said woodenly, and did not move when Catrin turned away. She glanced back before she left the nave, and they still stood there, rooted in their memories.

Catrin thought that the fastest way to re-join her escort on Candlewick Street was to circle the U-shaped cloister on the southern side of the cathedral, but realized her mistake when the building itself slowed her pace to a crawl. It was in a state of disrepair, having fallen out of use when the monks left, but it was still an impressive and fascinating structure. Three storeys of walkways, each open on one side so that they all looked down at the courtyard and the chapter house at its centre.

She was marvelling at the thickness of the walls and the beauty of their carvings when she nearly ran into a man dressed in priest's robes. "Oh! I do apologise."

The man chuckled, and only then did she recognize the precentor. "It is easy to forgive a Welsh beauty, my dear Lady Catrin."

"Oh, it's you! Good morrow, your reverence. I did not expect to see you here today."

"Nor I you, my lady." Owain Kyffin's eyes twinkled down on her from under his three-corner cap. "Why are you wandering the Walk today?"

"I am asking questions," Catrin responded easily. "Did you hear of the sad death that occurred at Greenwich Palace?"

"Aye, the queen's chaplain was here and he told all." The precentor urged Catrin to a seat on a bench in the cloister. "But why would that death lead you to the cathedral?"

"Not the cathedral, but to people within the cathedral." Catrin explained the connection between Thomas and Mathilda, and Owain Kyffin's merriment faded. He started playing with a crystal ring on his finger, turning it around and around.

"Poor child," he murmured. "And such a terrible shame about that boy. Penance! A useless notion. How could any of us make up for what we have done? If we could, the crucifixion would have been unnecessary."

"Agreed," Catrin murmured. She had never believed in either penance or purgatory, despite her faith. "But the old beliefs hold on still."

Owain Kyffin slid his finger over the inscription on his ring and gave a heavy sigh. "If only the people would accept the queen's religious settlement and simply worship God. It is a good faith, a good church. It could bring peace and stability to this realm, if people would only let it."

"There too, we are in agreement." Catrin rose to her feet. "But I must return to the palace, I'm afraid. The queen will want to know what I have learned."

Owain Kyffin's smile returned. "Please give her my humblest greetings. And I will pray for your success."

"I will." Catrin bowed her head. "And thank you, your reverence."

CHAPTER NINE

It took some searching, but Lucy finally found Lord Pierrick in the stables, feeding an apple to his horse. It was a lovely horse, all black but for a white sock on its left foreleg. She had always heard that a sock like that was a sign of an evil disposition in a horse, but when she said so he scowled at her. "I put no stock in such signs, Lady Lucy," he said. "Swiftsure is more brave and noble than many people of my acquaintance."

"I believe you," Lucy said hastily, not wanting to anger him further. "It's like Sir William Cecil always says — the only way to know the mettle of a man is to test it. Reputation matters little."

"*Oui, c'est un bon idée,*" the count said, and looked at her through narrowed eyes. "Perhaps you should consider taking this advice, my lady."

"Or you should."

"I believe I already attempted to test our mettle, so to speak," the count said loftily, and brushed a hand over Swiftsure's glossy back. "And I was firmly rebuffed."

Lucy took a deep breath for patience. "As I told you, *monsieur*, I was on an urgent errand for the queen."

"Yes, I remember." He paused. "I thought it an excuse."

"It was the truth."

He paused again. "Was the queen displeased?"

"She does not know yet that I failed." She fingered the lace on her cuff. "I had hoped that you would help me to rectify the situation before she learns of it."

"*Certainement,*" he said at once. "I did not mean to cause you grief, my lady."

"And I did not mean to anger you, *monsieur.*"

"Then let us start again." He drew Lucy's hand into the crook of his arm and led her out of the stables. "I am Pierrick de Bourbon, your champion, and you may call me Lord Pierrick."

"And I am Lady Lucy," Lucy said, and managed to push out the words she knew he wanted to hear. "Your future bride."

On their return to the palace, Catrin and Lord Heatherleigh left the stables together, and as they crossed the outer courtyard he put on a grave face. "My lady, may I confide in you?"

A question that inevitably led to awkwardness. "If you feel you must."

"I do, for I am deeply concerned." He dropped his voice. "I worry about the queen."

Considering the number of armed guards that surrounded them, Catrin could find some humour in that. "Do you think she is in danger from our false ghost?"

"No, but she is in danger nonetheless." He sent her a sideways glance. "A monarch without an heir is never steady on the throne."

"Some might say that a monarch *with* an heir is never steady on the throne."

"Is that what you say?"

It was too dangerous to answer, and thus it was high time the discussion came to an end. Besides, she had questions of her own. "Do you know the Ersfields well?"

"Why do you ask?"

"Lord Ersfield seemed to know you well enough to accept your guidance without question."

Lord Heatherleigh drew in air between his teeth. "He saw that it was good guidance. That is all."

"Is it? The wise woman knew your name, so she must have seen you there before. Have you visited often?"

It was his turn to change the subject, it seemed. He avoided answering by pointing to a struggle taking place not fifty feet away. "Behold! What is happening here?"

She followed his pointing finger and saw two guards converging on a small, ragged woman. They easily lifted her off her feet, and she twisted helplessly in their grip like a bird caught in a net. "The queen!" she cried. "Please, let me see the queen!"

Lord Heatherleigh seemed to find this no more than mildly interesting, but a twist of anger turned in Catrin's belly when she recognized the woman's wild dark eyes. She had tried to see the queen at least once before. Lady Lincoln had dismissed her with nothing but alms then, and now the guards would not even listen to her plea.

Catrin strode up to the struggling trio. "Let her go."

One of the guards sneered at her. "Says who?"

"Catrin, Countess of Ashbourne. I am a lady of the bedchamber, and I demand that you *let her go.*"

They released the woman so abruptly she landed in a heap on the ground, and immediately started to weep. "Thank you, my lady, thank you."

Catrin glared at the guards. "What do you mean by treating her thus? It was cruel and unnecessary."

"We was doin' what we're supposed to do," one of them said sullenly.

"Yeah," the other muttered, and scratched at his beard. "She was going to attack the queen."

Any fool could see that was not true, but there was no arguing with them. "You are dismissed," Catrin said instead. They slouched off, muttering, and Catrin bent down beside the weeping woman. "Fare you well, goodwife? Did they hurt you?"

The woman ran her hands down her arms as if to check. "No, good lady. I am well in body. 'Tis my heart that is broken."

"I'm not sure the queen can help with that sort of ailment."

"No, but Her Majesty can give me justice for my poor son. He was cursed, my lady. Cursed by a magician." Fresh tears trailed down her cheeks, leaving tracks in the dust. "Please, will you help me?"

"I will listen," Catrin said. "That is all I can promise until —"

"Lady Catrin!" Lord Heatherleigh strode over to them, one hand on the hilt of his dagger. It seemed he had at last decided to act. "Are you unable to handle the situation?"

"I'm perfectly —"

"I will take care of it. What-ho, wench? I doubt you are supposed to be here." He loomed over the woman, frowning ferociously. "What do you want?"

The woman quaked, and Catrin rose to her feet. "Lord Heatherleigh —"

"Speak, woman!" Lord Heatherleigh commanded. "Speak this instant, or leave this place!"

The woman squeaked in fright and ran, her bare feet leaving puffs of dust hanging in the air. Catrin clenched her fists tight enough to feel the nails bite into her palms. "Lord Heatherleigh, she wanted to petition the queen. What better reason to be at the palace?"

"And what better reason to stop her?" Lord Heatherleigh asked. "As courtiers, it is our duty to limit access to the queen."

"One duty, perhaps," Catrin murmured. "But not the only one."

He understood what she meant right away, and did not like it. "You have unusual ideas, my lady. They may well affect your chances of attracting suitors."

She sent him a cool glance. "One can only hope."

He understood that, too, and it made him scowl. "Do you intend to continue your enquiries into Mistress Mathilda's death this afternoon?"

She would continue until the day she died, if she had to. "Why do you ask?"

"I have various duties to perform, and must prepare. However, I am charged by the queen to help you."

"I see. As it happens, I have duties of my own. I will inform you if you are needed."

"Please ensure you do. And until then…" He bowed stiffly and turned away. "…farewell, my lady."

CHAPTER TEN

Most of the courtiers were busy with the tournament, and the queen knew that the loss of Mistress Mathilda weighed heavily on the maids, so she decided to let them be idle that afternoon. That was excellent news to Catrin, for it gave her an unexpected opportunity to talk to them all at once, without distractions. Surely they would know more about Mistress Mathilda, and possibly even her friendship with Thomas Starlyn. They might even know who had killed her, and not realise it.

The day had grown warm, so she was not surprised that they had chosen to be outside. Catrin found them sitting by the river, watching the swans glide by with their cygnets bobbing behind them. Some of the girls popped to their feet when they saw Catrin, obviously unsure whether or not they were required to curtsy, and sank back down when their fellows didn't move.

"Good afternoon, Lady Catrin," the sceptical one said. "Has the queen sent you to find us?"

"No; she will not require you until the evening meal," Catrin said, and sat down in front of them. "I came to ask you about Mistress Mathilda."

The littlest one immediately went teary, and another drew her into a tight embrace. "We don't want to talk about her."

"Why not? Did you not like her?"

"Of course we liked her — she was sweet, and very good at embroidery. She could finish her own work and still have lots of time to help other people."

"Then why not answer my questions?"

"Because it's sad," the littlest one said. "And if we talk about her, the green lady will know, and then she might sacrifice us too."

Catrin tamped down a flicker of impatience. "We can't allow that, can we? So I will only ask one thing. Did Mistress Mathilda feel guilty about anything?"

A couple of them giggled, and the sceptical one lifted her chin. "She felt guilty about Matthew, that is quite certain."

"Who is Matthew?"

"A *boy*," the littlest one said in a hushed tone of profound shock. "A boy with silver hair."

"He was a courtier," the sceptical one said. "Though he seems to have left court; I haven't seen him in over a week."

"Was he behaving badly towards her?"

"No, he seemed quite kind. He just … listened to her. They used to talk for hours." Tears rose in the girl's eyes and she determinedly blinked them away. "He was the only person who could make her laugh after her friend Thomas died."

"Then why would she feel guilty about him?"

The sceptical one shrugged. "She knew her parents wouldn't approve. He had very different ideas about religion than they did."

"I see." Catrin rose to her feet. "Thank you very much."

She hurried away from them, for they had given her an idea. It was something she could have handled herself, but she felt obliged to involve Lord Heatherleigh — and a frustrating obligation that proved to be. She could have done the task herself in the time it took to find him; she had searched most of the palace before she thought to check the middle court, where the combat-by-foot event of the tournament was about to begin.

There, a large square area for the match was marked off by scarlet and green ropes, with flags fluttering on tall poles at every corner. More ropes created a space for the spectators, and on the far side, nestled against the palace wall, was a high platform with a canopy and an elaborately carved chair. The queen was sitting in it, with Sir William Cecil standing behind her and Mistress Ashley at her feet. Guards stood at each corner, resplendent in royal livery.

Two men entered the combat area, fully clad in iron armour and carrying broadswords, and Catrin recognized their shields immediately. The snail and lamb was about to stand against the bear and ragged staff. Or, in other words, Lord Heatherleigh was about to fight Lord Robert.

He would do well to lose, and quickly.

A blast of a trumpet signalled the start of the bout, and the two men circled each other warily several times before the first blow landed heavily on Lord Robert's shoulder. All of the spectators heard the queen gasp, even amongst the cries of the crowd.

Lord Robert rallied quickly, dancing out of the way of a second blow and sending his sword crashing down on Lord Heatherleigh's helmet. The force of it drove Lord Heatherleigh to his knees, but he jumped up and spun out of the way of another blow. And another, and another. Finally he landed a blow against Lord Robert's breastplate, but paid a dear price for that minor victory. Lord Robert's sword flicked in between Lord Heatherleigh's breastplate and the plates covering his arm, and a spurt of blood was the result.

"First blood, Lord Robert," the herald shouted, and there was a burst of applause from the spectators.

Catrin laced her fingers together in front of her. The blow had weakened Lord Heatherleigh's grip, and he did not seem to be controlling his sword as well as he had. Lord Robert was quick to press his advantage, and began a fast series of blows that required Lord Heatherleigh to move his blade with speed and precision. He soon lagged, which proved his downfall. Mere seconds later, he had to let his sword drop in the sign of surrender.

Lord Robert raised his arms in victory, acknowledging the spectators who roared their support. Then he turned toward the queen and knelt down, crashing his gauntleted hand against his breastplate in a sign of devotion. It pleased her enormously, but not those around her.

Heatherleigh withdrew from the combat area and tossed his sword at his squire, who wisely let it fall to the ground before picking it up and sheathing it. Another boy came out with a roll of bandages, and hastily unbuckled Lord Heatherleigh's armour. Since blood was running freely down over the breastplate, his urgency seemed like a very good idea.

Catrin walked over to him, and he pulled his helmet from his head with his uninjured arm. "Lady Catrin," he said, somewhat warily. "I did not expect to see you so soon."

"Nor did I, my lord. I was not aware that you were competing."

"I was pressed into it when another knight withdrew. The joust is my preferred event." He winced as the arm-plates slid off, revealing leather padding that was liberally stained with blood. "Not this."

Catrin surveyed the wound. "May I help with that?"

"It is but a scratch," Lord Heatherleigh said bravely. "And I suspect you had another reason for searching me out."

"Indeed I do. I have discovered that poor Mathilda felt guilty before she died, just like Thomas Starlyn."

"Why guilty?"

"She was involved with a young courtier named Matthew who —"

"Ah!" He sucked air in through his teeth. "So she was unchaste."

"No, she was not."

"How do you know?"

"If she was unchaste, she would still be alive," Catrin said. "The altar required a virgin, remember?"

"Then why was she involved with a courtier?"

Catrin gritted her teeth. "If you would let me finish, my lord, I will tell you. I believe that the courtier, whose name was Matthew, knew something about Thomas Starlyn or his death, because the Mistress of the Maids heard the two of them mention Thomas' name before they left the palace. However, no one else has seen Matthew for several days."

Lord Heatherleigh tugged sharply on his beard. "I still don't know what Thomas Starlyn had to do with any of this. Did he not die before Niada even spoke the prophecy?"

"Beware of giving too much weight to the prophecy, my lord. It may explain some things, but it may also make us see things as they are not. Also, as Lord Robert said, words cannot kill."

"But these particular words might lead us to a killer. We should talk to Niada, and find out where she was when Mistress Mathilda was killed."

"You have seen Niada; you know she is nowhere near strong enough to lift a girl onto an altar. Moreover, her fingers are too bent and twisted to strangle anyone," Catrin said. "Forget about the prophecy for now; I suspect that we will learn more from this boy Matthew."

He sighed. "That is why you came; you want me to find him."

"I do." She let her gaze rest on his arm. "If you are well enough."

"I will be fine," he said, and hissed in a breath when the boy pulled the padding away from the wound. "And since I have now been eliminated from this event, I have plenty of time to make enquiries before the joust tomorrow."

"Very good. Thank you." She started to turn away, and then something else occurred to her. "And also, it might be wise to talk to the men who work in the gardens."

He made a frustrated sound and pulled off his gauntlet with his teeth. "By God's heart — why?"

"Lord St John saw someone in the corner of the garden where the altar was made. He said the man wore a stiff sort of hat," Catrin said. "The men who work in the gardens might know who it was."

"I understand." He bowed stiffly, his face awash with irritation. "I will look into it, my lady."

Catrin sunk into a curtsy and hid a smile. "Thank you, my lord."

The revels were subdued that evening, more a matter of cards and conversation than music and laughing. Catrin ended up at a backgammon table, with none other than Sir William Paulet. Her protests that she did not know how to play fell on deaf ears; the aged marquess promised at once that he would teach her.

"It is a very useful skill, my dear lady," he said in his pleasantly gravelly voice. "Perhaps you will meet your husband over the backgammon board."

She hid a smile. "And mayhap I will lose him when he sees my lack of skill."

"Practice will take care of that, my dear, just practice." He set up the board with precision and then beamed at her. "Now roll the dice, and we shall see who will begin."

Catrin rolled the dice, and came up with a three and a two. The marquess rolled and came up with two fours, which made him cackle with delight. "Oh, my lord, you have already taken a lead," Catrin said. "What chance do I have against such skill?"

"Ah — chance. That is the very thing," the marquess said, and moved one of his checkers four spaces. "It is chance, and chance alone, that keeps us in our place."

"I do not think so, my lord. You yourself have such skill and wisdom that you have managed to serve four sovereigns in your illustrious career, despite great changes and difficulty."

"I bend like the willow," the marquess said, and moved another checker four spaces. "As things change, so do I."

"That is very wise, my lord. I strive to do the same."

"Do you?" He dropped the dice into her hand. "Are you able to see which way the wind is blowing and adjust as needed?"

Catrin wrapped her fingers around the dice, the brittle bone cool against her palm. "I believe so."

"Then you must be able to see that the queen needs a husband and an heir."

Catrin restrained a sigh. "That sort of statement has more about it of the oak than the willow, my lord. There is little flexibility."

"It is the way the wind is blowing, I assure you." The marquess drew his hands into his sleeves and folded his arms. "And I am asking you, for the queen's sake, use your influence over her to make her see it too."

"I will think on it, my lord," Catrin said, and rolled the dice.

Lucy took a seat on the windowsill that offered the perfect vantage point. Below her was the river-walk, a gravel path with the palace on one side and a brick wall on the other, low enough for strolling couples to see the water flowing by. In front of her was the entire privy chamber, giving her a clear view of Lord Pierrick slowly working his way across it.

He talked to various people and joined in a game or two, and it seemed an age before he arrived at the corner of the room where Katherine Grey was playing cards with several other maids. Once he was there, though, the plan moved along very quickly. He soon had Katherine laughing and blushing, and they left the chamber together not long after that.

Lucy turned away from the room then, and fixed her eyes on the path below. Once again time slowed down terribly, until she saw their figures emerge from the dusk and pass close to the window. "The moon is waxing," Lord Pierrick murmured. "And I am glad, for you look beautiful in moonlight."

Katherine giggled, a high-pitched sound that Lucy had always found very irritating. "You are such a charming rogue," she said, and leaned so close to him she nearly fell. "All the ladies in France must have found you impossible to resist."

"Perhaps," Lord Pierrick said with a flash of a mischievous grin. "But I find only one lady impossible to resist."

Katherine pouted prettily. "Is it Lady Catrin? Most gentlemen fall at her feet."

Lord Pierrick chuckled. "No, *ma chérie*, it is you."

"Ooh, how lovely," she squealed, and wrapped her fingers around his forearm. "Perhaps we should —"

"Katherine! Get away!"

Katherine spun on her heel at the sound of her name, and Lucy leaned out the window to see who had spoken. All she could see was a twisted silhouette, but it was enough to identify her. Mary Grey was limping as fast as she could toward her sister.

"What are you doing here?" Katherine demanded.

"Saving you from yourself, as usual," Mary retorted. "Now come away. Right now."

Katherine held out pleading hands. "But he could help me."

"Hush!" Mary dropped her voice, but from her spot just above them Lucy could still hear. "It is too late for that, foolish girl."

"I suppose." Katherine dropped a reluctant curtsy in Lord Pierrick's direction. "Good evening, *Monsieur le comte*."

"Good evening, my lady," Lord Pierrick said thoughtfully, and watched the two of them hurry away. Only then did he look up at Lucy. "I am not sure if we have succeeded or failed, my lady."

"Let us call it a success, for I now have something to report at least," Lucy said. "Thank you, my lord."

Lord Pierrick gave the dramatic formal bow of the French court. "I live to be in your service, my lady."

For some reason, that made her blush. "Well … come in now, before the night air makes you ill."

"Very well," he said. "I have been told that you play chess. Will you join me in a game?"

She tilted her head to the side and considered him. "I will win, and you will sulk."

"You think so?" That mischievous smile flashed again. "We shall see about that."

Catrin untied the ribbons holding Lucy's sleeve to the bodice of her gown. "I still do not trust Lord Heatherleigh," she said. "He will not say how he knows Lord Ersfield, and I could tell that the wise woman does not like him."

"Perhaps she is jealous. Servants often don't like their master's friends." The sleeve slipped down her arm and Lucy caught it with her fingertips. "Nor do courtiers. Every day the queen's love for Lord Robert causes more resentment. Did you see her flirting with him today?"

"Tush," Catrin murmured, and glanced over her shoulder at the other ladies in the chamber. "'Tis a thing we must pretend not to notice."

"'Tis a dangerous thing," Lucy said, but she did drop her voice. "Sir William Cecil is very worried about it — even more worried than he was in September, before Lord Robert's wife Amy died. He knows that Lady Amy's manner of death will taint any new marriage Lord Robert makes, even if it is to the Queen of England."

Catrin untied the ribbons holding Lucy's other sleeve in place. "Their love is already thwarted, but they are the only two who do not see it."

Lucy caught the other sleeve as it started to slide. "Sir William keeps trying to make her see, but to no avail."

"Of course not. She is in love," Catrin said simply. "It is truly sad that the only man she wants to marry is the one man she cannot marry."

Lucy opened her mouth to answer, but before she could speak Mistress Blanche came in. Since Mistress Blanche was known for her ferocity whenever she heard Lord Robert's name, Lucy wisely changed what she was about to say. "I meant to tell you — one of the ladies saw Lord Heatherleigh speaking with Lady Mary Grey."

"Perhaps he is part of the latest plot the Grey sisters are hatching," Catrin said. "He is certainly ambitious enough."

"Is he foolish enough?"

"Perhaps. I will have to find out." Catrin passed a hand over her tired eyes. "Tomorrow."

CHAPTER ELEVEN

Catrin was spinning through darkness. Voices echoed around her — her father, telling her to look for miracles — her stepfather, scornfully telling her she was worth less than the clothes he had given her — her mother, singing lullabies — Lucy, gently encouraging. Then her feet touched ground and the voices abruptly stopped. She opened her eyes and found herself in a narrow passage lined with walls of plaster and wood. There were doors scattered around the passage, but when she tried to open them they resisted her. She moved forward, wanting to run but hampered by a weight at her side that held her back.

Moving slowly, she found a break in the passage. She went down it, only to find herself facing a brick wall. Retreat led her to a second side path, which snaked and twisted around several corners until it, too, ended in nothing.

She understood then. It was a maze, and she had no way of knowing how to break free. There were no hints or riddles … just the maze, and the smell of rot, and that dead weight at her side that seemed to have no form or shape.

She was trapped.

Catrin woke up with a gasp and took firm hold of the linen sheet beneath her. It brought her back to reality, back to the scent of lavender in the air and the gentle breath of Lucy beside her. All was well; none of that was real. But it seemed as if her nightmares had taken a different turn; no longer were they centred around her lost home in Wales. This was a new dream, and it reflected a new dilemma.

The death of a young girl, and a killer she might never find.

The early-morning mist was still rising in Greenwich Park when the queen emerged from her bedchamber, fully dressed. The determination of her pace made everyone in the room go quiet. "We shall walk in the gardens," she said, and her use of the formal royal 'we' further emphasized the intensity of her mood. "And we wish to be accompanied only by Lady Catrin and Lady Lucy."

Surprise slackened the jaws of Mistress Blanche and Mistress Ashley, but they obediently hung back. Catrin and Lucy fell in behind the queen, but neither of them dared to speak. The click-click-click of three pairs of court shoes was all that broke the silence until they were in the orchard.

There the queen stopped and took a deep breath of the cool fresh air. "I did not sleep," she said. "Did you?"

Lucy nodded, her eyes wide. Catrin shrugged. "Moderately well, Your Majesty."

The queen looked back over her shoulder and her dark gaze pinned Lucy in place. "Have you anything to tell me?"

Lucy glanced at Catrin. "Oh — ah — perhaps —"

"Speak," the queen said impatiently.

"I have discovered that it is certain that Lady Katherine is in trouble of some sort, for she tried to convince my betrothed to help her. Her sister said it was too late for him to help."

The queen scowled. "Is that all?"

Lucy quaked. "Thus far, Your Majesty."

"Then return to the palace and find out more."

"Yes, Your Majesty."

Lucy darted around the three guards who followed them and disappeared into the distance. Catrin watched her go in mingled amusement and concern. "She is trying her best, Your Majesty, but intrigue is not really her forte."

"She must learn," the queen said. "Intrigue may well be our only way forward."

Catrin looked at her, taking in the set jaw and balled fists, and restrained a sigh. "Especially if the path is dishonourable."

The queen sent her a sharp glance. "There is no dishonour," she said. "Only the petty arguments of stupid men."

"Which occasionally have a grain of truth."

The queen whirled to face her, and a diamond flew off the high collar of her gown. She let it fall glittering to the ground without so much as a glance. "I thought you of all people would support me."

"If you were not an empire, I would," Catrin said quietly. "I long to see you happy, Your Majesty, but I fear that marriage to Lord Robert would mean only that you lose the place your mother fought so hard to give you."

The queen winced. "Ah, a sword thrust well-aimed," she said, and moved on at the same restless pace. "It is not just Lord Robert. It's — everyone. I feel they are all against me."

"Not all of them, Your Majesty."

"No? Even Sir William Cecil presses me daily to choose my successor. It is like being forced to choose my own winding-sheet."

"It certainly is, and I support your refusal whole-heartedly," Catrin said. "Whatever trouble it may cause to rule a kingdom without an heir can be handled."

"Or avoided." Her face brightened. "I look forward to going on progress next month ... perhaps we will be able to leave all this behind."

Catrin bent to retrieve the jewel, to save Mistress Blanche from having to look for it later. "Until the autumn, at least."

"Aye, there's the rub. Only until the autumn. And we still must perform our duties today." The queen sighed. "Tell me how your task is progressing. Do you know any more about the death of Mistress Mathilda?"

"More about Mistress Mathilda, but little about who killed her," Catrin said. "Do you know a silver-haired courtier named Matthew?"

"There is Matthew Dyer, heir to Viscount Cotherston," the queen said. "He took up a place at court when he turned sixteen … not long ago."

Ahead of them, Mistress Ashley emerged from a side path and sent Catrin an enquiring look. She shook her head and Mistress Ashley withdrew with an understanding nod. "Have you seen him lately?"

"Not that I recall; forsooth, there are too many courtiers to notice them all on a daily basis."

"That is certainly true." Catrin paused by a rosebush and stroked her fingers along the delicate petals of a new bud. "I ask only because no one seems to have seen him for many days, but the Mistress of the Maids is sure he and Mistress Mathilda left the palace together on the night she died."

"Ask Sir William Cecil; he may have a record of the boy asking to leave, which would give you a clearer idea of his movements."

"I will, Your Majesty. Thank you."

The queen let out a long breath. "It is time to return to the palace; I too must speak to Sir William."

Excitement was high for the second round of the joust. Lord Heatherleigh was set against Lord Pierrick, and speculation was rife over which of them would prevail. The *comte*'s youth and inexperience spoke against him, but Heatherleigh's injury was a disadvantage that his opponent might well exploit.

Everyone had their opinion, and backed it up with their money. Even the queen had wagered a few shillings — and she had chosen to support Lord Pierrick.

Catrin watched as Lord Heatherleigh mounted his horse and signalled his squire to lead the horse to the starting point. The crowd let out a roar of anticipation, and everywhere small azure flags started to wave. At the far end of the tilt, Lord Pierrick took his position, and a similar roar went up for him as crimson flags rose up in every direction.

The flag-bearer stepped out to the centre of the tilt, holding the green start flag, and the crowd went silent. The flag wavered — held — then dropped to the bearer's side when a man leapt over the fence holding back the spectators. He ran toward the viewing-gallery where the queen could be seen through the windows, and dropped to his knees on the sand. "I must speak to you, Your Majesty," the man cried, and shrunk a bit when the guards closed in. "I must ask you to choose an heir — an heir of the true faith — the Protestant faith."

The queen leapt to her feet, strode forward and flung open a window so all could hear her. "Leave our presence at once, you knave. Indeed, leave our court! At once, I say!"

The man pleaded for mercy, but two of the guards lifted him up by hooking their arms under his. Their grim expressions and the furious face of the queen boded ill for his survival, and Catrin saw Lucy drop her gaze.

Lord Heatherleigh urged his horse toward them and held up a hand. "Hold, both of you. Allow my men to take custody of him."

One of the guards snorted. "I think not, my lord. Did you not hear? The queen ordered him removed from her court."

"Yes, and my men will remove him," Lord Heatherleigh said. "You must remain with the queen; it is not good for her to be in the open without a full complement of guards. Any further incidents might have great consequence."

The guards faded back, and Heatherleigh's men appeared to drag the intruder away. A cheer arose from the crowd as the man was removed, and the queen gave a girlish smile as she closed the window. "It seems I have more than one champion today."

"So it does," Catrin said, and felt her shoulders prickle with sudden unease. "Lord Heatherleigh was certainly quick to intervene, was he not?"

"Yes, he was most chivalrous. Perhaps I must change my mind about who is likely to win this contest," the queen said, and waved coyly as Heatherleigh returned to the starting point.

"Perhaps you must," Catrin agreed, and wondered if she should do the same. She had treated Heatherleigh as a minor irritant in her quest, but now she wondered if there was more to him. Why would he offer to take charge of such a man? The only reason she could think of was that they had a prior connection … and that was suspicious.

The time had come to find out more about the man charged to help her find a murderer.

After the jousts came a service, with a sermon by the precentor himself. Catrin and Lucy sat near the front of the chapel, which allowed them a good view of everyone who was there. Lucy was focused on Sir William Cecil, who wore his long black scholar's gown as always and listened gravely to the sermon, taking notes on a thick sheet of paper with a short simple quill. The Marquess of Winchester sat next to him, his chin resting on his chest and his eyes closed.

Lord Pierrick was sitting further away, on the opposite side of the communion table, and he had eyes only for Lucy. Behind him, and obviously very uncomfortable, was Lord Heatherleigh. He looked irritated, and never opened his prayer book, which Catrin assumed was due to the injuries sustained in his defeat. He had proven no match for the *comte*.

Catrin drew in a deep breath scented with incense and ancient polished wood and tilted her head back. The high arches above them gathered cold air that slid down over her head and neck, a blessed relief from the afternoon heat. The words of the liturgy washed over her, elegant and beautiful and already so familiar that she could drift along with them. And then, finally, '... the blessing of God almighty, the Father, the Son and the Holy Ghost, be amongst you and remain with you always.'

Amen.

The crowd rose in quiet reverence and left the chapel, groups forming in the flow of people like eddies in a river-current. The careful separation by status could not be maintained in such a situation, and dark simple robes and dull doublets soon blended with the colourful finery of court. Velvet caps with proud feathers mingled with graceful French hoods and simple white wimples. And then she saw it — a cap was knocked askew and for a second silver-blond hair gleamed like a beacon. Catrin gasped. "Matthew Dyer!"

Lucy strained up on her tiptoes, trying to see. "Where?"

She had no chance to answer. A woman screamed and a man shouted, and then the crowd scattered like geese before the prow of a boat, revealing a man in dark robes lying prone on the chapel floor. Blood poured out from his side, spreading in a red pool over the black-and-white tiles.

Sir William Cecil was bending over him, pressing his own robes against the wound. He was shouting orders in a voice that shook, and a second later the queen herself burst in from the door that led up to her private closet above the chapel. "God's wounds," she gasped. "What has happened?"

"A foul, cowardly attack," Sir William said brusquely. "Someone has stabbed the Marquess of Winchester."

CHAPTER TWELVE

Catrin reported seeing Matthew Dyer in the chapel, and the queen sent guards to search the entire palace while two surgeons worked desperately to save the marquess' life. Catrin herself went on a different sort of search — one which took her around the outside of the chapel, along the water-wall, and finally into the foul-smelling jakes outside the lodgings in the outer court. There she found what she was looking for, but could not retrieve it.

Frustrated, Catrin went looking for the one man she knew might have an insight into the events of the day. She found him in the presence chamber, strumming absently on a lute while he stared out the window. "Good afternoon, *Monsieur le comte*."

He set the lute aside and gave a stiff and formal bow. "Good afternoon, Lady Catrin."

She offered her sweetest smile. "Congratulations on your victory in the joust."

"*Merci.*" He straightened, holding himself stiffly upright. "I suspect that I know why you come to see me. It is about *Monsieur* Matthew, is it not?"

She folded her hands in front of her. "You were the last person to see him at court, save for Mistress Mathilda."

"I believe I was, but I cannot help you."

Catrin's eyes narrowed. "Why not?"

"I have nothing to say."

"You had much to say when you spoke to him several days ago. He said something that made you angry. You said that you would not be part of anything dishonourable. What did he want you to do that you found so objectionable?"

Lord Pierrick lowered his gaze. "I fear I cannot tell you that.."

"Why not?"

"To reveal another's secret … it is dishonourable."

"But it is honourable to help capture a man who tried to kill a venerable member of this court, and may well have succeeded."

"Are you sure that he was the attacker?"

"We must assume so. The nature of the wound meant that the attacker must have gotten blood on him, so the queen ordered that everyone in the chapel at the time submit to a search. No one there had any such stain, so the attacker must have escaped. I saw Matthew Dyer right before the attack, but he was gone before we could question him."

"So it must have been him." Lord Pierrick shook his head in sorrow. "Once *Monsieur* Matthew was simple and honest, kind and true. Once I would have sworn on my honour that he was a danger to no one."

"Evidently, that is no longer the case. And still you keep his secrets."

Lord Pierrick pressed his fist to his heart. "I swear to you, my lady, if the secret would help capture him, I would tell you. But it has nothing to do with his fiendish attack, and to reveal it would hurt others as well. So I will not — cannot — tell you."

Catrin sighed. "I will have to report your refusal to the queen — you know that, don't you?"

"I do."

"Then that is all there is to say," Catrin said, and walked away from him. She admired the man's sense of honour, but it was terribly troublesome. The strangest detail could prove significant in these circumstances; anything Lord Pierrick knew could lead to Matthew Dyer's capture. It was impossible to know that his secret would not help her.

She would have to find out another way, and she already knew what it would be.

The room was dim and shadowed, and smelled of rose oil and turpentine. It threw Catrin back to a very unpleasant time for a brief, hideous moment, but she pushed the past aside and walked over to the canopied bed. Sir William Paulet laid there unmoving, his thin hair sticking up in wisps against the pillow and his face an unnatural grey. Catrin rested her hand on the silken coverlet next to him and his eyes opened, his gaze wandering aimlessly for a minute or so before he managed to focus on her face. "Lady Catrin."

"Good morrow, my lord," she asked lightly. "I heard you asked for me?"

"I did." He closed his eyes again. "I knew you would have questions."

"Indeed I do."

"I fear I saw nothing. My head was turned away, toward the windows, because I saw my son returning." He paused to catch his breath. "Just as he turned his horse toward the stables, I heard a thud and felt this terrible heavy pressure in my side."

Catrin tugged the coverlet away from his throat, hoping he would find it easier to breathe. "Do you know Matthew Dyer, the heir to the Viscount of Cotherston?"

"I met him once, when he first came to court. He seemed an honest lad, eager to learn."

"Do you know Mistress Mathilda, who was killed a few days ago?"

He paused again. "I used to know her grandfather, but when she arrived at court I confess that I did not strike up an acquaintance. Her father has strange ideas, and I feared he had passed them along."

Perhaps he had. "What about Thomas Starlyn?"

The marquess shook his head wearily. "I do not know that name."

She could tell he was growing tired, but she had to ask. "My lord, my last question is somewhat impertinent. Will you indulge me?"

"Be quick," he murmured. "I feel a great urge to sleep."

"Yes, my lord. I only want to ask if there is anything you regret — anything you feel guilty about?"

"Margery Roos," he murmured, and then his eyes snapped open. "What? No, nothing. No guilt. I regret nothing, in all my years of service. Nothing."

"Very well, my lord, very well. I just had an idea, that's all, but I see I'm wrong," she said hastily. "Please, don't agitate yourself."

"I'm seventy-eight years old, child. I will agitate myself if I so wish," he muttered, and promptly fell asleep.

The door swung open and his son rushed in, sweat beading on his forehead.

"Why are you bothering him? My father needs to rest." He dropped into a seat beside the bed and took gentle hold of his father's hand. "The surgeons said he is in a very delicate state."

"I apologise, my lord. I would not have intruded, but he asked for me."

"He's not asking for you now," Lord St John said. "So please, leave him alone."

Catrin bowed her head. "Of course, my lord," she murmured, and backed slowly out of the room. Her last image was of Lord St John brushing a wisp of hair from his father's face, before he bent his head in silent prayer.

The queen was with Lord Robert in the privy chamber, rocking back and forth on her heels while the maids whispered together in one corner and the ladies in another. She looked up at once when Catrin walked in. "Have you seen the marquess? Does he live?"

At once Catrin found herself the centre of attention; every eye turned to her. "He lives," she said, and a collective sigh of relief wafted through the room. "He was badly injured, but there is hope that he will survive."

"Oh, he will survive. There is no one stronger than Lord Winchester," Lord Robert said with a gentle smile. "Forsooth, he will outlive us all."

Catrin crossed to the queen and sunk into a curtsy. "May I speak with you both, Your Majesty?"

"Certainly, my talisman," the queen said, and led her to a quiet corner. Mistress Ashley and Mistress Blanche shooed everyone away, and stood nearby to guard their privacy.

"Do we have a new problem, my lady?" Lord Robert asked. "Your eyes are full of fresh worry."

"Fresh worry, but a familiar tale," Catrin said. "I found the knife that was used to stab Lord Winchester."

The queen gasped. "Where?"

"Lord Winchester's attacker threw it in the jakes. It was too deep in the muck to retrieve, but I was able to see that its handle was made of hawthorn."

The queen drew in a sharp breath. "Like the altar on which poor Mathilda was laid."

"Yes. There is little doubt that Matthew Dyer is involved in both attacks: he was seen with Mistress Mathilda and he was in the chapel today. But everyone who knew him here at court agrees that he was not a villain. He was a simple, honest boy who enjoyed being a courtier."

Lord Robert frowned. "People can change."

"Especially when they fall under a malign influence," Catrin said. "Do you remember what Lord St John saw? A man in the garden, where the altar was later found. A man, not a boy."

"Ah, I see," the queen said. "You think Matthew Dyer is acting on someone else's orders."

"Someone who has a very specific plan." Catrin's fingers wandered almost of their own volition to trace the outline of the *stiletto* knife she hid under her sleeve. "I know that I have advised against this up till now, but I think the time has come to pay closer attention to the prophecy Mistress Mathilda recited. The fourth line, after all, is 'fell the ancient pillar'."

The queen went a little pale. "That must mean Lord Winchester."

"Yes. And both his death and a virgin's death was needed to save the green lady."

Lord Robert frowned. "So we must speak to Lady Ingolde."

"I will do so this evening," Catrin said. "And until then, I think we need to redouble our efforts to find Matthew Dyer."

"Well and good," the queen said. "Lord Robert will lead the search."

Lord Robert bowed. "Yes, Your Majesty."

That evening, Lucy had to prepare the queen's table. She started with the freshly ironed linen tablecloth, laying it carefully in place. Then she collected a silver plate and spoon, and dropped them both when Lady Mary Grey suddenly appeared in the doorway. "Lucy Howard."

Her name, not her title. Lady Mary should have had more respect for Lucy's status, but Lucy did not dare say so when Lady Mary's eyes were spitting fire. "What is the trouble, *Lady Mary?*"

"I want you to stay away from Katherine."

Oh, how Lucy wished she could. "Why?"

Mary pointed an accusing finger directly at Lucy's face. "You are still angry with us for what happened after Lady Amy Dudley died, last autumn. You are looking for any excuse to hurt us."

"No, I am not. That all lies in the past, and if the queen can forgive you, so can I."

"Then it's jealousy." She laughed an ugly triumphant laugh. "That's the truth of it! You're jealous of Katherine. She could take your betrothed away from you in a second, and it infuriates you. So you're following her — bothering her —"

The injustice of it stung. "I'm not jealous! Quite frankly, Katherine could marry Lord Pierrick tomorrow and I wouldn't protest. I — I was just trying to be friendly."

The excuse fell flat. Lucy did not blame Mary for giving her a blazing look of disbelief before she turned and stomped away in that awkward gait of hers. But she did blame herself for her own thoughtlessness when she saw who stood behind her.

Lord Pierrick himself.

His eyes were full of such hurt that it rent at Lucy's heart. He turned and walked away, and Lucy stood frozen in horror for a full second before she could force her limbs to move. Then she dashed after him, dodging laughing courtiers and bored ladies-in-waiting, and finally caught up with him by the great staircase.

"Lord Pierrick — Lord Pierrick, please —"

He raised one hand and let it fall. "Catch your breath, my lady."

She leaned on the balustrade, grateful for its solid strength, and drew in air until she no longer felt like her lungs were burning. "I'm so sorry — I did not mean you to hear that."

"But you did mean to say it." He turned sideways, leaning one hip on the balustrade so he could face her. "Tell me, my lady, why is it such a burden to marry me?"

Because my heart belongs to another. The words were right there, and with them Lucy saw the image of Sir William Cecil smiling when she remembered a particularly obscure heraldic symbol. But somehow, she couldn't say them. Was she ashamed of her love? Was it because she knew it could never be? Regardless, she could not tell Lord Pierrick about it. So she dropped her gaze to the wide wooden boards beneath their feet and cast around for another reason. It seemed an age before she finally came up with: "I am afraid."

He straightened. "Do you think I will be cruel? I swear, my lady, I would never lay a hand on you in anger."

"No, I don't think that." That, at least, was true. "I just … don't want to leave the court. I have friends here, and I love being part of everything. I love serving the queen."

He rested his hands on her upper arms. "I understand. This is your home."

"It is." She looked around at the smooth plaster walls, heard the buzz of a dozen conversations, smelled heavenly spices rising up from the kitchens below them. "I will miss it terribly."

"Then we shall not leave it." Lucy looked up at him in surprise and he smiled — a gentler, kinder smile than she had yet seen. "Not until you are ready."

"And what if I'm never ready?"

"*Chaque chose en son temps.*" He slid his hands downward until they could wrap around hers. "Each thing in its time."

Her own meal complete, Catrin went down to the banquet hall on the floor below the royal chambers, where Lady Ingolde could usually be found. She was still sitting at the table, gazing mournfully into a cup of red wine. And judging from the way she was swaying slightly on the bench, Catrin judged that it was not her first.

Catrin sat down across from her and refilled her own cup from the jug on the table. "Good evening, my lady."

Lady Ingolde glanced up at her suspiciously. "What do you want? I've done nothing wrong."

"I never said you did."

"Then you're the first. Five people — five! — told me tonight that I should have let myself die to save that girl."

"But you have no power over who lives or dies."

"Of course I don't."

Catrin sipped her wine. "And you have no idea who hurt Mistress Mathilda."

"Of course I don't."

"Nor do you know who would try to kill Lord Winchester." She snorted. "No."

"And you don't know why Thomas Starlyn killed himself."

"Of course I — did you say Thomas Starlyn?"

"Yes, I did. He was Mistress Mathilda's friend."

Lady Ingolde stared at her through watery eyes. "What does he have to do with all this?"

"I don't know yet."

Lady Ingolde started turning her cup in circles between her hands. "I know his parents, God help them," she said. "They are good people, and I am very sure they had nothing to do with either his or Mathilda's death."

"How do you know his parents?"

"Family … connections." She dropped her gaze to her cup and took a long drink. "Who told you to ask me all these questions? Was it Griffin Petre?"

"Lord Heatherleigh? No," Catrin said easily. "Why would he send me to ask you questions?"

"He knows I would not tell *him* anything, even if it would save my life." She set the cup down with a thump. "Two pounds fourpence."

"I beg your pardon?"

"That is what that green gown cost me. I had other expenses where the money could have gone, but I spent it on the gown so I would fit in at court." She gave a great sigh and shuffled slowly away from the table, her cane dragging along the floor until she could set it in place. *Clunk, thud, whomp.* "And now I dare not wear it."

For once, Catrin retired before Lucy. She did not manage to get to sleep before Lucy came in, though, so she rose again to help her friend undress.

Unusually, Lucy was grumpy. "Sir William Cecil did not come to play chess this evening; I had to play with the Spanish ambassador, and he does not like to lose."

"Perhaps you should lose on purpose, to keep him in good humour."

"Never. It's bad enough when I lose by accident."

Catrin loosened the ribbons on her friend's sleeves. "Did that happen tonight?"

"Not even once."

"How clever you are."

"Thank you. I —" Lucy stopped and turned to face Catrin. "You're about to ask me for something, aren't you?"

"Why do you suspect that? I tell you that you're clever all the time."

"True, but that half-smile means you're up to something." Lucy set her hands on her hips. "What do you want?"

It seemed there was no point in dissembling. "I want you to find out how Lord Pierrick knows Matthew Dyer."

"Oh." Lucy bit her lip. "I'm not sure I can. He did not come to play chess tonight, either."

"Truly?" Catrin started loosening the ribbons on her friend's bodice and hid a smile. "This bothers you more than I expected."

Lucy lifted her chin. "It does, but not for the reason you think."

"I see."

"Oh, no you don't. You just think you do."

"What do you think I think?"

"That I have … tender feelings for Lord Pierrick, and I don't."

"Of course you don't."

"I *don't*." Lucy stamped her foot. "Stop smiling!"

Catrin twisted her face into a solemn expression. "Yes, my lady."

"Oh, you — you —" Suddenly Lucy's anger dissolved into a giggle. "You look like one of the monkeys in the Tower menagerie."

"Alas, you wound me," Catrin said cheerfully. "After such an insult, the least you can do now is fulfil my small request."

"It wasn't an insult, it was an observation," Lucy said haughtily, but she laughed again when Catrin pouted. "Oh, very well. Put your face back in order. I will try."

CHAPTER THIRTEEN

The next morning, the sky was an ominous red and clouds were building at the horizon, but such threatening signs did not deter the spectators who had arrived to see the third round of the joust. Indeed, they seemed all the more vigorous in their appreciation of their favoured knights — who were, in the first bout, Lord Pierrick and Lord Robert himself.

Catrin was with the queen, who was as wildly anxious as she always was when Lord Robert was competing. She sat rigid in her chair, her eyes fixed on him while his squire led his black stallion to the starting-point. He accepted his lance from one of his men, and sat waiting until Lord Pierrick had accepted his.

The flag-bearer stepped out with his green flag and held it out, pointing downward. The tiltyard went silent — so silent that Catrin could hear the queen's agitated breathing. And then a single voice rang out: "Hold!"

"Hold, hold!" the flag-bearer responded in clear ringing tones, and let the flag go limp.

"What has happened?" the queen asked, and Catrin moved closer to the window to see.

"Someone has brought Lord Robert a note," she said. "He is reading it — and he is dismounting!"

Hope blazed in the queen's eyes. "So he will not joust?"

"It seems not — but he is coming here, so he can explain."

The queen relaxed only slightly, waiting until Lord Robert himself arrived in the viewing-gallery. He had discarded his armour, but wore heavy riding boots and a cloak. "Your Majesty, I must go to London."

The queen frowned, but it was easy to see that she was not truly displeased. "What is more important than participating in my tournament?"

"Obeying my sovereign," he said with a twinkle in his eye. "She charged me with finding out who is encouraging the old superstitions to rise, and I have just now heard of a man in the city who claims that pressing the Host to his eyes cured his blindness. Now he is telling all who will listen that they must repent of the new religion and go back to the old ways."

"I can see how that is a more pressing matter," the queen said graciously. "You may go, Robin."

"May I go with him, Your Majesty?" Catrin asked. "Repentance is something that greatly concerned our victims; this man may know more about the person who gives Matthew Dyer his orders."

"Yes, you may," the queen said. "And return as soon as possible with news."

"Yes, Your Majesty," Catrin said, and left the gallery with Lord Robert. The joust was continuing, with another knight preparing to take Lord Robert's place, but she was not sorry to miss it.

She was, however, sorry to leave the fresh country air. As always, the smell of the city hit her as soon as they drew near — a blend of hot steel, coal, damp and excrement. Many courtiers of her status had a house in the city, but she could not imagine why. It would be impossible to live with that stench every day.

They rode directly to St Paul's churchyard, where at least the scent of the bookstalls held back the worst of it. And there, sitting on the bottom tier of the Paul's Cross pulpit, was a man in a ragged tunic and loose-fitting hose. His face was dirty but for a line across his eyes, which had been scrubbed so ferociously that it was pink and shiny.

They dismounted, and one of Lord Robert's men came forward to take the horses' reins while Lord Robert himself approached the man. "I would speak to you, goodman."

The man beamed at them and nudged a collecting-cup with his foot. "Are you here to talk about the miracle? My eyes were healed, my lord! Healed!"

"So I have heard. With the Host."

He nudged the cup again. "Yes, indeed. A man came and laid the Host on my eyes. It was damp, for he carried it away from the Mass in his mouth. But in moments I could see!"

Lord Robert's voice grew stern. "There is no Mass in the Church of England, and no Host. Just the Communion bread and wine."

The man's jaw set stubbornly. "The Communion bread is just bread — your own Prayer Book says that. The Host is the body and blood of Christ. It is holy. I had forgotten that, until my blindness was cured, and now I must repent. We must all repent."

Lord Robert straightened. "You speak against the new church."

"No, my lord. I just tell people what happened to me, and what I think it means."

Catrin stepped forward. "Do you know the man who laid the Host on your eyes?"

He shook his head vigorously. "I never saw him. By the time my eyes were opened, he was gone."

"How very opportune that is," Lord Robert murmured. "Now think, fellow. Are you sure you can't tell us anything about him?"

He folded his arms and the ragged sleeves of his tunic fell back to his elbows. "Nothing. I don't know nothing."

"You may know nothing about the man, but you must know about that," Catrin asked, and pointed to an ink drawing on the man's forearm. "Who drew it?"

"The man did, before he laid the Host on my eyes," the man said, and twisted his arm around, trying to see it. "I can't tell what it is."

"I can. It's a lamb," Catrin said, and looked at Lord Robert. "And it looks just like the drawing I saw at London Stone, carved into the pillar where Thomas Starlyn killed himself."

The rain started to fall midmorning, and by the afternoon the royal chambers were unpleasantly damp and cool. The queen ordered fires lit, and settled down contentedly before the dancing flames. "I hear a lute in the presence chamber. Lady Lucy, fetch the musician."

Lucy rose at once and hurried from the relative peace of the privy chamber to the noise of the chamber beyond, where the majority of courtiers spent their days, forming alliances and trying to gain the attention of important patrons.

She wove her way amongst them all, following the music, until she finally found the player. To her surprise, it was none other than Lord Pierrick. He rose up and bowed when he saw her, and that charming smile lit up his features. "Ah, my lady. Glad I am to see you, for your light banishes the shadows of this grey day."

The smile made her blush, and the words made her fidget. "I am not the one to flatter, my lord. The queen requests that you play for her."

"*Certainement.* I would be honoured," he said, and followed her back to the privy chamber.

The queen ordered him to a spot in the window-seat closest to her, so she could hear properly, and he bowed low before he settled in and began to play. Lucy resumed her seat and took up her sewing, but she did not pick up the needle. She could not help but watch Lord Pierrick's fingers dance over the strings, drawing out sweet light tones that blended with the beat of the rain on the windows and the crackle of the fire. The queen's eyelids soon started to droop, and several of the maids laid down their heads in their friends' laps and fell asleep. Even the noise outside the door seemed to fade away into a mere hum in the distance.

Then Lord Pierrick brushed his foot on the floor, a small movement that Lucy would not have noticed had she not been so intent on him. She raised her eyes to his and he inclined his head toward the far side of the room. She glanced over just in time to see the hem of Katherine Grey's skirt vanish through the door.

Lucy did not want to follow; the music had wrapped her in its gentle folds and she wanted nothing more but to remain. But she knew where her duty lay, so she rose as quietly as she could and tiptoed back into the presence chamber. Katherine Grey was moving toward the main door, her gown of pale yellow showing clearly amid the courtiers' darker clothes. It was easy to follow her out to the grand staircase and down one floor to the banquet hall.

The hall was dim and quiet at that time of day, for the midmorning meal was long over and preparations for supper would have only just begun. Indeed, it was so empty that Lucy dared not follow Katherine into the room, but hid herself behind the hangings near the first window. Meanwhile,

Katherine walked to the very centre of the room, gazing up at the painted ceiling as if the answers to life's questions were there, hovering above her.

And then came another set of footsteps, and Lucy knew from their uneven pattern that it was Katherine's sister Mary. She had not been in the privy chamber, she realized then. Where had she been?

"Why did you want to talk here?" Katherine asked, and Lucy jumped at the sudden sound. Katherine had not modulated her voice; she did not seem to be in any fear of discovery. When Lucy peeked out between the tapestries, however, she could tell that Mary did not feel the same.

"Tush, you'll bring the guards down on us," Mary said, and took a small vial out of the purse she wore at her belt. "Here. I stole it from the ladies' chamber."

Katherine took the vial and held it up to the light. "What is it?"

Mary glanced from side to side and went up on her tiptoes to whisper in Katherine's ear. Katherine gave a great cry and flung the vial away. "I cannot! I will not!"

"Foolish girl!" Mary cried. "You've broken it!"

"It is an evil thing!"

Mary seized her sister's arm. "It is the only way."

"No!" Katherine cried, and ran from the room. Mary limped after her, and Lucy emerged from her hiding-place to hurry over to the spot where she could see glints of broken glass. And there she found a strange yellow powder spreading along the seam between wall and floor like mould. It made the skin crawl on the back of her neck.

She knew she needed to save it if she was going to find out what it was, but did she dare touch it? It could easily be poison, and she had nothing with her to carry it in. So she shifted one of the rush mats to cover it all and hurried back to the ladies' chamber.

She had a ring, given to her by her mother, that opened to reveal tiny portraits of her parents. She rarely wore it, for it was too large and heavy for her hand, but for the first time she was grateful for its size. She was able to collect a goodly portion of the powder in the hollow between the two portraits without getting any on her fingers, and latch it safely so none could spill out. She then scattered the rest with her foot and hid the glass beneath the mat, and hurried back to the privy chamber with the ring safely on her finger.

Lord Pierrick was still playing as she settled back into her place. Her heart was fluttering from that burst of activity, and she was all the more anxious when she noticed that Katherine and Mary Grey had not returned. What were they up to? What if Mary had more of that powder, and was even now persuading Katherine that they had to use it? Did they intend to harm someone — and if so, who?

With such thoughts swirling about in her head, Lord Pierrick's music did not have the soothing effect it once had. Lucy was almost grateful when the queen raised her hand. "Enough for now, my lord, we must begin our preparations for supper," she said. "I hope to see you there."

Lord Pierrick rose and bowed low. "As you wish, Your Majesty."

He started toward the door as the maids and ladies reluctantly roused themselves, and Lucy rose as he passed her by. "Good my lord, may I have a word?"

He expected her to ask, she could tell, and escorted her to a quiet corner with a speed and ease which told her he had planned out the path. They settled together in a window-seat, and Lucy carefully pressed the ring into his hand. "Do not open it," she murmured. "Inside is a powder Lady Mary Grey tried to give to her sister. Lady Katherine refused to take it, calling it an evil thing."

He tucked the ring into his belt, but did not look at it. "Poison?"

"What else?"

"I will find someone to identify it. Did they say for whom it was meant?"

"No, or I would have cause to speak to the queen immediately." Lucy glanced over at the ladies she spent her days with. They were laughing at their own sleepiness, praising the music, looking forward to the evening. "I cannot imagine why the Grey sisters would want anyone dead."

"Nor I — except the queen herself." Lord Pierrick pursed his lips. "Perhaps they want to kill Her Majesty before she names an heir."

"Yes … if they did, Lady Katherine has the bloodline to become queen. But she would have rivals — the French queen dowager, Mary, for one. The Earl of Huntingdon, for another. It would likely end in civil war."

"So it would be wiser to be named the queen's heir than to kill the queen and risk losing everything."

"Yes, it would."

Lord Pierrick's gaze rose thoughtfully to the ceiling. "Perhaps, then, their intention is merely to encourage the queen to choose an heir."

It was an arresting thought. "So the powder wouldn't kill the queen; it would just make her ill enough to make her see that it is wise to determine who will come after her."

"And they themselves could nurse her back to health, hoping that in her gratitude the queen chooses Lady Katherine." He spread his hands wide. "I must admit, it would be a clever scheme."

Lucy pressed cold fingers to her forehead. "And an evil thing."

CHAPTER FOURTEEN

When Catrin and Lord Robert arrived back at the palace stables, one of the page boys was waiting for them in a state of great agitation. His urgency was such that he didn't even wait for them to dismount, but came running up to Lord Robert in blatant disregard of the stallion's flying hooves. "Lord Robert, Lord Robert! The queen needs you right away."

Lord Robert jumped off the horse. "Is she ill?"

"No, but she is very upset. They're all upset — all the ladies, all the maids."

"What has happened?" Catrin asked, but the boy didn't wait to answer. He took off running, and they followed as quickly as they could, leaving the horses in the care of the stable boys.

The boy led them directly to the royal lodgings through the chapel, where they found Sir William Cecil waiting for them on the second floor of the great staircase. "This way," he said grimly, and took them into the banquet hall. It was completely empty, bar one yeoman standing by the fireplace looking somewhat pale and shaky. He was guarding a wooden box that lay on the hearth — a small, narrow box that looked disconcertingly like an infant's coffin.

Catrin and Lord Robert both came to an abrupt halt, staring at the thing as if it might come alive. "Has anyone opened it?" Catrin asked.

"Not yet," Sir William said. "One of the maids found it and they all went hysterical. They're sure it's another sacrifice."

Catrin knelt before the box and brushed her fingers along the grain of the wood. It was rough and pitted, suggesting it had not been carefully prepared. "It's ash, not hawthorn," she murmured, and lifted the lid. The guard hastily looked away, and Lord Robert laid a hand on his sword hilt.

Inside lay a human figure formed from wax, with exaggerated features twisted into an expression of agony. It wore a green gown, awkwardly sewn as if by an inexperienced hand. The feet and hands had been blackened by flame, and two bright red hawthorns pierced the figure, one at the stomach and the other at the heart.

"This is a threat against Lady Ingolde," Sir William said.

"Worse than that," Lord Robert said. "It's image-magic; cursing a person by cursing their image. There are people who claim they can make a person waste away by slowly destroying their image."

"Evil magic," Sir William said gloomily. "Just the thing to frighten people into abandoning a new religious settlement."

"This must be the same person who killed Mathilda and attacked the marquess. Those thorns are from the hawthorn tree, and there are also these." Catrin lifted the figure so they could see the white blossoms that lay beneath it, releasing an awful scent that reminded her of the sickroom. "I was told that it is unlucky to bring hawthorn blossoms inside; it leads to illness and death."

Sir William plugged his nose. "I can see why; they smell like the plague. Prithee close the box, my lady."

Catrin let the figure rest on the blossoms again and shut the box. She stared at it a moment, considering. "If no one has seen this yet, we have a chance to avoid any consequence," she said thoughtfully. "Let us tell people that the box was empty — a mere trick to frighten people. That will save Lady Ingolde from any further unwanted attention."

"And may even save her life," Lord Robert said dryly. "I have often heard that people who believe they are about to die soon do."

"Yes, that is a fine plan," Sir William decided, and directed his intense grey gaze at the guard. "You are sworn to secrecy."

The young man nodded mutely, his face still somewhat clammy.

"Very good," Lord Robert said. "You may leave us."

That was an order the young man was happy to obey; in seconds they were alone. "For the green lady to live, there must be a sacrifice," Catrin murmured. "A new altar, a new virgin. Fell the ancient pillar."

"But it did not fall," Lord Robert said thoughtfully. "Lord Winchester still lives."

Catrin rose to her feet and dusted off her hands. "And perhaps, if he recovers, that is when the green lady will die."

"Yes, I can see a twisted logic to that," Lord Robert said. "It would explain why there was a threat today, not an action."

"Hmm." Sir William stroked a hand down his beard. "Perhaps I should assign someone to watch our green lady."

"Yes," Catrin murmured. "I think that would be wise."

Lucy saw Sir William Cecil ere the evening meal was done, but he did not stay to eat. He spoke with the queen but avoided conversation with Lord Robert, drew several men aside to speak to them in whispers, and left again. It was only after, when the revels had begun, that he returned to the privy chamber. For a moment he watched the dancers with a faint air of bemusement, and then he turned toward the chess tables. Lucy waited with bated breath as he drew closer, the game already set up on a low table in front of her.

His eyes fell on that first, and then alighted on her. Strangely, he did not smile. "Good evening, Lady Lucy."

"Good evening, Sir William."

He settled down on a cushion on the other side of the table and his grey eyes looked deep into hers. "You need a partner, my lady."

Pleasure glowed warm within her. "I do, my lord. 'Tis a better game that way."

He picked up a pawn and held it within his hand. "Life is a better game that way, too."

Her heart skipped a beat. "Not all think so."

"Not all are meant to have a partner." He set the pawn down, delicately, and picked up the queen. "But I do not believe that you, dear one, are meant to spend your life alone."

Suddenly his grey eyes saw too much, and Lucy lowered her gaze to hide what she could. "I have recently been betrothed, my lord."

"I am pleased to hear it." He set down the piece and rose to his feet. "I hope you embrace this adventure, my lady. Please … do not let any ties you may have made here at the palace restrain you."

Tears rose in her eyes and Lucy tried hard to hold them back. "I will do my best, my lord."

"I have no doubt, my lady." He bowed low. "Fare thee well."

"Fare thee well." She whispered it, and did not know if he heard, for he moved swiftly away and left her. She picked up the piece he had held and wrapped her fingers tight around it, breathing deeply to keep the tears from falling.

Someone approached her and she blinked her vision clear. It was Lord Pierrick, holding two tankards in his hands and grinning. "Good evening, my lady. Shall we have a match?"

"Very well." Lucy set the piece back in place. "Why not?"

Their game got tangled into a stalemate, which was interesting. Lucy and Lord Pierrick finally gave up and tried to analyse how it had happened, tracing their moves back to the beginning. Neither of them could figure it out, and they were both growing quite annoyed, so it seemed best to set the game aside. Lord Pierrick asked her to walk by the river instead, and she accepted. The rain had stopped, after all, and the fresh damp air might cool her cheeks.

They had just started along the path when he drew the ring from his belt and opened it. "Do not touch it," Lucy warned. "The powder inside could be dangerous."

"I am pleased by your concern," Lord Pierrick murmured, and tilted the open ring so the moonlight fell on the powder. "I have never seen such a powder, but it does not smell of poison."

Lucy tilted her head. "Does poison always smell?"

The question seemed to take him aback for a moment. "You're right, that was a false assumption," he said. "My tutor of Logic would be most disappointed in me."

"You have a tutor?"

"I did. Peregrinus was his name," Lord Pierrick said fondly. "He would not leave France, for all that I begged him to come with us. He said his bones were too old to travel so far."

Lucy knew that she should return to the topic of the powder, but she was curious. "How long was the journey?"

"From Brittany to my uncle's home in the north? Many days. I fear I cannot answer more clearly, for I do not remember much. We arrived three years ago, when I was but fourteen, and it was mere weeks after my father died so I was much distracted by grief."

She could see that distress in his eyes, and it moved her to reach out and rest her hand on his forearm. "I am so sorry."

"He died in battle, like the warrior he was." He closed the ring and held it tight. "I would have missed him far more had it not been for my uncle, Baron Audley. He has taken care of my mother and I very well, and taught me much that a father should teach his son."

"Is it just you and your mother? Do you have any brothers or sisters?"

He spread his hands wide. "Not a one, I'm afraid."

"Was it lonely?"

"Not at all. My dog Brutus and I —"

"You have a dog?" Lucy couldn't stop a little jump of delight. "I have always wanted a dog, but my father refused. What does he look like?"

"He is a spaniel, and a fine hunter."

"Why didn't you bring him?"

"He needs the woods and the wild, not the confines of my quarters in a palace."

"Yes, I can understand that." As disappointing as it was. "I will meet him eventually, will I not?"

He took her hand in his. "Of course, my lady."

The touch of his hand made shivers run up and down her spine. "Good," she said awkwardly. "I ... I look forward to that."

He smiled that gentle smile. "As do I."

They wandered on, and she looked up at him in mingled curiosity and apprehension. There was much about him to commend him, but she knew so little about him that she was still afraid. She did not know how he reacted when he was stopped from doing what he wanted to do. She did not know how carefully — or how recklessly — he spent money. She did not know how he would respond if she asked him a question he did not want to answer.

But that, at least, it was possible to test. "May I ask a question, my lord?"

"*Certainement*, my lady."

"How do you know Matthew Dyer?"

His only reaction was a hitch in his step. "I suspect it is not you who wants the answer to this question, but your friend Lady Catrin."

"It is true that she asked me to ask, but false that I do not want to know. Matthew Dyer may have been the one who attacked Lord Winchester, and if you know anything —"

"I know nothing." He hesitated. "About the attack."

"But you know something about him."

Lord Pierrick stopped walking and sucked in his cheeks so that hollows appeared under his cheekbones. "I cannot tell you more, my lady. Loath as I am to keep secrets from you, I am honour-bound to protect the innocent. And if I told you what that man was doing, it may have great consequences."

"It may have great consequences if you do not."

"Perhaps. That is the burden I must bear," Lord Pierrick said sadly. "I pray, though, that it does not make you think less of me."

"No, it doesn't," Lucy said thoughtfully. "But may I ask that you tell me, if it is ever honourable for you to do so?"

He squeezed her hand. "You may indeed."

CHAPTER FIFTEEN

The next morning, Catrin was amusing herself by reading *The Book of the Courtier* when Lord Heatherleigh walked up to her and bowed. "Lady Catrin."

"My lord." She closed the book with a snap. "A woman of discreet modesty. That is the ideal court lady, according to Castiglione — if Sir Thomas Hoby has translated him aright."

"I think that he makes a fine point, my lady."

She was not at all surprised by that. "Perhaps, but I suspect that none of the Italian court ladies have ever been asked to find a murderer. It requires a rather different set of skills."

"Not in this case, it seems," Heatherleigh said stiffly. "A silver-haired boy in court clothes was just seen at Paul's Walk, and I believe that it would be very helpful to have a woman of discreet modesty on hand to convince him to return to the palace. Will you come?"

She rose at once. "Shall we bring horses?"

"It will be faster to walk up from the wharf at this time of day."

"Excellent; I will meet you at the water-steps."

They were soon moving upstream in smooth, controlled bursts as the water-man rowed with the usual strength and speed. Lord Heatherleigh rested his chin on his linked fingers and his elbows on his knees. "I was thinking about the last line of the prophecy, 'And the falcon will rise once more'. Perhaps the falcon refers to England's warrior kings."

Catrin raised one eyebrow. "It is true that the falcon was used as a symbol for Edward III and Edward IV —"

"Yes, it was."

Catrin turned her head away. " — but I doubt those warrior kings will ever rise again, falcon or no."

Lord Heatherleigh huffed out an irritated breath. "Then what do you think it means?"

"I try not to speculate." She drew her fingers over the boat's weathered wood. "Are you acquainted with the Grey sisters?"

He straightened his shoulders. "I am."

"Are you one of those who thinks Lady Katherine should be queen?"

"No." He folded his arms. "Are you?"

"Not in the least." She gazed out over the side of the boat. "Forsooth, that is why I avoid talking to either sister in an intimate setting. Speaking to Lady Mary Grey in an isolated spot in the garden, for example, would make people wonder if there is a purpose behind the conversation."

"Garden conversations tend to revolve around the weather and the flowers."

Catrin stared at him. "Do they?"

He stared back at her defiantly, but his gaze soon wavered. He seemed about to answer when he suddenly turned his head toward the riverbank. "Listen."

A strange sound was coming from the Tower. Catrin listened hard, trying to distinguish it over the slapping of the water and the rattle of the oars. It was like thunder, but it came from within the Tower, not above. And it ended in snarling cries, each one full of a fierce savagery that resonated in sickening waves within her.

"Lions. It's the lions in the Tower menagerie." Catrin took hold of the edge of her seat to steady herself. "They are roaring."

"Yes … yes, it must be that," Lord Heatherleigh said. The wild, angry sound rose from the Tower once again and he shifted on his seat. "What do you think it means?"

"Probably that they are hungry," Catrin said, but she could not help but wonder. That line in the prophecy … 'let the lions roar and the fires burn'. Could the sound mean something more … ominous?

Lord Heatherleigh seemed equally as uneasy as she; he remained silent and wary even after they alighted at Paul's Wharf and walked the short distance up Paul's Hill to the cathedral. The houses there were crowded closely together, the streets dark even in mid-day, and vile-smelling mud was caked deep in every gutter. Catrin had to resort to the use of her pomander — a pewter ball pierced in floral patterns and packed with rose petals. It usually hung at her belt, but it spent most of that journey in her hand, pressed tight to her nose.

It did not get much better when they arrived at the cathedral. Owain Kyffin bustled up just as they walked through the arched doorway, and he smelled of dust and sweat. "My lord — my lady — did you come to see me?" he asked, breathing hard. "I have just now returned, so I am not prepared to offer you the welcome you deserve. Perhaps my —"

"Do not trouble yourself, your reverence; we are here for information, not spiritual solace," Lord Heatherleigh said. "Where have you travelled that has exhausted you so?"

"A crossroads outside the city," the precentor said, and glanced at Catrin. "Where poor young Thomas Starlyn was laid to rest."

Lord Heatherleigh's eyes narrowed. "Did you bless the burial of a suicide?"

Owain Kyffin set his feet apart, his shoulders bunching. "I blessed the gravesite of a poor sick boy."

"How dare you!" Lord Heatherleigh jumped backwards, his face suffused with anger. "I shall ensure that the queen hears of this."

"I fear the wrath of the Almighty more than the wrath of our blessed sovereign," the precentor retorted. "It was the right thing to do."

"It was not!" Lord Heatherleigh's shout was so loud and so sudden that a nearby horse reared up and its rider had to fight for control. "Traitors and suicides should have no grave!"

Catrin felt a wave of anger rise up inside her, and struggled to hold it back. "No grave near yours perhaps — but I doubt they would want such a position," she snapped. "I am glad it is not you who determines whether or not someone is deserving of heaven, Lord Heatherleigh. You are singularly lacking in compassion."

Lord Heatherleigh let loose an oath and strode off, scattering children and chickens before him. Owain Kyffin's eyes went very wide. "You have angered a man who may have great influence at court someday, my lady."

"Great influence or none, I could not let him say such things." Her anger kept the tears that threatened to fall burning in her throat. "Some traitors are only people who did the right thing at the wrong time."

Owain Kyffin's voice gentled. "You know of such a one?"

"My father." She raised her gaze to the very top of the cathedral's spire and watched the eagle weathervane wobble in the wind. "He was executed by Queen Mary."

"Ah, that is a pain I know well. I lost a brother to Mary's burnings." Owain Kyffin patted her arm. "Hopefully, such terrible times are over now."

Catrin managed a smile. "Hopefully."

The Walk was just as full as it had been the morning Catrin came to see Master and Mistress Starlyn, but this time the floor was slick and muddy from the rain the day before. She lifted her skirt with one hand and managed to dodge the worst of it as she and Owain Kyffin wove their way through the chattering crowds, looking in all directions for anyone with silver hair who was dressed for court. Catrin was not surprised that they found nothing. It had taken them too long to get there, and too long to start the search.

The precentor soon had to attend to other duties, so he left her under the care of one of the chaplains and trotted off to fulfil them. Catrin circled the nave once more, without any expectation of success, and was surprised when she ran into someone she knew well. He seemed to be trying to give a ring to a wizened old man, who was shaking his head. "*Monsieur le comte!* What are you doing here?"

Lord Pierrick seemed taken aback by the question. "Ah — praying. And you?"

"I was searching for an old friend of yours," Catrin said dryly. "I don't suppose you've seen a young man with silver hair wandering about?"

"I have not," he said stiffly. "Are you here without an escort, my lady?"

"Alas, I am. My companion grew angry with me and left; I have not seen him since."

It was to his credit that he was visibly irritated by that. "A lady should not have to travel through this city alone; it is not safe. I am about to return to the palace, if you would like to come with me."

"I would — thank you," Catrin said, and followed him out of the nave with a word of farewell to the long-suffering chaplain. "I hope your prayer brought you comfort?"

"Prayer always brings comfort." He drew his lip between his teeth in a way that reminded her of Lucy. "I regret that you did not find your quarry."

"As do I," she said, and followed him through the rows of printing booths. They soon emerged into a street market, where fabric of every sort and colour were on display. Quality silks and satins sat along humble muslin and thin summer wool. And in the middle of it all, something she had never seen before. "But perhaps it is not a wasted journey after all."

He followed her gaze. "You wish to purchase cloth?"

"Not exactly." She walked over to one booth that displayed a thin light linen, dyed whiter than she had ever seen before. Indeed, it was so white that it seemed to glow, even in the dim light under the booth's canopy. "This is amazing, my goodman. However did you make your cloth so white?"

The seller glowed nearly as brightly as his cloth at the compliment. "I cannot tell you all my secrets, my lady, but I will say that it takes many baths of acid and alkaline."

"It's beautiful," Catrin said, and lifted her purse suggestively. "Have you sold much of it to gentlemen of the court?"

"No, not much to gentlemen." He gave a gallant bow. "Mostly to fine ladies such as yourself."

"Have any gentlemen purchased it recently?" She sent him a winsome smile. "I ask because my betrothed is the type of man who would purchase this for me secretly, and I do not wish to ruin his surprise."

"Ah, young love." The seller chuckled. "I can tell you this, my lady — if your betrothed has hair of the finest blond, he has been by this booth before."

Catrin clapped her hands. "He has! Oh, how lovely. How much did he purchase?"

"Several yards."

"Was this recently?"

"Within the fortnight, my lady."

She glanced hopefully toward a booth displaying shimmering silk. "And has he bought anything since?"

"No, my lady. I have not seen him since. Indeed, I thought he was leaving the city — he said something to his companion about not returning to court." Catrin let her face fall and the seller hastened to add, "But I'm sure he didn't mean it."

"That rather depends. Did you know his companion?"

"I fear not, my lady. It was an older gentleman. I could not see him well; he stayed far back."

"I shall find out who it is," Catrin said, and did not have to pretend to be resolute. "Thank you, goodman. I shall send someone to purchase more of this fine fabric if his gift does not arrive."

The seller bowed. "Thank you, my lady."

Catrin re-joined Lord Pierrick and they resumed their path toward the river.

"You are not betrothed," Lord Pierrick said. "Why such deception?"

"I believe Matthew Dyer bought that cloth."

"I assumed that from your description. But it was not for you."

"No, it was so he could pretend to be Thomas Starlyn's ghost," Catrin said. "I noticed when Mistress Mathilda and I saw the apparition in the outer court that it had an unearthly glow I had never seen before, and seemed to float. Well, I found out how he managed to float, and now I know how he could glow."

"And now you have learned something of his companion, as well," Lord Pierrick said, and a satisfied smile spread over his face. "*Bien joué*, my lady."

Catrin retired to her chamber when they returned to the palace, telling Lord Pierrick that she needed to prepare for the evening revels. However, what she truly needed to do was think. She had learned so much, and yet she could not make sense of any of it.

Catrin sat down in the window-seat and stared out at the village in the distance without seeing anything, her mind filled with ideas and images. She knew that Matthew Dyer had become the instrument of an older gentleman, a gentleman who had a clear and violent plan. For some reason, that gentleman felt the need to kill — and to kill by following a prophecy spoken by a wise woman who lived ten miles away and seemed to have nothing to do with any of it.

She also knew that the gentleman used hawthorn as a sort of signature. Hawthorn ... used in May Day revelry for the 'god' of spring, the Green Man who held the cycle of death and rebirth in his hands. Did this gentleman consider himself such a god? Did he hold pagan beliefs? Holding to such traditions might explain the elaborate sacrifice of poor young Mathilda, but not the attack on Lord Winchester, or the use of image-magic to threaten Lady Ingolde.

Magic. They had seen an uprising of the old superstitions recently — holy candles, healing with the Host, the nocturnal vigil — all of which had been part of the 'magical' traditions of the old church, and often seemed to involve the ancient Christian symbol of the lamb. Could it be that this older gentleman who controlled Matthew Dyer considered himself a magician?

If so, it would explain the use of deception and illusion to frighten people, such as the false ghost and the dramatic display of the wax figure. It did not, however, shed any light on the great obstacle she had yet to overcome: namely, what this magician might do next.

But it was a start.

CHAPTER SIXTEEN

The evening meal was over, and most of the queen's favourites already partaking of the evening's amusements, when Lord Heatherleigh came into the room and glowered most ferociously at Catrin.

Amused by his sour expression, she skipped through the last steps of a galliard and bowed to her partner, then walked over to him. "You look as if you suffer much disquiet, my lord," she said. "Has your supper settled poorly?"

"I have had no time for supper," he said sourly. "And it is you who causes my distemper."

"I?" She said innocently. "Why, what have I done?"

"I am willing to wager that you told the queen that I left you at the cathedral."

"Did you expect me to keep it secret?"

"And you told her that a magician — a *magician* — was responsible for the death of that girl."

"I believe a magician *is* responsible for the death of that girl."

"Then you should have told *me* about it — before you told the queen. Just as you should have told me about the wax figure that I heard about only today. We are supposed to work together."

"No, you are supposed to help me," Catrin said coolly.

A trill from the pipes and recorders announced that they were about to play La Volta, and a cry of delight arose around the room. Lord Heatherleigh ignored the noise. "How can I assist you if I am not included?"

"How can you assist me if you are not even present? A dilemma indeed. Alas that I cannot solve it right now." Catrin sent a come-hither smile to a courtier hovering nearby. "I much prefer to dance."

"Fine." Lord Heatherleigh swept her up into the crowd of dancers and took her hand in a tight grip. "Dance you shall, and as you dance you will listen."

Catrin attempted to pull her hand away but could not. "I do not wish to converse further with you, my lord. Do let me go."

"I will not," he said grimly, and bowed toward her as the music began.

She returned the bow without thinking, but her face felt tight with fury. "Did you find Matthew Dyer after you left the cathedral in a temper?"

They both drew back one step and then skipped forward so they fell in with the other dancers. "I did not."

"Did you save the green lady from her tormentors?"

"The green lady is not the innocent you think she is." He led her around in a wide circle. "I know her to be a thief and a liar."

She spun once, her skirts swirling around her, and set her hand on his shoulder. "Without proof, that is mere slander, and I —"

He set his hands at her waist and threw her into the air, turning at the same time so the room spun around them. "No more from you. Listen."

Catrin landed somewhat harder than the other women, and glowered at him as she tried to catch her breath. He took the opportunity to continue. "You should have told the queen that the lions were roaring."

"Oh? Should I have mentioned that the swans were swimming as well?"

"You know perfectly well that it is the lions which are significant, not the swans. I heard them roar again as I returned

149

to the palace." They spun together and then he flung her into the air once more. "It means that we need to focus on the prophecy. We must speak to the wise woman."

A final spin, and then Catrin managed to speak. "We have already done so, remember? Niada knows nothing; even to her, the prophecy was mere words."

He turned away from her, moving in a circle until their steps brought them together again. "We spoke to her kindly then. When we return, I shall speak with more ... purpose."

"I will not allow —" He threw her in the air once again and she lost her words in a gasp. She landed with a thump and tore herself free of his hold. "Enough. I will not be treated thus."

He took hold of her arm and pulled her into the alcove by a window-seat. "I am not finished with you."

Her right hand flashed to her left sleeve, but she had no time to draw her *stiletto*. Lord Robert had suddenly appeared, and taken a firm grip of Lord Heatherleigh's shoulder. "Let the lady go."

"Lord Robert." Lord Heatherleigh released his hold and bowed before the man. "This is a private matter."

"Less private than you think. You have drawn much attention," Lord Robert said grimly. "Are you well, my lady?"

"Well enough," Catrin said tightly. "Did you have need of me, my lord, or shall I retire?"

Lord Robert bowed. "I have need only of Lord Heatherleigh, my lady."

She curtsied in return and walked away without another word. Furious, her arm aching and her fingers still itching to plunge her *stiletto* into any part of Lord Heatherleigh she could reach, she strode down the stairs, bypassed the privy dining chamber and marched into the banquet hall, which was still half-full of people lingering over their plates. Lady Ingolde was there, but she was the only one Catrin knew. Everyone else was at best vaguely familiar, and most were deeply into their cups. One pair was feeding each other strawberries, while a group behind them played a strange game that involved stacking crusts of bread and knocking them over. In the far corner, two courtiers were singing their own version of a minstrel song.

Catrin was passing the tables when the sudden scrape of a bench over the stone floors made her jump. She swivelled in time to see Lady Ingolde lurch to her feet. Her mouth was working as if she was choking, but there was no noise. And then, even as Catrin watched, she collapsed to the floor.

The minstrel song continued unabated, even when some women sitting near Lady Ingolde started shrieking. Catrin rushed to the lady's side and dropped to her knees. "Lady Ingolde — tell me what's wrong. I'll get help."

Vomit leaked from the lady's mouth, and she started pressing both hands to her heart. "No ... regrets..." she whispered. "I followed..."

"Lady Ingolde, please. Is it your stomach? Your chest?"

"Cannot ... breathe..." Her body arched and then collapsed; Catrin felt the woman's heart and was astonished at its fast, irregular rhythm. "I followed ... my faith..."

"Lady Ingolde —"

"...to the end." She said it on a long sigh, and her whole body went limp. Catrin raised her voice, demanding that the shrieking ladies find Lord Robert at once. They rushed out, and several other people quietly slunk away.

Catrin gently laid the Lady Ingolde flat on the floor and crossed her hands over her chest, and it was then that she saw the knotted string around the lady's neck. She pulled on it gently, and a grey wax disc slid out of its place beneath her bodice. It had Latin written on one side, and the other held the imprint of a lamb.

Catrin gently removed the necklace from the lady's neck, just as Lord Robert rushed in. "Lady Catrin, are you hurt? What has happened?"

Catrin hid the necklace in her own purse. "What we expected, I'm afraid."

His gaze fell on the elderly woman lying before them and he swallowed hard. "The green lady no longer lives."

"No, she doesn't." Catrin's gaze fell on the trenchers and tin plates still scattered over the table, the remnants of a last lonely meal. "Despite the sacrifice."

"It was the magician."

The man in guard's livery sat stiffly upright on the bench. Lady Ingolde's body was no longer on the floor, but aside from that the banquet hall had changed little. Catrin sat in Lady Ingolde's place, while Lord Robert prowled the room, too restless to stand still.

Sir William Cecil circled the guard, his hands clasped behind him. "And how did this magician manage to kill a woman who was under your direct protection?"

"He cursed her. I can't do anything against a curse, my lord."

"And how do you know that he cursed her?"

The man shifted uneasily. "The figure of wax, my lord. The one in the coffin."

Lord Robert's head came up. "How did you know about the wax figure?"

"Everybody knows, milord," the man said. "One of the maids saw it and told the tale far and wide. She said there were thorns in the figure's stomach and heart."

"And so there was," Sir William confirmed thoughtfully. "Does that have any bearing on her manner of death?"

Catrin kept her eyes on the tin plate in front of her. "It was indeed her heart that gave out, my lord, and her stomach that felt the most pain. But — may I ask a question?"

"Of course, my lady."

Catrin raised her gaze to the guard. "Did she eat with anyone?"

"No, my lady. No one came near her after Lord Heatherleigh left."

Catrin's eyes narrowed. "Why was Lord Heatherleigh here?"

"I don't know, but he told me the lady was dangerous." The man dropped his gaze. "I didn't believe him. She was just a little old lady."

"Lord Robert, if you would," Sir William said quietly.

"With pleasure," Lord Robert snarled, and left the room.

"Are you sure there was no one else?" Catrin asked.

"Only the people who brought the food and wine, and I knew all of them. None of them is a magician."

"I'm sure they aren't," Sir William said dryly, pointing to the door. "Wait outside."

The man popped to his feet. "Yes, my lord," he mumbled, was gone in seconds.

Sir William gazed thoughtfully at the door as it swung ponderously shut behind him. "Lord Winchester is better today."

"So I assumed," Catrin said.

"He was even able to take a bit of food." Sir William rocked back and forth on his heels. "We must ensure that he does not hear of Lady Ingolde's fate."

"No; it could be damaging."

"Exactly." He turned in a circle, as if searching for something in the empty room. "The man who did this killed quickly both times ... but it was easy to tell how Mistress Mathilda died. The cause of this death is not so clear. How does one die by a curse?"

"She did not die by a curse, my lord." Catrin tilted the plate toward him so he could see the torn green leaves scattered across it. "She died by poison."

"Poison?" Sir William's eyes flared wide. "Are you sure?"

"I fear so. There are wolfsbane leaves on this plate, but they look so much like the fresh herbs that I wager she would never have recognized them."

Sir William crossed over to examine the leaves more closely. "How did you recognize them?"

"My father taught me about wolfsbane when I was a child. I found signs of the powdered roots at the bottom of her cup, as well."

"So she was doubly dosed. And once the remnants of the meal were disposed of, no one would have been able to tell that there had ever been poison." Lord William shook his head. "A curse would seem a likely explanation, in such a circumstance."

The door opened and Sir Robert strode in, pulling Lord Heatherleigh along with him. The man did not look happy: his hair was tousled and his doublet unbuttoned, and he only wore one boot.

"What indignity is this?" he demanded. "I do not take kindly to being so treated."

Sir William gazed at him for a long moment. "We do not take kindly to men misbehaving toward ladies."

Lord Heatherleigh scowled. "If necessary, I will apologise to Lady Catrin."

"You should apologise to Lady Catrin whether it is necessary or not," Lord Robert said. "But that is not why you are here."

"Then why am I here?"

"I wish to know," Sir William said mildly, "why you spoke to Lady Ingolde this evening."

Lord Heatherleigh pulled himself free of Lord Robert and started buttoning up his doublet. "She stole something valuable from my father, and I confronted her."

"What was it?"

Lord Heatherleigh averted his gaze. "An ancient heirloom, which we obviously do not use any more but did not wish to sell."

Sir William spread his fingers out on the table and leaned forward. "From such a description, I wager it was something the queen has outlawed. A rosary, perhaps? A saint's shrine?"

Lord Heatherleigh deliberately did not look up. "Something of that sort, yes."

"Why did she steal it from him?"

Lord Heatherleigh scowled. "The only explanation is insanity. She was raving — she said her 'family' wanted to protect the item, and she has none. Then she called Matthew Dyer an innocent young boy."

"Did you see the people who brought her food or wine?" Catrin asked.

He shot her an irritated glance. "Not the food, but I saw the boy who brought wine. He was wearing his cap incorrectly — pulled down tight over his head."

Catrin let out a sigh. "As if, perhaps, he was trying to hide silver hair?"

Lord Robert closed his eyes as if in dread of the answer. Lord Heatherleigh opened his mouth to deny it, and then his shoulders slumped in abject defeat. "Yes, that could very well be the truth of it. But why — why would Matthew Dyer come to the palace and pose as a page boy?"

"To act as an instrument to the magician, of course," Lord Robert snapped. "And he succeeded in his quest, for Lady Ingolde is dead."

Lord Heatherleigh stared at him in horror. "I am sorry, my lords. I was so focused on the theft that I missed the greater crime."

"Agreed," Sir William said. His voice was calm, but his eyes flashed with irritation. "We must consult with the queen — you may leave."

Lord Heatherleigh left with all haste, and Sir William offered to take charge of the cup and plate that was their only evidence. Catrin surrendered it nearly without thought, for something else had occurred to her. "That is the second time that Lady Ingolde has claimed the bond of family," she murmured. "First she said that she had family connections to the Starlyns, and tonight she said her family wanted the item she stole."

Sir William shook his head. "She had no living relations; if she did, she would not have been a burden of the court while Sir Thomas Chaloner is away."

"Then she must be referring to a family she chose," Catrin said. "And that makes me wonder what it could be."

CHAPTER SEVENTEEN

Catrin was trapped once again. The ground shifted under her feet, and rocks rattled, fell, rolled until they thumped against crumbling plaster walls. Circles of light broke the darkness, bathing a series of scenes in pools of deep yellow. A woman sitting at a window. A man urinating against a doorpost. A child in rags sitting on the street, playing with a rat.

The weight at her side dragged her down. She still did not know what it was, but now she knew it was precious. She could not lose hold of it, could not let it go. There was danger in it, but there was also safety and comfort. Somehow she was sure of that, but could not understand how it could be.

Ahead of her, a dark figure. He moved with purpose, and she knew her task was to follow. But she did not know where he was going — she did not know whether she could trust him. Should she take one of the other paths that snaked off on either side? Would that be the better course?

She could not decide. And so she simply followed, plodding on, on, on through the maze.

Catrin was required in the queen's cabinet the next morning. She and Lucy rose early, and moved silently about the room getting dressed because many of the ladies were still in bed. Some were weeping; others were buried in the blankets, hiding from the day like children.

Catrin and Lucy left the room and walked together along the gallery, their footsteps echoing in the empty space. "Where is everyone?" Lucy wondered. "Even the river-walk is empty."

"Still a-bed, I wager. They were all probably up quite late discussing Lady Ingolde's death," Catrin said. "I wonder if any of them felt genuine grief."

"We barely knew her; she had just arrived at court." Lucy knit her brow. "How sad, that no one will mourn her."

"Perhaps she was thinking the same thing, and that is why she told me that she had her faith."

"I hope so." Lucy took hold of Catrin's hand. "I'm glad you were there... I'm glad she wasn't alone."

"As am I." Catrin paused outside the door to the queen's cabinet. "Remember, dearest — no matter what people think, it was not a curse, but a poison. Be careful what you eat and drink today."

Lucy squeezed her hand. "I will, I promise. And I will see you anon."

"Anon, my dear."

Lucy continued on to the bedchamber, where she was due to help Mistress Blanche freshen the room for the day. Catrin slipped into the cabinet, and found Lord Robert Dudley and Sir William Cecil already there. They were not speaking, which did not surprise her. They rarely had anything to say to each other.

She curtsied and greeted them both, just as the queen came in. She seemed agitated, and kept adjusting her clothing as if it did not fit her properly. "Sending my ladies to collect the washing-water and toothcloths themselves made my morning preparations very slow, Sir William."

"But it ensured that they knew where everything had come from, Your Majesty," Sir William said. "Methinks we should be additionally careful right now, with a known case of poison to contend with."

The queen scowled. "It is remarkable, how few people accept that it *was* a case of poison," she said. "I have seen a dozen people going to London this morning in search of protective amulets and counter-curses. They would do better to purchase bezoar stones and unicorn horns."

"Yes; we must restore order as soon as possible," Sir William said. "Have you any insights, Lady Catrin?"

"I believe that there are connections between all these deaths, my lord," Catrin said. "Thomas Starlyn and Mistress Mathilda were both struggling with regret, and even Lord Winchester confessed to a single regret in his life. However, Lady Ingolde told me as she died that she did not have any regrets because she held fast to her faith." Catrin retrieved the wax disc from her purse and held it up so they could all see the figure of the lamb. "And Lady Ingolde was the only one of the four of them who had this symbol."

Lord Robert took the disc. "I have seen many of these. It is the *agnus dei*, something long associated with the old Church of Rome."

"I think the symbol has been usurped by the magician I told you about yesterday," Catrin said. "He uses it to claim people, so to speak, such as Lady Ingolde, the man who is telling everyone that his blindness was healed, and young Thomas Starlyn. Those who are claimed believe that they can live without regret."

The queen frowned. "But Starlyn had regrets."

"Not at first. He was enthralled by the magician, and during that time, as Mistress Mathilda told me, he used to greatly value a wax pendant on a string. I think young Thomas became the magician's assistant, and gradually came to regret it. He rejected the magician and killed himself in remorse, but the magician still claimed him, and that is why the symbol was found not on Thomas' body, but on the board where he killed himself."

"An assistant," Sir William murmured. "Just like Matthew Dyer, who the magician is now using to attack and kill on his behalf."

"Yes. I believe Master Dyer took Thomas Starlyn's place," Catrin agreed. "After Thomas' death, he started to change. He stopped coming regularly to court, and tried to convince Lord Pierrick to join him."

"There is one problem," the queen said. "The magician claimed Lady Ingolde, you say, but still killed her."

"She must have angered him somehow, and didn't know it," Catrin said. "Perhaps by the theft that Lord Heatherleigh mentioned."

"That is possible. I agree with you thus far," Sir William said slowly. "But what if this magician you speak of is but an assistant himself, and simply kills those he is told to kill?"

"I did not consider that." Catrin raised one eyebrow. "Who could be his master?"

"Another magician: namely, Niada."

"That is a significant possibility," Lord Robert said. "After all, it does seem like he is following her prophecy with dog-like devotion."

"But Niada lives and works in Ersfield, and never comes to London, while the magician's work is exclusively in the city," Catrin said. "When would they have met?"

"That is a question you can only answer if you speak to her again," the queen said. "I will arrange for Lord Heatherleigh to accompany you to Ersfield, Lady Catrin."

Catrin felt a cold twist of anger in her stomach. "Lord Heatherleigh, Your Majesty? But he has not been ... helpful of late."

"I am aware," the queen said. "This will be his one chance for redemption."

Lord Robert's eyes narrowed. "I'm not sure that is possible, Your Majesty."

"Nor am I, and I intend to tell him so. Believe me, Robin, he will know the stakes." The queen knocked on the wall of the cabinet and Mistress Blanche poked her head in inquiringly. "Send for Lord Heatherleigh."

"Yes, Your Majesty."

The queen turned back to Lord Robert. "While Lady Catrin is in Ersfield, you must continue to look for this magician, Robin. He must be stopped."

"Yes, Your Majesty."

"And as for you, Sir William, you must find Matthew Dyer. It may be helpful to look into his family; he might try to contact them."

"I will look into it right away," Sir William promised, and rose to leave.

"Hold — there is one last thing," the queen said. "What was Lord Winchester's one regret?"

"I do not really know," Catrin said. "He said the name 'Margery Roos' when I asked if he had any regrets, and then denied it."

"I know that name … I have heard it before … but where?" Sir William said thoughtfully. "Ah yes — the records of the Court of Wards. I recently took over from Sir Thomas Parry and had all the records brought here so that I might peruse them before I preside over my first session. Margery Roos was once a ward of the state."

Catrin's spine tingled. "When?"

"I do not recall, I'm afraid."

"May I look?" Catrin turned to the queen. "It should not take long, Your Majesty, and then I will go to Ersfield."

The queen considered. "Very well."

Lucy was waiting for the queen in the privy chamber when Lord Pierrick came in. "Good morrow, my lady," he said.

"Good morrow." Lucy tilted her head and regarded him thoughtfully. "You seem very excited."

"I have been asked to join the men searching for Matthew Dyer," he said. "We will take to horse within the hour."

Lucy studied his flushed cheeks and the tension in his shoulders. "So you *want* to join this search?"

"Of course! It means that I have been noticed by men of influence at court."

"But it could be dangerous."

He laughed a joyful, reckless laugh. "Fear not, my lady, I will return safe and triumphant."

She gave in to an impulse she didn't even understand and removed one of the jewels on her neckline, pinning it over his heart. "See that you do."

Something flared in his eyes, and he took her hand, brushing his thumb over the back. "Yes, my lady," he murmured, and kissed her hand before he left the room. Lucy found herself watching him go, and again she really didn't know why.

Fortunately, she didn't have time to think about it for long. The queen entered her privy chamber then, dressed and ready to grant an audience. Or perhaps 'braced' to grant an audience might be a better word, Lucy thought. She seemed to be almost dreading something.

"Has anyone besides Lady Ingolde fallen ill?" she asked.

Lady Mary Sidney sunk into a curtsy. "No, Your Majesty."

The queen rose from her chair and paced in a quick circle. "You think it silly to ask, but it is I who failed to protect Lady Ingolde, even though Lord Robert informed me about the wax figure. I do not want to make any more such mistakes."

"What happened to Lady Ingolde is not your fault, Your Majesty," Lucy said. "And I'm sure Lady Catrin will soon prove it."

"Yes, I believe she will. I have never known anyone so determined, bar perhaps my own mother." The queen sank into her chair. "I believe that I could eat something, Lady Mary."

"Yes, Your Majesty. Are you willing to have a guest while you break your fast? His Reverence Owain Kyffin has arrived; he heard there was a death and wanted to offer succour," Lady Mary said. "Shall I show him in?"

"Yes, do," the queen said. "His good humour would be a comfort in this time."

Lady Mary bowed and backed out of the room, and a moment later the precentor came in, walking as if he was bouncing on the soles of his feet. He always did that, and Lucy found it quite amusing.

He bowed low before the queen with a beaming smile. "I pray God's blessings upon you, beloved Majesty."

"And I upon you, my trusty and well-beloved friend," the queen said. "Please, rise, and break your fast with us."

"It would be an honour, Your Majesty." He straightened and glanced around at the half-full room. "I am pleased to see that these delightful ladies are in good health. How many have died?"

"Only one," the queen said, over the sound of a trail of servants busily setting up a table and loading it with food.

"Truly? I heard that several were struck down — and by a curse, no less."

"It seems the extent of our troubles have been exaggerated," Lord Robert said. "How did you hear about it, your reverence?"

"There were many members of court at the cathedral early this morning," Owain Kyffin said. "They were in such a state of agitation that I thought the situation rather urgent."

"Rumours get out of control so quickly," Lucy said, with one hungry eye on a basket of fresh white mancet bread.

"Yes — as we say in my home of Denbighshire, *tyfid maban, ni thyf ei gadachan*." Owain Kyffin looked around and chuckled. "Apologies — I thought Lady Catrin was here to translate. It means that the child will grow, but his clothes will not."

"Just like a rumour grows bigger, while the truth stays the same," Lucy said. "I've never heard that before, but I like it. Did you say Denbighshire?"

"Yes, I did."

"That is where Lady Catrin's mother was born — near Valle Crucis Abbey."

Owain Kyffin's face lit up with delight. "I was born in the abbey itself — the monks had a small hospital there. It is a lovely place."

"That is what Lady Catrin says. She used to tell me about its old ruins and great mounds of earth."

"Used to? Why no longer?"

"Sadly, she has not mentioned them since she discovered her mother is dead."

"Alas; that must have been painful for her." His gaze drifted downward. "Was the death recent?"

"No, it happened several years ago."

"And it left her with no family? No one to care for her?"

Lucy started to answer, but the queen's voice cut through her words. "Why do you ask, Master Kyffin?"

The precentor jumped, as if he had been caught somewhere he should not be. "No ... ah, no reason in particular."

"Are you sure? Lady Catrin seems to make even the most chaste of men think of marriage."

Owain Kyffin blushed. "I am sure she does, Your Majesty, but I … I cannot think that way."

"Cannot, or should not?" The queen lifted her chin, eyes narrowed in that way that made her dark gaze disconcertingly piercing. "You know my views on married clergy, and women living on the cathedral grounds."

He blushed all the deeper. "I do."

"Then put Lady Catrin out of your mind and come. You as well, little Lucy. Let us break our fast."

Sir William had had the records laid out in the queen's viewing chamber, for it boasted a long table and plenty of windows — and it was never in use, for the queen used the king's viewing chamber if she ever felt the need.

Catrin walked the length of the table, reading each carefully lettered title. "The Court of Wards goes back to 1526, does it not?"

"Yes, and Lord Winchester was joint Master of Wards from 1526 to 1534."

That could be useful. Catrin moved directly to the oldest books, and started flipping through each entry. Much of it was about feudal dues, but every now and then she found a reference to one of the 'wards of the state' — meaning children who had inherited a title and estate before they were old enough to take responsibility. The court was supposed to manage it for them, and appoint a guardian to look after the young heir's interests.

It did not always prove beneficial for the heir.

Catrin had to wonder if that was the sort of thing that had happened with Margery Roos. Had her estate been mismanaged? Had she emerged from her minority — often referred to as 'suing out her livery' — with less than she had when it began?

It took only a few minutes' search to find the record. "1527: Margery Roos, heir to Baron Wicke, thirteen years of age. Her guardian was Lord Boltoph... I don't know that name."

"He was a viscount who died fighting for Lady Jane Grey in 1553," Sir William said. "His estate was forfeited to the Crown. Mary's court used the land exclusively for hunting, so his manor is now derelict."

"Where is it?"

"Approximately five miles from Ersfield Manor. I imagine the families were friends, but the old Lord Ersfield died soon after King Edward did, so neither he nor his son — the current earl — took part in the troubles. Their title and lands survived intact."

"How long would Mistress Margery have been with Lord Boltoph?"

"Female heirs can sue out their livery when they are fourteen." Sir William took the ledger from Catrin and flipped forward several pages. "And she did, so she would have been there for a year at most. It says that Lord Winchester visited her several times, but nothing further."

"Is she still alive? I don't remember ever meeting a female baron."

"I don't know. She may have died without issue, so the title reverted to the Crown. Or, her title may have been absorbed into her husband's title when she married." He closed the book with a snap. "That is all the information we have, I'm afraid."

Catrin's lip quirked. "Then it is time for me to write a letter."

CHAPTER EIGHTEEN

Lord Heatherleigh was sulky and silent the whole way to Ersfield, which suggested that his conversation with the queen had not been to his liking. Catrin remained wilfully cordial and polite, but did not allow him near her person. Even when they arrived, she allowed a stableboy to help her dismount rather than accepting him.

He jumped down from his horse scowling fiercely, but she did not think it was because of her. Rather, his ire was focused on a group walking toward them from the direction of the village. It was an unusual group, made up of both men and women, young and old, poor and quite wealthy. And one of them Catrin knew. "Is that not the Earl of Huntingdon?"

"I don't think so," Lord Heatherleigh said abruptly. "Look here; our hosts have come."

Lord and Lady Ersfield had emerged from the front door, wearing mourning black and moving listlessly. They did not look pleased to see them. "Good afternoon, my lady," Lord Ersfield mumbled. "Why have you returned?"

"I wanted to speak to you about your daughter's last day," Catrin said gently. "Is there somewhere we could talk?"

Lady Ersfield simply turned around and went back into the house, leading them to a privy chamber off the great hall. She sat down on a bench against the wall without another word and directed her gaze to the floor.

"Prithee, sit," Lord Ersfield said, and sat down next to his wife.

"Thank you," Catrin said, and she and Lord Heatherleigh chose some chairs nearby. "Do either of you know the name Matthew Dyer? He is heir to the Viscount of Cotherston."

"Yes, we do." Lord Ersfield's face tightened slowly. "Did he kill my child?"

"Not that we know of," Catrin said. "But he was seen with Mistress Mathilda on the evening of her death."

"She was fascinated by him, just like she was fascinated by that Thomas Starlyn," Lady Ersfield said. "I told her to stay far away from him."

"I think she obeyed you … for the most part," Catrin said. "But did you have a specific reason for disliking him?"

"His family hold outdated beliefs," Lord Ersfield said venomously. "We didn't want our girl to have anything to do with them."

"Did those beliefs include magic?" They glanced at each other, and their silence spoke for them. "And did Mistress Mathilda ever mention magic — or a magician?"

Lord Ersfield dismissed the idea with a wave of his hand. "She knew better. There's no such thing."

A faint light dawned on Lady Ersfield's face. "She did ask whether I believed in magicians once, after Niada had been here to help birth a baby," she said. "I said that magic was nothing but old superstition and pagan ritual."

Lord Ersfield grunted his approval. Lord Heatherleigh sent Catrin a considering glance. "The timing of that question is interesting. Perhaps Mistress Mathilda suspected that Niada herself was a magician."

"Perhaps; I will ask Niada about that when I go to see her," Catrin said. "But first, one last question. Do you know Margery Roos? Or Lady Wicke, as she may have called herself?"

"I know the name, but not the person," Lady Ersfield said. "She caused quite the scandal back in the old earl's day."

"What scandal?"

"She came to live on a neighbouring estate after her father died, and within a month or two her belly started to swell," Lady Ersfield said. "Everyone knew that there was a babe coming, but then — nothing happened. Her belly fell again and no one ever talked about it."

"The child was probably stillborn, and I imagine the girl was glad of it," Lord Ersfield said. "When she turned fourteen she left, and no one in her home town would have known she was ever pregnant."

"Who was the father?" Catrin asked.

Lord Ersfield averted his eyes. "No one knew."

He could not have said more clearly that he did know. "Are you sure? Did she never mention his name?"

"She never talked at all," Lord Ersfield said.

Lady Ersfield nodded. "People thought she might have been born that way, but that's probably just a rumour."

"Do you know what happened to her?"

"Married, I think, but I don't know what happened after that," Lady Ersfield said. "I'm not even sure she's still alive."

"Nor am I," Catrin murmured. "But it will be interesting to find out."

The queen decided to go riding that afternoon, so Lucy went in to help her change her clothes. Mistress Ashley sent Katherine Grey in as well, even though the girl did not seem up to the task. Her face was ashen and a faint sheen of sweat stood out on her forehead.

Inevitably, the queen noticed. "Lady Katherine, are you ill?"

Katherine brought over the queen's riding costume, and the fabric trembled from the shaking of her hands. "No, Your Majesty. I am … a little over-warm, that is all."

"Of course you are; you are wearing velvet in May," the queen snapped. "Go at once and change into something more suited to summer."

Katherine set down the clothes most carefully. "Yes, Your Majesty."

She left the room, and it suddenly occurred to Lucy that the situation offered the best chance yet to glean information from Katherine Grey. Her sister Mary was nowhere in sight, and Katherine herself might be prevailed upon to offer confidences in her present state. "Your Majesty, may I go assist her?"

The queen's dark eyes gleamed. "You may."

With a hopeful heart, Lucy hurried out of the bedchamber through the back door and arrived in the gallery. Katherine was only a few paces ahead of her, sitting on a chest bound with iron, and she looked ghastly. Not a kind thing to say, but definitely accurate. The poor girl was miserable. "Lady Katherine, can I help you?"

Tears trembled on her eyelashes. "I want to lie down."

"Very well, my lady. We're not far from the maids' chamber; lean on me and I will take you there."

Katherine lifted one arm and rested it over Lucy's shoulder, but made no more effort to rouse herself. "Everything is terrible."

"Why do you say that?" Lucy asked, and put her arm around Katherine's waist so she could lift her to her feet. "Has something happened?"

Her head fell against Lucy's shoulder with a thump. "I am all alone. Abandoned."

"That is terrible." Lucy urged her onwards, and she shuffled forward with great reluctance. "Who has abandoned you?"

"All love, all life," she said, and broke down weeping.

Lucy could no longer keep her going, and they both collapsed onto a low bench that creaked under their combined weight.

Lucy was the first to catch her breath. "How can that be?"

The only answer was a gurgle. Then Katherine suddenly pitched forward and vomited — all over Lucy, all over herself, all over the bench and the floor. Lucy could not believe that so much could come out of one person, and she could not stop a cry of disgust.

"I am sorry, I am sorry," Katherine wept. "Oh, has there ever been a woman as cursed as I?"

"Katherine!"

For once, Lucy was glad to see Mary Grey. She hurried over to them as fast as her twisted back would let her, glaring at Lucy. "What have you done?"

"Nothing, nothing. She was kind," Katherine sobbed. "Oh, Mary, I'm so sorry — look what I've done."

"I will get someone to clean it, and I will take care of you," Mary said gently, then sent Lucy a scornful glance. "*You* can take care of yourself."

Lucy rose to her feet, sticky and stinking and starting to feel rather ill. "I certainly intend to."

Catrin and Lord Heatherleigh found the wise woman in her cottage, humming to herself as she set a mortar and pestle on the square wooden table by the fire. She glanced up when they entered, and picked up the bunch of dried leaves resting at her right hand. "Adder's-tongue fern," she said. "It's fine for curing ulcers of the skin, but it must be gathered in April."

"We're not here to talk about herbs," Lord Heatherleigh said. "There are evil things afoot at the queen's court, and they are all related to your prophecy."

"My prophecy has nothing to do with evil things," Niada said, and plucked some leaves and spores from the bunch. "It is only meant to illuminate the future."

Catrin looked around the room. The flagstone floor was uneven, but clean and well swept. There was a cot in one corner, neatly made, and a domed chest at its foot. The room smelled fresh and light, probably from the bunches of dried flowers and herbs hanging from the rafters. "Do you know any magicians, Niada?"

The twinkle in Niada's eyes slowly faded. "I hope not."

Lord Heatherleigh glanced uneasily at the white cat who watched them from a perch on the window sill. "Why do you say that? After all, you're somewhat of a magician yourself, aren't you?"

Niada abandoned the mortar and pestle and moved instead to a tall cupboard standing by the fire. "No. What I do is not magic; it is the collected wisdom of a hundred generations of women such as myself. I learned from a woman named Zophia. She learned from her mother, who learned from *her* mother. We use what comes from nature and the faith, but we do not try to manipulate either the natural or the spiritual world."

Catrin watched, fascinated, as Niada opened the doors of the cupboard and revealed dozens of vials, jars and urns, each with a label attached with twine. "And magicians do?" she asked.

"Yes, in different ways." She took out a glass bottle and carefully tipped something that looked like tiny white and purple blossoms into a linen pouch. "Some work with celestial magic, taking meaning from star charts and constellations.

Some work with protective magic, making charms and amulets."

"There is someone in London now doing that sort of protective magic," Catrin said. "He cured blindness with the Host, protected animals with holy candles, tried to hold a nocturnal vigil, and uses the *agnus dei* to make people believe they can live without regret."

Niada tied the pouch tightly with a piece of twine, and threaded a long piece of thin black leather through the loops. "He's benevolent, then." She set the pouch on the table and returned to the cupboard to retrieve a small wooden box. "Probably a soothsayer who clings to the old ways."

"Benevolent, he is not," Lord Heatherleigh said, his wary gaze still fixed on the cat. "He's also using your prophecy as a lesson-book for murder. First Mistress Mathilda was killed and placed on an altar. Then Lord Winchester was attacked, and when he started to recover Lady Ingolde was killed by a curse."

Catrin sighed. "She was poisoned, Lord Heatherleigh."

"Her death began with a curse." The cat's gleaming green eyes narrowed and Heatherleigh took a nervous step away from it. "You saw the wax figure yourself."

Niada set the box on the table next to the pouch. "That is ceremonial magic, and it is dangerous because it makes connections with the spirit world that are unstable and uncontrollable. It always involves sacrifice, but rarely on the part of the magician. Instead, the magician mutilates innocents, kills helpless animals such as cats or chickens, or draws blood from the unwilling. They use such sacrifices to conjure spirits, trap familiars in items such as rings or amulets, and create wax figures to concentrate evil and help destroy the people portrayed."

"Could a magician be both benevolent and evil?" Catrin asked. "Could he use both protective and ceremonial magic?"

"At first, he certainly could," Niada said. "But it requires great strength to maintain that balance, and once a magician has started to kill, it is all too easy to continue."

The cat let out a low hiss and Lord Heatherleigh jumped. "So who do you think will be next?"

"The next line in the prophecy is 'let the lions roar and the fires burn', but the lions' roars we heard have not yet led to anything, and there has been no fire," Catrin said thoughtfully. Then a sudden thought tickled her sense of humour. "Lord Heatherleigh ... isn't your first name Griffin?"

"Yes ... I was named after a family friend," Lord Heatherleigh said absently. Then he realized the significance of what he had said and went very still. "Griffins ... are half lion."

Catrin nodded solemnly. "So I've heard."

"And some say griffins pulled the chariot of the sun-god across the sky," Niada said. "That is quite a fire in which to burn."

The cat flicked its tail and Lord Heatherleigh swallowed hard. "But it's only a story. A legend. It's... not real."

"No, it's not. To us, at least." Catrin laced her fingers together. "But to the magician, who is looking for another sacrifice..."

Lord Heatherleigh turned pale. "I do not believe it."

"That's very brave, my lord. But still ... you should beware of what you eat," Niada said solemnly, and tapped the box. "And perhaps you should take this."

"What is it?"

"A blend of leaves, essentially. My own antidote to poison. Boil them with vinegar and drink it, and it will counter all effects." She smiled sweetly. "Cheap at sixpence."

He produced the coins at once, and Catrin hid a smile. "Thank you for your help, Niada."

"You're very welcome, my lady." She waited until Lord Heatherleigh had taken the box and hurried out the door, then held out the pouch. "Please, take it, and wear it every day."

Catrin watched the pouch twist lazily on the end of its leather tie, feeling strangely drawn to the embroidered pattern on the linen. "What is it?"

"Vervain. It will protect you."

"You think I need protection?"

"I know you need protection." Niada pressed the pouch into Catrin's hand. "You are tracking a man who does not hesitate to kill, and I wager you will find him."

Catrin hung the pouch around her neck. "Yes, I will."

CHAPTER NINETEEN

The evening meal was well underway by the time Catrin arrived back at the palace. She changed her clothes without enthusiasm and went into the privy dining chamber, where Sir William and Lord Robert were sitting on either side of the queen. Her thirst was such that she accepted a cup of wine and downed it hastily, but she did not feel particularly hungry. It was enough to find a seat next to Lucy and take a piece of bread from the basket in the centre of the table.

"Catrin!" Lucy gave her a hug, evidently relieved. "Did you learn anything new?"

"Quite a lot — including that Lord Heatherleigh is rather gullible," Catrin said. "Niada and I convinced him that he was the next victim without even making much of an effort. He went immediately from the stables to his rooms, and I hear he barred the door."

Lucy giggled. "Clever you. That might stop him from interfering for a day or two."

"Hopefully, he will hide for as many days as it takes to find our magician," Catrin said. "Has anything happened here?"

Lucy gave a little shudder. "Nothing you would like to hear while we are eating, I assure you. Did the wise woman give you any insights?"

"She mentioned that there are different types of magicians, and only one attacks the innocent," Catrin said. "It reminded me of a goodwife I met in the outer court, who claimed that a magician cursed her son. I think I will try to find her."

"Without Lord Heatherleigh?"

"Definitely without Lord Heatherleigh. I will find another escort."

"Make sure you do; it isn't safe to go into the city alone." Lucy glanced up as Lord Pierrick came in, and her face lit up in a way that made Catrin's heart ache. "But it may be slightly safer than it was; Lord Pierrick went to help capture Matthew Dyer, and has just returned."

Lord Pierrick came over and bowed low. "My lady. I return as promised."

Lucy tilted her head. "Safe, I can see. But triumphant?"

He grinned, his eyes alight with the fire of battle. "Yes. *La victoire!* We found Matthew Dyer in the stews of London and conveyed him to the Tower. He is under guard there until morning, when Sir William Cecil will question him."

"Well done," Lucy said with pleasure. "Come and take your ease, my lord. You have earned it."

Catrin went to London Stone the next morning, with one of the yeomen of the guard serving as escort. It was crowded, mostly with people just passing through, but some paused to look at the advertisements on the wooden proclamation boards surrounding the Stone. Others gazed at the Stone itself, sometimes placing a hand on the iron bands that held it upright. One person chipped a piece away, letting it fall into a wooden box that he then hastily hid in the folds of his clothing.

"Good morrow, my lady."

The voice came from close to Catrin's side, and she looked down to see the blue-eyed boy she had spoken to before. His vivacity was all the more intense that morning; even his freckles looked ready to leap into action. "Good morrow."

"Can I be of service today?"

"I believe so. But first, what is your name?"

He grinned at her, as if delighted by the question. "I'm Finn, my lady."

"Finn." Catrin retrieved some coins and held them out. "I'm looking for a lady who says that her son was cursed by a magician. Do you know anyone like that?"

"I surely do." The coins disappeared into the folds of his clothes. "Follow me, my lady."

Catrin indicated that the guard should follow them, and then did her best to keep up with Finn's slight young figure as he slipped effortlessly through the crowd. They passed Old Fullers' Hall, and soon after left the cobbled streets for a lane that was naught but rough earth. No gravel had been laid in many a month, and a trench down the middle of it was filled with stagnant water and human waste, mixed with the fat and gristle of old cuts of meat and the bloated remains of mouldy loaves of bread.

Catrin picked her way through delicately, and stopped about halfway down the street, when Finn pointed at a door that hung loosely on its hinges. "In there. I'll wait here for ye, my lady, and keep an eye out."

"Thank you," Catrin said, and stepped inside. It took a moment for her eyes to adjust to the dark, but then she could see that it was an empty space, with a staircase to the left and a hole in the stone floor to the right that stank of a cesspit. An elderly man was lying near it, his head resting on a mat of rushes that was easily two years old. It turned Catrin's stomach, and she had to raise her pomander to her nose.

"Who's there?"

The voice came from the top of the stairs. It was a woman, small and thin. Catrin knew her as soon as she saw the wild dark eyes.

"I am Lady Catrin — the lady from court. The one you asked for aid."

"And you gave it. After a fashion." The woman descended one stair, then two, with great caution. Her tiny bare feet stuck out from under the ragged hem of her skirt. "So why are you here?"

"I wish to talk about the magician. The one you said cursed your son."

A great shudder ran through her. "Come with me."

She climbed the stairs again. Catrin went to follow, but the guard held her back and ascended before her, one hand on his sword-hilt.

They emerged into a large room with several doors branching off of it. Before them sat a loom and several baskets of wool, which told them how the woman earned her living. In the corner was a fireplace, and a young boy sat in front of it, staring at flames that were not there.

The woman sat down on the floor and held out her arms. "Come here, my sweeting."

The boy rose as if controlled by strings and walked in short jerky bursts toward her. His right hand was swathed in linen wrappings, and his eyes were wide and round. He did not blink as he moved, and buried himself in her embrace with no change of expression. "My son," she said, and her voice broke. "The magician ... did this to him."

"Did what?" Catrin asked, and the boy cringed away from the sound of her voice.

"I do not know everything." The woman rocked the boy gently and pressed a kiss to his limp brown hair. "But I know he ... he cut off his thumb."

Catrin's stomach rolled and she pressed her hand hard against it. "That is why you tried to get an audience with the queen."

"Yes; I wanted the magician caught. Stopped."

"So do I," Catrin said, and had never meant it more. "I will find this evil man. One way or another. I promise you."

"Thank you," the woman murmured.

Catrin knelt down in front of them, where she could see one of the boy's big brown eyes peeking at her from under his mother's arm. "Hello. I'm Lady Catrin. Can I ask you a few questions?" He stared at her for a minute, then gave a small nod. "Do you know a lady named Mathilda?" A blink was his only response, but she decided that meant 'no'. "Do you know a tall lady in a green dress?" Another blink. "How about a man named Thomas? Thomas Starlyn."

The boy immediately burst into tears. "Thomas not my friend anymore."

Catrin's heart skipped a beat. "Why not?"

"We went to see big magician," the boy wept. "And magician caught me — kept me."

The woman rocked him gently and tears flowed free down her cheeks. "He was gone for three days."

Catrin's heart ached. "Do you know where he kept you, sweeting?"

"No," he sobbed. "I was with dolls — lots of dolls — all white and slippery — and great big barrels. And it smelled like pee all the time."

"Were there any drawings of lambs?"

"No … but I saw sheep once. Big sheep dancing at a fair."

The poor child must have had a nightmare. "Did Thomas stay with you?"

180

"Sometimes." He sniffed back his tears. "He said bezzen not like what the magician was doing."

"Bezzen?" She had to think about that for a minute. "Do you mean brethren?"

He nodded and buried his face in his mother's chest. "The magician shouted at him. Told Thomas that he would burn the whole house if Thomas told anyone."

"How did you get away?"

"Thomas took me away, after…" He started to cry again and the woman pointed silently at the boy's mutilated hand.

"After that," she said, and hopeless fury burned in her eyes. "Thomas brought him home and told me about the magician."

"Even though it was a secret," the boy said tearfully. "We weren't supposed to tell the secret."

"Some secrets need to be told, and this is definitely one of them. Thank you," Catrin told him, and set her entire purse of coins at their feet. "You have been a good, brave boy."

The final pageant for the tournament was meant to be a great spectacle, so all the ladies of the bedchamber were expected to participate. Lucy was playing one of six maidens who were defending their castle from dishonourable knights — the castle being a massive structure built on an oxcart. It had three levels and several windows, and she had been placed on the second level on the right. All she had to do was throw flowers, so she did not understand why she had to go to so many rehearsals.

That morning, it was all so boring that she could not hold back her yawns. Indeed, she had to choke one back rather hastily when she saw Lord Pierrick approaching, lest he think her rude.

He doffed his cap and bowed before her. "Good morrow, my lady."

Lucy felt her cheeks turn pink. "Good morrow, my lord."

"Might I have the great honour of your company for a walk?"

"Oh, yes, please," Lucy said, and jumped down from her small seat at the window to the level below, which led to the castle 'door'. A set of steps led from the 'door' at the side of the oxcart to the ground, but Lord Pierrick set his hands at her waist before she could use them and lifted her down. It was a bold thing to do, and made Lucy blush all the more. "My lord! I could have used the stairs."

"They did not seem safe," he said solemnly, but his eyes twinkled with mischief. "Do forgive me for taking such liberties with your person."

That thought tangled her tongue entirely. By the time she was calm enough to respond, they had left the palace behind. "Did you have a reason for suggesting this small journey, my lord?"

"Besides the pleasure of your company?"

She sent him a stern look. "Yes, besides that. Now behave yourself."

He laughed, but the amusement faded quickly. They passed under the arch into the gardens, and he glanced back to ensure they were alone before he drew the ring from his pocket. "I can now tell you what you captured in this ring."

"How do you know?"

"I have taken it to Paul's Walk several times without success. However, while we were looking for Master Dyer, I decided to show it to a woman selling herbs and bandages, and she identified it easily. It is balsaminta."

"How strange." Lucy took the ring and looked at the powder again. "Balsaminta makes women deliver their babies."

He blinked in surprise. "Truly?"

"Yes; my cousin took some when her child was late arriving, and just a few hours later she was the lighter of a healthy son."

Lord Pierrick stopped walking. "And what would happen," he asked slowly, "if you took it when the child was not yet due?"

"The same thing, I would imagine, but —" Lucy understood then, and the thought made her heart clutch in her chest. "But the baby would die."

Their eyes locked. "That is why Lady Katherine called it an evil thing," Lord Pierrick said. "Her sister was trying to make her rid herself of a child."

"Yes; and I understand why her sister wanted her to do it, too. Lady Katherine is a relation of the queen's. She cannot marry or … ally herself with a man without royal permission."

"Which she does not have?"

"Which she does not have." Lucy pressed her fingers against her lips. "That is her secret. She truly has been plotting against the queen."

"Though not in the way the queen suspected." Lord Pierrick took her arm again. "We must tell Her Majesty."

"Yes; if she discovered that we knew and did not tell her…" Lucy turned back to the palace. "Let us go at once."

CHAPTER TWENTY

Catrin found her pace increasing as she approached the queen's chamber. A sense of unease was building within her, as if she could see clouds gathering on the horizon and knew there was no way to stop the storm.

Lord Robert was there when she went in, which was reassuring, as was the familiar solid, sensible presence of Sir William Cecil. There were several ladies scattered about, and the queen herself was there, playing the virginals so her back was to the room.

The queen glanced over her shoulder as Catrin lowered herself to her knees, and abruptly the music stopped. "You look pale, my talisman. Are you quite well?"

"I have much to tell you, Your Majesty."

The queen turned away from the keys and folded her hands in her lap. "Speak."

"I now know why Thomas Starlyn thought he needed to do penance," Catrin said, and told the story of the poor boy and his missing thumb. "His role in the theft of that child must have smote his conscience terribly."

The queen rose, pale and trembling. "And so it should. Have that woman cared for, Sir William."

Sir William nodded to a clerk, who made a note. "Yes, Your Majesty."

"Why didn't the mother tell anyone about this?" Lady Mary Sidney asked. "Then all of this evil might have been avoided."

"She came twice to the palace, but was thwarted each time," Catrin said. "I do not know why she did not tell her parish officials."

"Fear, I wager," Lord Robert said quietly. "I would be living in terror if I were she."

"Yes, so would I," Catrin said. "And to save us all from living that nightmare, I intend to search for more examples of the *agnus dei*."

"Was the child marked with the lamb symbol?" Sir William asked.

"No, my lord; the magician used him, but did not claim him. I intend to look for people the magician has claimed, and try to convince them to tell us who and where he is."

"Perhaps you can begin with Master Dyer," Sir William said. "When I spoke to him at the Tower this morning, I noticed an *agnus dei* around his neck — an old one, well worn."

Catrin caught her breath. "Did he tell you anything?"

"He would not speak, except to ask for the presence of a certain Maurice Webb."

"Who is that?"

"As yet, we do not know. My men are searching London for him, and I am sure they will succeed," Sir William said. "But while we wait, I suggest you speak to Master Dyer. You may be able to persuade him to tell us what he knows, and I would prefer not to resort to the rack."

"I will speak to him, and I will do my utmost to ensure he speaks back," Catrin said. "He may be our only chance to find the magician."

"Indeed," Lord Robert said wryly. "The next line in the prophecy refers to Death crossing the waters, and since I have not seen that name on any passenger manifests lately, it seems we cannot yet ask him to help."

The queen smiled at the image. "Nor can we trust the falcons. In the last line, they are said to rise. Perhaps I should put them all under guard while we wait, to stop such a rebellion before it starts."

"Yes, indeed you should. Guard every last one," Lord Robert said solemnly. "Clip those tiny wings."

That made her laugh, but Catrin could not appreciate the jest. A sound had come to her ears that spoke of violence, and she turned her head so she could identify it. "Someone is coming — and they are moving quickly."

Lord Robert shifted closer to the queen and set a hand on his sword-hilt, and at the door the guards straightened. They moved to stop the two people who burst in, but saw at the last minute that it was Lucy and Lord Pierrick and fell uneasily back.

"Your Majesty," Lucy said, and fell to her knees beside Catrin, breathing hard. "We have something we must tell you right away."

Lord Pierrick knelt by her side. "And, if I may be so bold, it is something best heard by as few ears as possible."

"Lord Robert, Sir William, and Lady Catrin may stay," the queen said, and the ladies at her feet immediately got up and moved away. "Now speak."

Lucy swallowed hard. "We believe that Lady Katherine Grey is pregnant, Your Majesty."

"That is why she and her sister have been behaving so strangely," Lord Pierrick added.

The queen's face went white, then flushed an angry red. "I knew they were against me! I knew they would betray me! Damn them both to hell!"

Lord Robert sank to his knees. "Your Majesty, I beg you —"

She spun around and strode toward them at such speed that her skirts spread wide like wings. "Do not plead for them, Robin! It is your mercy that has kept them free this long — but no more! Sir William, have them dragged to the Tower in chains!"

Lucy blanched, and even as Catrin was reaching for her hand to soothe her Lord Pierrick did the same. "Your Majesty, if I may?" he said. "Perhaps it would be best not to let them know that you are aware of this."

"Nay, indeed! They will know — they will know the cost of incurring our anger!"

"At what cost for your reign?" Sir William asked quietly. "We might learn much if we observe the Grey sisters and those who interact with them over the next few months."

The queen stopped abruptly and started squeezing her hands together. She said nothing for a long moment, but then nodded abruptly. "We must learn who else is involved. Lucy, who else knows of this pregnancy?"

Lucy's small frame started to tremble. "As far as we know, no one but Lady Mary Grey, Your Majesty. She is protecting her sister, and tried to get rid of the child using balsaminta."

Catrin straightened. "Did she steal the balsaminta from the ladies' chamber?"

"Yes, but I found it and hid it in a ring so it could be identified." Lucy sent her a sharp glance. "How did you know?"

"I will tell you anon," Catrin murmured, for the queen was raging once again. She spun in a furious half-circle and swore at the ceiling above them, then fixed her gaze on Lucy once more.

"Who is the father?"

"We do not know, Your Majesty."

"I will find him," Lord Robert said grimly.

"Then I will wait to punish them." The queen clenched her fists and drew in several deep breaths. "But I tell you now, that child will be born in the Tower and raised a bastard."

Sir William nodded. "And so it should be, Your Majesty."

One would have thought that was enough excitement for one day. Lucy settled into a window-seat with a book, and even Catrin was looking forward to an afternoon spent in quiet industry amongst the queen's ladies. But it was not to be. She had hemmed no more than a handsbreadth of the pillowcase assigned to her by Mistress Ashley when a page boy came in bearing a letter on a silver platter. She considered ignoring it, but changed her mind when she saw the seal.

Baron Wicke had answered at last.

She opened it quickly, hoping that the letter might solve at least one of the puzzles that pained her: namely, why Lord Winchester considered Margery Roos his one regret. She found only a few sentences, written in a shaky hand with thin ink.

To Catrin, Countess of Ashbourne, his lordship Baron Wicke sends greetings.

I was much surprised to receive your letter, and more surprised still to read that you suspected Margery Roos of lewd behaviour before she reached her majority. I can assure you that this was not the case. She married my father in 1528 and had two sons, the eldest of which inherited my father's title. I, as the younger son, inherited her title.

She has no other children, either by the nobleman of the court you mentioned or by anyone else. Indeed, she claims that said nobleman helped and protected her, and she does not like hearing his name used in such a dishonourable fashion.

I would thank you not to share your unfounded suspicions.

Your humble servant, John, Baron Wicke

Hmm. Lady Margery's confirmation of Lord Winchester's honourable behaviour suggested that he was not the father of her bastard child, but it did not convince Catrin that the child never existed. Who else would know about it? Who else could she ask? She still suspected Lord Ersfield knew more than he had said, but he was in the country and she did not have time to make the journey. Lord Winchester knew, of course. But his health was still delicate, and his son Lord St John still ferociously guarded his sickroom. She would have difficulty gaining access, but it was not impossible. She was sure she could convince them both that she needed to know.

She folded the letter and stored it in her purse, just as Sir William Cecil came hurrying in. He bent low beside the queen and whispered in her ear, and she drew in a sharp breath. "We have need of you, Lady Catrin."

Catrin set the pillowcase aside and started to go to the queen, but Sir William beckoned urgently to her and hurried out of the room again. Catrin altered her path to follow him instead, and found Lord Robert outside, fastening his cloak around his throat. "We must go to the Tower," he said. "The keepers have found something."

She went with him at once, and they travelled by water-ferry the short distance between the palace and the Tower. Lord Robert requested that they be left at the dock just past St Martin's Tower, so they had to go around several outbuildings and through the bulwark gate. That led them to the west entrance and the Lion Tower, where much of the Tower of London's menagerie was housed.

"They found him when they went to give the beasts their afternoon meal," Lord Robert said, as they climbed the stairs.

"Found who?" Catrin asked, but they reached the top before he could answer. They were in the section that looked down on the lion pit, and below them three lions were pacing back and forth on the straw; one male, with his massive shaggy mane, and two females. All three had blood caked on their muzzles.

Beside them on the platform, three men in royal livery stood next to a ladder, looking down into the pit. The senior man saw Lord Robert first and bowed awkwardly, as if he didn't have complete control of his limbs. "Lord Robert — it is good of you to come," he said. "I do not — we do not — know quite what to do."

"It seems to me you are doing exactly what you should, lieutenant," Lord Robert said. "Retrieving the body."

The lieutenant straightened shakily. "Yes, that must come first."

Catrin returned her gaze to the pit, which was ruthlessly lit in every corner by the afternoon sun. Two men were down there, holding massive shields made of heavy wood. They advanced toward the lions, making soothing sounds as they crowded them away from the corner filled with a raw red pile of flesh that she initially thought was a dead pig. Only when a third man descended into the pit and turned it over did she realize it was the remains of a man. Deep slices had torn open his abdomen, and his neck was nothing but a bloody pulp. His eyes, though — his eyes were open, staring sightlessly up at them.

"It is Matthew Dyer, the prisoner," the lieutenant said blankly. "I don't know how he ended up ... down there."

One of the men gagged, and even Catrin had a moment of light-headedness. Only Lord Robert stayed steady, watching without comment as the third man wrapped the remains in a length of burlap and attached a length of rope to each end. "When was he last seen in his cell?"

The third man threw the ends of the rope upward, and the two men with the lieutenant caught them and started hauling it up. The lieutenant made a gurgling sound in this throat, as if he was trying hard to hold onto the contents of his stomach. "Right after Sir William spoke to him."

"That does not leave much time unaccounted for," Lord Robert murmured.

The lieutenant didn't seem able to answer, and Catrin did not blame him. It was obscene, the way that burlap bundle swayed and bumped against the stone, and the smell of blood soon became overwhelming. Catrin lifted her pomander to her nose and gave in to the urge to turn away. Which was why she saw a man in a friar's smock rushing across the drawbridge.

"Please do excuse me," Catrin said, and hurried back to the stairs. She was over the drawbridge just in time to see the man pass by the Bloody Tower. The sun shone on his white hair, telling her he was elderly, but he moved remarkably quickly for a man of his age. He seemed completely determined to reach the opposite end of the Tower from the gate where he had entered.

Catrin quickened her pace to keep up with him and he stopped short, so quickly that his shoes scraped in the gravel. He threw a glance over his shoulder and Catrin jumped backward, flattening herself against the wall. She was regrettably sure that she had not moved quickly enough, and even more sure that the dark red of her gown showed nicely against the stone of the inner walls. So when she finally dared to tilt her head forward far enough to see the path, she was not surprised that her quarry had disappeared. The only question was — where? She would have to search further, but not right then.

First, she needed to know what happened to Matthew Dyer.

She retraced her steps back to the Lion Tower, and found all three of the men back on the walkway and the lions moving restlessly about beneath them. Lord Robert was holding a velvet pouch in one hand — gingerly, for it was spattered with blood. "It is Master Dyer's purse," he said. "It was far away from the body; I thought he may have had the presence of mind to fling it away when he was attacked."

"So you assume there is something of importance in it."

"I hope, rather than assume," he said dryly, and opened the drawstring. He first withdrew a pouch full of coins, and a string of beads. And finally, a few sprigs of hawthorn.

Catrin took it from Lord Robert's hand. "Our magician claimed Master Dyer; the *agnus dei* he wore shows that. And yet he killed him, and left this symbol of his evil behind."

"What if he did not come here intending to kill Master Dyer?" Lord Robert asked. "Perhaps the hawthorn was for someone else."

Catrin considered that, and a sudden thought made her tighten her grip on the sprigs in her hand. Several blossoms drifted to the ground. "Where are the men who were supposed to be guarding Master Dyer?"

"I have not seen them yet," the lieutenant confessed, and his gaze rested on the bloodied bundle at his feet. "This ... this manner of death has ... distracted us all."

Catrin handed the hawthorn back to Lord Robert. "Perhaps this was meant for them."

Lord Robert dropped the items back into the pouch, his face bleak. "Lieutenant, you had better take us to Dyer's cell right away. There might be more bodies to bury."

The lieutenant led them to the cell where Dyer had been kept, and it was a path through so many walkways and tunnels that Catrin knew she could never remember how to get back to it. All the cells they passed were empty, which was strangely disconcerting. Door after door hung open, and not a single human soul was about.

Finally, at the end of a long arched corridor, the lieutenant turned to the left. A cell had been carved out of the stone wall and an iron gate stretched across it. Unlike all the others, it was firmly closed. And, also unlike the others, there were two chairs outside it, with a table between, sitting below a barred window.

Two men were sprawled on the stone floor inside the cell, both wearing livery. There were no visible injuries to their bodies, and no blood around them. Also, they were making a strange sound … a whistling, growling sound. Catrin recognized it in an instant, and had to press a hand to her mouth to hold back a cry of amusement.

They were snoring.

"Hampson! O'Connor!" The lieutenant roared their names and hauled on the cell door, which was firmly locked. "Wake up, sirrah! You blackguards! Rouse yourselves!"

They stirred, blinking. "Lieutenant?" one of them mumbled. "Why you'n m'house?"

The lieutenant tore a ring of keys from his belt and unlocked the door, flinging it open as if it was made of gossamer rather than cast iron. He dived on them both, lifting them up by their sword-belts and flinging them out of the cell with such ferocity that they both stumbled and cracked their heads on the opposite wall.

"Ow," O'Connor mumbled, rubbing his pate.

"Why'd you do that?" Hampson asked, but he was rapidly growing more alert. His eyes swung from the empty cell to the window to the group standing around, horror growing with every second. "God's heart — what's happened?"

"Dyer is dead," the lieutenant said through clenched teeth. "And he escaped on _your_ watch."

"No, he didn'," O'Connor said. "The magician freed him."

The lieutenant drew in breath to shout some more, but Lord Robert stopped him. "We have heard much about this magician," he said. "What did he look like?"

"Huge," O'Connor said, just as Hampson said, "Skinny." They looked at each other in confusion and Catrin hid a smile.

"Perhaps you should start at the beginning," she said. "When did you last see Master Dyer?"

"When we brought him back from the room where Sir William was talkin' to him," O'Connor said. "We locked 'im up and sat down, and then one of the boys brought some bread from me wife."

The lieutenant sputtered. "Your wife sends you food when you're on duty?"

"Sometimes," O'Connor said. "If she knows we won't be free to go get our mess."

"So we ate the bread," Hampson said, and indicated an empty tin plate on the table between the chairs. "And then, all of a sudden, someone flew in that window."

"Don' know how," O'Connor said, and tested one of the bars dubiously. "But I saw it with me own eyes. A man with a great black robe and grey wings flew in and held out his hand."

"And then my keys rose up from my belt and floated toward him," Hampson said. "It was like he was calling them. I tried to take them back but they darted out of the way of my fingers, like they were alive. He caught them and used them on the cell door, and Dyer walked out. He said something about killing us, but the magician said it wasn't necessary."

"Then he put us into the cell without touching us," O'Connor said. "Tongues of fire came out of his fingers and wrapped around me, pulling me into the cell."

"No, it wasn't fire," Hampson said. "It was water. Ribbons of water, all around me from my neck to my ankles. I had to tiptoe into the cell; I couldn't move my legs."

"And that's all I can recall, my lords," O'Connor said, and leaned back in his chair.

For a few seconds there was silence — a blank, confused silence. And then the lieutenant started to bellow again.

"You pair of churls! Do you really expect me to believe —"

"I think it may be true," Catrin said quietly. Lord Robert and the lieutenant stared at her in astonishment, and she crossed the room to take up the tin plate. Seeds were scattered liberally across it. "Or, true to them at least."

"Are you sure?" Lord Robert asked. "It seems the sort of fancy to arise from a few too many tankards."

"We drink no tankards on duty," Hampson said indignantly. "We would never."

"Never," O'Connor agreed, and put a hand to his head. "But me 'ead is spinnin', I gotta say."

"I suspect another form of poison, not alcohol," Catrin said. "Lieutenant, may I request a small clean vessel to collect these seeds in?"

"Yes, my lady," the lieutenant said, and started down the corridor.

"Prithee be quick about it, goodman," Lord Robert said. "We must return to the palace as soon as possible."

"Yes, but we have one more task before we go," Catrin said, and sent him a winsome smile. "We have to find a friar."

CHAPTER TWENTY-ONE

The lieutenant's presence gave them access to the buildings under the bell tower and the long wooden building where Catrin had lost sight of the man in the friar's robe, but he seemed reluctant to take them there. He moved more and more slowly as they passed St Thomas' Tower, and jumped at the sound of moaning emanating from one of the cells. Catrin glanced into the room and immediately understood why the sound made him nervous.

There was no one in the cell.

"Just one of the Tower spectres," Lord Robert said dismissively, and followed Catrin down the path that led to the queen's gallery. "Are you sure this is where he was going, Lady Catrin?"

"As sure as I can be," Catrin said. She understood his scepticism; the gallery was a strange place for anyone to go, for everyone knew that the queen was not fond of the Tower and rarely visited it. That meant that the queen's gallery had been essentially out of use for years.

It was a plain building, made of flat stone with no windows on the ground floor. The door was padlocked, but the lock itself hung open; Lord Robert unhooked it and tossed it aside, and then stepped in ahead of Catrin with one hand on his sword-hilt.

The air inside was heavy with dust, and the place smelled of old linen and weathered wood. A squeak and a scurry told Catrin that they had startled a mouse, but she didn't see it. Her eyes were riveted on the white-draped figures all around the room. They were slim and narrow, and as tall as she was.

"I have seen these before." Catrin reached out to one, but did not dare touch. "I thought they were people."

"Where did you see them?" Lord Robert asked.

"On a barge that seemed to move without rowers. The maids called it the ghost ship."

Lord Robert scowled. "I grow weary of such fantastical tales," he said, and pulled off the cloth that covered the nearest figure. To Catrin's relief, it wasn't a figure at all. It was a stone jar with a domed top, and etched into the stone was the outline of a lamb. Catrin pried the top loose on the one nearest her, and found a jumble inside. Wooden beads were mixed with more *agnus dei* pendants. They rested on a pile of rings and small vials filled with dirt.

Catrin replaced the top and opened another jar. Inside were dozens of tiny bells on leather cords, with words inscribed on them that the light was too dim to read. They looked just like the bell that Master Starlyn had been wearing on his wrist.

"They are charms … charms and amulets," she murmured, and the words seemed to hang heavy in the air. "Meant to save people from anything that might hurt them, be it fire, fever, or caterpillars in the garden."

Lord Robert pivoted on his heel and pinned the lieutenant to the wall with the ferocity of his gaze. "You must have known about this."

The lieutenant nodded miserably. "I supervised the delivery from the barge, nearly a week ago."

"Who delivered them?"

The lieutenant averted his eyes. "I don't know. They were strangers."

"Where are they going?"

"To people who need them."

"How?"

The lieutenant folded his lips as if to stop himself from speaking, but the answer came burbling out anyway when Lord Robert took one threatening step forward. "The father is supposed to come and collect them, as always. Master Dyer used to come with him to help."

"The father? What father?"

The lieutenant crumbled, sliding slowly down the wall. "Father Webb. The magician."

"Webb." Lord Robert's jaw tightened. "So you knew exactly who Master Dyer meant when he asked for Maurice Webb, and you didn't say anything."

"Father Webb is a good man — a kind man. I did not want to risk him falling foul of the queen's men."

"Too late for that, I'm afraid," Catrin said. "How do we find Father Webb?"

"Ask around at London Stone," the lieutenant whispered. "He will come if you ask for him."

They agreed that Lord Robert should stay hidden in the crowds while Catrin asked for Father Webb, for he and his men were an intimidating sight whether they intended to be or not. She asked several people milling around the Stone for Father Webb, and then asked several more who were standing by the noticeboards. About ten minutes later, a man emerged from the far side of the Stone and stood before her. He had a long beard that was the same grey as his eyes and the white hair she had noticed before. He wore a friar's smock which was worn and thin, and his face was not so much wrinkled as creased with care. He could have been anywhere from thirty to fifty. "Good afternoon, my lady. You asked for me?"

"Good afternoon, Father," Catrin said, and held out the pouch she carried. "I believe these belong to you."

He took the pouch and opened it with long thin fingers, then glanced down at the *agnus dei* discs she had placed within it. "I am only their guardian; soon enough they will be given away."

"For what purpose?"

"To help those who suffer." The grey eyes gazed steadily into hers. "Are you in need of such succour, my child?"

"Let us say that I need something else," Catrin said. "Wax figures, in the shape of —"

"I do not make such abominations," Father Webb said abruptly. "I will not have any part in curses, and I will not associate with those who do. It is dangerous dark magic."

That took her aback. "Is there someone in the city who does?"

"I think there must be," Father Webb said. "There have been evil deeds in this city of late."

"Such as pushing a boy to suicide?" Father Webb blanched and Catrin pressed her advantage. "Thomas Starlyn died here, by his own hand, out of guilt for what he had done at the behest of a magician."

His gaze veered abruptly away. "I cannot explain his guilt, nor do I know the magician."

"But you know Thomas."

"Yes … I found him." Father Webb sat wearily down on the base of the noticeboard. "And I knew him, for it was I who baptized him. And then, as he grew … he left the faith and took on other beliefs. Beliefs that took him to a manor outside the city, with people who were not his own."

Catrin glanced up at the crude drawing in the rough wood. "Did you put the carving of the lamb there?"

"Yes. I blessed him before they took him away, and put my symbol there in remembrance. I could not let him go to his grave without a blessing."

Catrin narrowed her eyes. "Did you also bless Matthew Dyer?" she asked. "Did he die by the lamb as well as the lion?"

"No!" Father Webb held up a hand, palm out. "I have done no murder."

"Matthew Dyer asked for you when he was arrested. His guards are convinced a magician set him free. I saw you at the Tower, not long after he was killed. And yet you, a self-confessed magician, deny involvement?"

"I do."

Catrin retrieved the vial of seeds she had collected at the Tower. "Do you know what these are?"

He took the vial, peered through the glass, opened the stopper and sniffed. "They are datura seeds. They make you see strange visions. Then they make you happy, and then they make you sleep." He handed back the vial. "And sometimes you never wake up."

"They were used to impair the guards outside Master Dyer's cell — to make them think the keys floated away from them and they were immobilized by tongues of fire and water. That's how the magician made it possible to get Master Dyer out of his cell and take him to the lion pit."

"I understand." She gazed at him for a long second and he smiled a patient smile. "My lady, just because I know what they are does not mean I used them."

"I'm not sure I believe you."

"You should believe me. I could never kill that boy." A new knot of people came to look at the Stone, and he drew Catrin closer to the noticeboards, out of their earshot. "Once, he and I were part of the same family. Once, he was pleased to watch me bless the amulets and charms that I make. And then he started to want more magic — stronger magic. And he began to fade away from the true faith."

Part of the same family. She understood then. It was a rosary in Master Dyer's purse, not a mere string of beads. "Was Lady Ingolde part of this family as well?"

"Yes, she was. She brought us a golden crucifix from the Heatherleigh family, which now has a place of honour on our altar." He bowed his head in fresh grief. "*Requiescat in pace,* my lady."

A cold shiver ran down Catrin's spine. "You are all of the religion of Queen Mary."

He lifted his chin. "Yes."

"So you are against the queen's religious settlement."

"Yes, but not against the queen. We are willing to live out our faith in secret, for the sake of peace."

"Who is 'we'? How many people —"

"I will not tell you that." He folded his arms, hiding the pouch between them. "I will not break the seal of the confessional."

"So you would risk a murderer escaping justice?"

"There is no one with such an evil heart among our number."

"How can you be sure?"

A faint smile eased the worry-lines around his eyes. "I know them well."

"You do not know me," Catrin said. "And yet you tell me this."

"I do not see an evil heart in you, either," Father Webb said simply. "I trust you will keep our secret."

Catrin pinched the bridge of her nose between her fingers. "I cannot promise that."

The smile strengthened. "I understand, my lady, and I believe that you will do what is right."

"What I believe is right is very different from what you believe."

"I understand that, too." Suddenly the grey eyes shone with light. "But still, I have faith."

The wind on the Thames ruffled the silk of Catrin's hood and teased a lock of hair out of place. She tucked it back absently, and the motion drew Lord Robert's gaze from the buildings downstream. "You are very quiet, my lady."

"I am facing the fact that I was wrong, my lord."

He chuckled. "It takes a strong soul to admit it, so take heart from that. What do you think you were wrong about?"

"It seems there is no one magician with a benevolent and an evil side, but two entirely different men: one who wants to help, and another who wants to harm. One who uses the *agnus dei* lamb as his signature, and one who uses hawthorn."

Lord Robert stroked his hand over his beard. "So you are assuming that Father Webb is telling the truth."

"I believe he was, yes. He seemed truly repulsed by what this other magician is doing — and he considers himself a soothsayer, not a magician. He claims to make protective charms and tell the future, with the sole aim of encouraging and supporting his flock. No image-magic, no curses, no poison."

"I wager his visions of the future predict a Catholic monarch on the throne, though, and that is a dangerous thing," Lord Robert said grimly. "Mary the Dowager Queen of France already claims that she is the legitimate heir — and not to our queen, but to Henry VIII. If she could, she would remove Elizabeth from the throne this very day."

"I doubt that Father Webb has such a political bent."

"But it is not impossible."

"It is not impossible," Catrin agreed with a sigh. "But I am more concerned with finding the other magician. I think he might be involved in what is happening at Ersfield Manor."

Lord Robert sent her a sharp glance. "What *is* happening at Ersfield Manor?"

"I do not know exactly. Lady Ingolde was the first to tell me of strange happenings there, and then Sir William Cecil confirmed it. And I myself saw an odd group of people gathering there when I last visited with Lord Heatherleigh. That makes me wonder if Lord Ersfield knows the magician – or worse, is harbouring him there."

"Indeed. Perhaps Lord Ersfield angered him, and that is why Mistress Mathilda was the first victim."

Catrin shivered. "If that is the case, it is no wonder that Lord and Lady Ersfield are so devastated by this death. Perhaps it is guilt."

"That could very well be the case." Lord Robert watched a seagull dive for a piece of bread floating in the water. "Methinks I must ask the queen to imprison the guard O'Connor."

"Why? The seeds show that they were incapacitated. The bread must have been sent by the magician, not O'Connor's wife, so he was not responsible for his actions."

"Not those actions, no. But I saw him outside the Tower, telling all and sundry that he was the victim of an evil magician who uses lions to kill men. Until now, most of the actions of this magician have been confined to court, but now … rumours could spread, and with rumours come riots."

"That is probably what the magician wants." Catrin pondered. "The first lines of the prophecy were aimed at individuals. The next lines — 'let the fires burn', 'halt the death that crosses the waters' — are not. Nor would they be as easy to contain. More people could be affected by what the magician does next than by the acts thus far."

"That is a grim thought. We must warn the queen."

Greenwich Palace rose up on their left, and a strange sound arose. It was like chanting, or shouting ... or both.

Lord Robert peered through the half-open water-door and his face tightened with anger. "It seems we are too late. There is a crowd in the outer court."

"Doing what?"

"God knows." Lord Robert placed some coins on the wooden plank he sat on. "Take us to the water-steps, goodman, we do not have time to go all the way to the landing stage."

"Yes, milord," the water-man muttered, and smoothly maneuvered the boat across the current. Lord Robert leapt out without waiting for him to tie up, and Catrin gathered her skirts and jumped out after him, because there was no time to behave like a delicate maiden who needed help.

They both ran down the path and darted through the water-door, and the muffled noise became clear almost at once. It was a man's voice — Lord Ersfield's voice — shouting above a crowd that was cheering and roaring in response. "A new altar, a new virgin — and my daughter died! Fell the ancient pillar — and Lord Winchester, a great and noble statesman, was attacked! But he did not die, so the green lady was the next victim. She died in agony! And today — this very day — a boy was killed by lions. And what does the prophecy say? 'Let the lions roar!' My friends, I assure you, the lions roared as they tore him apart."

"He should have been a preacher," Catrin said dryly. "He has the speaking style for it."

"He's drawn a crowd *to the palace*," Lord Robert said. "This puts the queen in great danger."

"Why aren't the guards doing something about it?"

"That is what I intend to find out," Lord Robert said, and vanished into the crowd.

Catrin pushed her way forward, jostling and being jostled, and eventually got close enough to see Lord Ersfield himself. He was standing on a mounting-block, and two of his men stood at his feet, guarding him. They watched the crowd, impassive and uncaring, as Lord Ersfield's voice rose up again.

"And despite all this death and sorrow, the prophecy is not entirely fulfilled! There are still more plagues to come. The falcon will rise, it says! Halt the death that crosses the waters, it says! What falcon? What death? We do not know — BUT SHE DOES."

The sudden roar made Catrin jump. She? Was he referring to the queen? She pushed herself forward until Lord Ersfield was right above her. His cap was askew and his hair a matted mess beneath it; he looked like he hadn't eaten or bathed in days. "Lord Ersfield! This is not seemly! Prithee come down from there."

He continued as if he hadn't even heard her. "SHE KNOWS. The witch who first spoke the prophecy. The evil sorceress who holds us all in the palm of a gnarled hand while her familiar prowls the world looking for a chance to pounce. SHE KNOWS. The queen must force her to reveal her secrets! She must imprison her while there is still time!"

Sudden anger made Catrin bold. She strode forward and swatted Lord Ersfield's knee, forcing him to look down at her. "Good my lord, you are telling tales. Speak the truth, or cease speaking." She said it loudly, so as many people as possible could hear, but Lord Ersfield merely laughed.

"The queen's slave wants me to stop speaking! She wants me to give in and allow the queen to do nothing! But I will not! I WILL NOT!"

"Lady Catrin!" It was Lord Robert, arriving with a large contingent of guards. "Remove yourself, please — neither Her Majesty nor I want to see you harmed."

"Yes, my lord," Catrin said, and immediately withdrew to the safety of a nearby doorway. There she watched as three guards swept Lord Ersfield from his perch, and several others advanced toward the crowd with menace on their faces. People scattered before them, some running to the road that led to London and others rushing for the water-door.

In no time the courtyard was empty, leaving Lord Robert alone in the vast space. His sword was out, and his face red with exertion, but still he bowed a courtly bow when Catrin stepped out of her shelter. "My lady."

"My lord." Catrin brushed some dust from her skirt. "Shall we go to the queen?"

"Aye." He sheathed the sword. "To the queen."

CHAPTER TWENTY-TWO

As Catrin and Lord Robert walked into the privy chamber, it was easy to tell that the queen was upset. Her chest rose and fell in quick short bursts over the constraints of her bodice and her dark eyes were snapping with apprehension. Her voice, however, was calm. "Well done, my lord," she said. "The threat was well handled."

Lord Robert knelt before her. "Thank you, Your Majesty."

"Where is Lord Ersfield now?"

"Held under guard, awaiting your will."

"I wish to speak to him anon. Lady Catrin, I applaud your bravery."

Catrin knelt before her. "Thank you, Your Majesty."

"I hear you have managed to explain why the guards let Master Dyer out of his cell."

"After a fashion," Catrin said, and explained about the datura seeds. "So, once again, what seemed like magic was just a poisoning under a mask."

"This magician must know herbs and medicine very well, to create such illusions," the queen said thoughtfully. "Could this Father Webb be he?"

"He recognized the seeds, but did not seem to have any deeper knowledge, Your Majesty. I am more inclined to think that we have two magicians, and one is working out of Ersfield Manor."

"Why do you think that?"

"Father Webb said that Thomas Starlyn was drawn to a group who met at a manor outside the city — a group with different beliefs. And his parents told me that he met a magician, who drew him into unsavoury activities."

The queen's hands clenched on the arms of her chair. "We need to know what is going on at Ersfield Manor."

"Yes, Your Majesty, and I believe that we have a source," Catrin said. "Lord Heatherleigh seems to understand a lot about what is going on there, but when I ask he avoids the question."

The queen's gaze took on a steely glint. "He will not avoid *my* questions. Lady Mary, prithee fetch the man from his rooms ... and impress upon him that this is not a request."

"Yes, Your Majesty."

Lady Mary Sidney glided out of the room, and Catrin sat back on her heels. "If I may speculate for a moment, Your Majesty... I think the arrest of Master Dyer greatly frightened the magician, for Master Dyer could have chosen to reveal all and led our men directly to him."

"So the magician killed him," the queen murmured. "Horrifically."

"Horrifically, yes, but logically," Catrin said. "I think all his murders are for a purpose. He may be using the prophecy to determine the time and manner of death, but I don't think he is a zealot killing merely to fulfil a prophecy."

"No, I would agree," Lord Robert said. "His actions show a clear-headedness and a level of planning that does not reflect the actions of a zealot."

"Again, well reasoned, but I do not see how it helps us stop him," the queen said, and lifted her chin when Lord Heatherleigh came in. His movements were small and cautious, and he avoided getting close to anyone. It was very unlike the way he used to stride, and Catrin felt a small twinge of guilt.

Just a small one.

"Welcome, Lord Heatherleigh," Lord Robert said dryly. "The queen has questions for you."

Lord Heatherleigh knelt down gingerly before the queen's chair. "I am willing to be of service, Your Majesty."

"Good. Then tell us what is going on at Ersfield Manor," the queen said brusquely. "And do not attempt to deny any knowledge of it; we are aware of your involvement."

Lord Heatherleigh quaked. "There is nothing going on there, Your Majesty. Nothing, I should say, of any import. It is merely a meeting of minds — intellectual exercises between men who are like brothers."

"Brothers?" Catrin said, and glanced at Lord Robert. "Do you call yourself the brethren?"

He quaked. "How did you know?"

"The mutilated boy," Catrin told the queen. "He said that Thomas told the magician that the brethren would not like what he was doing. The magician then threatened to burn the whole house down if they thwarted him."

Lord Robert rose to his feet and stood over Lord Heatherleigh, his face like thunder. "We need to know who is part of this brethren. Right now."

"I — I do not know all their names. We call each other only 'brother' and 'sister'."

The queen sent him an icy glance. "Tell us the names you do know."

Lord Heatherleigh glanced at Catrin. "As you saw, Lord Huntingdon recently joined us. And Lord and Lady Ersfield, of course. Sir Thomas Chaloner, when he is in the country."

"But not his relative, Lady Ingolde," Catrin said. "She was a member of Father Webb's flock."

Lord Heatherleigh's face suddenly suffused with colour. "Do not call them a 'flock'," he spat. "They are not sheep but wolves. Wolves! Waiting to destroy us one by one. To burn us to death, like they once did, every day."

Catrin sent the queen a wry glance. "And here I thought one could burn to death only once."

The queen's lip quirked, and Lord Robert hid a smile.

Lord Heatherleigh jumped to his feet, trembling from head to toe. "You jest — you jest! You do not see the danger! At any moment men such as Webb could invade this palace and put us all to the sword. We live a hairsbreadth from disaster every moment. Enemies are all around — waiting — itching to destroy us. Beware! Beware!"

"Enough," the queen said harshly, and the echo of her voice chased his around the corners of the chamber. "Return to your chamber, Lord Heatherleigh. We will recall you in the morning, and expect that you will have more names to share with us."

"Yes, Your Majesty," he mumbled. He pushed himself to his feet and backed away.

The queen shook her head in disbelief and turned to one of the yeomen standing nearby. "Bring Lord Ersfield to us immediately."

The man hesitated. "Your Majesty, I have heard that he is raving like a madman. I doubt you will get anything coherent out of him."

"We wish to see him all the same," the queen said. "And call the master of the revels. He must cancel the rest of the tournament; this is not a time for celebrations. Our guests may stay if they wish, but let it be known that there will be no further events."

"Yes, Your Majesty."

Catrin shifted her weight, unease rising within her, and the queen's sharp knowing gaze rested on her at once. "Fare you well, Lady Catrin?"

"Well enough, Your Majesty, but I feel there is somewhere I need to be."

The queen nodded. "You may go, my talisman."

Catrin rose to her feet. "Thank you, Your Majesty."

Catrin made her plans quickly, and gathered the necessary materials more swiftly still. Then she paused in the middle of her chamber and considered. She felt like one of the knights in the precentor's story, forcing the white and red dragons to finish their battle so the fortress would be safe. Like them, she did not know how the battle would end, but she had one advantage at least: she knew which dragon to support. It was time to act.

First things first: she needed to speak to Lord Winchester while there was still time. So she left her chamber and hurried through the corridors to his.

A hasty knock, and it swung open to reveal Lord St John, his doublet loose and his fingers stained with ink. "Lady Catrin! What are you doing here?"

"I need to speak to his lordship."

Lord St John buttoned his doublet, fumbling in his haste. "He is not well enough for visitors."

"I'm fine," came a weak voice from behind him. "Do not fuss so."

Lord St John rolled his eyes and stood aside, allowing Catrin to go in. "The doctor said —"

"The doctor is younger than my second-best hosen; what does he know?" Lord Winchester said, and held out a hand to Catrin. "One should never reject a visit from someone so beautiful, my son. Remember that when I am gone."

"You are not going anywhere, Father," Lord St John said, and cast himself somewhat wearily onto a pile of cushions on the floor. "As you said yourself, you still have work to do."

"I'm sure you do," Catrin said. "But it is about work you have already done that I need to speak to you. Your work as the Master of Wards."

Lord Winchester tensed. "What do you want to know?"

"What happened to Margery Roos."

Lord Winchester gasped, and his son rose up in instant concern. "Father — are you ill?"

"No, not at all," Lord Winchester said, but he looked dangerously pale. "Nothing happened to Margery Roos, my lady. She sued out her livery, returned to her ancestral home, married and had children. That is all."

"That is not all." Catrin was not about to be so easily dissuaded. "She became pregnant while she was still a ward, didn't she?"

"Why would you say that?"

"Her son told me that you helped and protected her."

Lord Winchester looked away. "Not enough. I did not protect her enough."

"Do you know who the father was?"

"There was no father. There was no child."

Catrin folded her arms. "I don't believe you."

"That is your choice."

"I think she had a child, and you found a family to take it in."

He gave a little jump, and his gaze darted up to hers and then away. Then he gave a long sigh. "My lady, when one is an official at court, one does what one must."

Catrin nodded. "As you said before, one must bend like the willow."

"Aye. And sometimes, a breeze with far more power than you pushes you in a direction you do not want to go, and forces you to leave a helpless sapling unprotected." He leaned his head back wearily. "I did what I could, and I will say no more."

"Your lordship, was the child —"

"No more," Lord Winchester said, and closed his eyes.

"But I need to know —"

Lord Winchester gave a weary sigh. "*No more.*"

"That is enough," Lord St John said firmly. "I'd like you to leave, Lady Catrin. Before you damage his health."

"But I —"

"Leave now, my lady." Lord St John escorted her to the door with a firm hand on her back. "And please do not return."

Catrin left the room, but turned back to face him. "I cannot promise that."

He laughed an unpleasant laugh. "Oh, yes you can," he said, and leaned down so that his nose was nearly touching hers. "Because I promise you, my lady, if your questions hurt my father in any way, there will be another death at court. Is that understood?"

"That is a dangerous thing to say in the current circumstances."

His nostrils flared. "I am a dangerous man, when necessary."

Catrin narrowed her eyes, considering. Could she be looking at the magician? Not likely, but possible. "We shall see."

Her escort of guards was waiting for her in the stable yard, with the horses saddled and lanterns ready even though the moon was nearly full. They rode as fast as they dared through the city and urged the horses to a gallop once they reached the open fields. The countryside sped by, and no one spoke until the walls of Ersfield Manor rose up before them.

Catrin reined in and slid down from her horse. "Take care of the horses while I speak to Lady Ersfield."

"Yes, my lady," one of the guards replied, and the three of them turned their mounts toward the stables. Catrin left her lantern behind and circled the ancient guard tower with only the moonlight to guide her, moving silently through the blue-black world.

The house was dark, but for a single circle of candlelight in one of the upper rooms. Catrin tried the door, hoping to enter silently, but it was locked. She had no choice but to knock, and then step back and watch as that circle of candlelight rose up, faded, and then grew stronger again, lighting up the window beside the door.

A hand set the candle in the windowsill, creating a flickering circle of light. Then the door creaked open and Lady Ersfield filled the space. Shock chased disappointment on her heavy oval face: evidently, Catrin was not the person she had hoped to see.

"Good evening, my lady," Catrin said easily, as if this was not a highly unusual time to visit. "You are about to have a visitor, methinks, and I must come in before he arrives."

Lady Ersfield cast her eyes down. "It is my husband who receives visitors, not I."

"Glad I am to hear it," Catrin said, and pushed her way inside. "Prithee send a page with some food and drink to the stables for my escort, and offer them a place to sleep."

Lady Ersfield seemed about to protest, but in the end she simply did as she was told. Shutting the door with a thump, she walked away carrying the candle with her.

Catrin moved silently to the window and waited. Slowly the dark outlines of the trees blended with the darkening sky and the light of the stars grew stronger. The pebbled path glowed in the moonlight, pristine and undisturbed, until a creeping shadow warned of the approach of a visitor.

Lady Ersfield returned in time to see it coming, and set the candle in the window with a faint whimper. Catrin retreated into the shadow of a tapestry. "Answer the knock."

Lady Ersfield whimpered again, but when the knock came she answered. She did not have the chance to speak: a harsh whisper broke the silence. "The brethren are discovered. They are in danger."

A tic started flickering beneath Lady Ersfield's left eye. "I don't care — I don't have anything to do with all that."

"Your husband is being held at Her Majesty's pleasure, so *you* must act. He is raving — at any minute he could betray us all."

"He doesn't know anything. He didn't do anything."

"It is what he might do that is of concern right now." There was a rustle of paper, and Catrin moved closer to the door. "These are for the brethren. Your pages know how to find them all; prithee, send them right away."

Lady Ersfield let out a soft moan and took the bundle. Catrin plucked it from her hand and swung the door open. She knew who would be standing there, long and thin in his green cloak with his forked beard. "Thank you, Lord Heatherleigh," she said coolly. "I wager these will prove very useful."

CHAPTER TWENTY-THREE

When morning dawned, it brought with it several of the queen's guards, a half-dozen messengers, and two of Sir William Cecil's secretaries, all prepared to unearth every secret ever kept at Ersfield Manor. Catrin met them in the great hall, a lack of sleep making her feel like she had been run over by all their horses at once. She recognized one of the secretaries from a previous adventure, so she approached him first. "Good morrow, Master Christopher. I trust you are well?"

He bowed low. "I am, thank you, Lady Ashbourne."

"Good. I suggest you begin by securing Lord Heatherleigh. He is locked in the privy chamber," she said, pointing, "and will not speak."

"Yet," Master Christopher said bleakly. "I have been told that his only chance to escape the executioner's block is to help us as much as possible."

Catrin shivered, and in her mind's eye a blade flashed in the sun as it fell. It was a vision of her father's death that she had not suffered in many months. "Let's hope it will not come to that," she said. "Did my messenger tell you about the notes I took from Lord Heatherleigh?"

"Yes; the queen wants to see them right away." He waved one of the messengers closer, a slim young lad with eyes that sparkled with excitement. "Galen will take them."

"I made a list of the names; I hope it is acceptable if I keep it," she said. "I have reason to believe that a man I wish to find is one of them."

"Yes, that is perfectly fine, my lady, but it would be a helpful start for us if I could see it."

"Of course." She retrieved the paper from her purse and handed it over. In truth, she did not need it anymore; she had already memorized the names. The Earl of Huntingdon, as they knew. Tristan Kelly, the man who had begged the queen to choose an heir during the joust. Lord Ersfield, of course. Lord St John, Lord Winchester's hostile son. The Earl of Bedford. The vicar of St Mary Overy in Bankside. And, surprisingly, one of the queen's own chaplains.

Master Christopher read the list several times, then glanced back at the others and jerked his chin in the direction of the privy chamber. "Thank you, my lady. We will start our work now, with apologies for our tardiness."

Catrin glanced out at the horizon, where the pinks and greens of a summer sunrise had only recently faded. "Tardiness?"

"Sir William wanted us to leave right after your note arrived, but we had difficulty getting out of the palace." Master Christopher rested a hand on the inkhorn strapped to his belt, as if assuring himself it was still there. "A crowd has gathered, demanding the release of Father Webb."

Catrin went dizzy for a second and had to lean against the door jamb. "Father Webb has been arrested?"

"He is in the pillory at Charing Cross. The queen and Sir William thought it might allay the fears of the populace regarding the prophecy to see a soothsayer punished." He tugged on the brim of his hat. "Thus far, it has not. And Lord Ersfield is making it worse, encouraging the rioters by shouting from the room where he is being held."

Catrin forced herself upright. "Can you continue here on your own?"

"Yes, my lady."

"Good." Catrin turned and headed for the stairs, bent on retrieving her things with all speed. "I must get to London right away."

A crowd had gathered at Charing Cross by the time Catrin arrived. Men, women and children surrounded the pillories that stood at the base of the cross, shouting abuse. Amongst them carters swore at the people blocking their path, while their horses shook their manes and whinnied with distress. The air stank of the rotten vegetables and horse dung that people flung at the three men in the pillories, and Catrin winced when an apple landed with a thump on a young man's forehead.

She knew exactly how much that would hurt.

Sickened and annoyed, she pushed her way through the crowd. At first people scowled and swore at her, but they soon noticed the jewels on her collar and hood and recognized the fine silk of a court gown. It was enough to part the crowds, and — to her relief — stop all the rubbish flying toward the pillories. She was able to approach without risk, although she had to step carefully.

Father Webb was in the centre pillory, bound at the neck and wrists and standing upright. He was covered in unidentifiable sludge, and his eyes were full of heartbreak. "My lady," he said. "Has this lesson in humility come via your hand?"

"No, and I wanted you to know that," Catrin said, and lifted a leather pouch full of water to his lips. She remembered how thirsty she had been when she had spent a whole terrible night pilloried that way. "I am on my way to the palace; I will intercede for you with the queen."

Father Webb gave a great sigh, but he drank. "I doubt it will have any effect. The crowd demands a villain when evil has been done."

Catrin took the water to one of Father Webb's companions. "I believe it is the evil yet to come that they fear," she said. "Namely, the death that comes over the waters."

"Crosses the waters," Father Webb said, and a tear trickled down his cheek. "I was told the prophecy said 'crosses the waters'."

"Yes, that is true," Catrin said, and took the water to the young man whose forehead was already swelling from the apple. "Does it matter?"

"Some think that it must refer to those who practice the old faith, because we make the sign of the cross over the Holy Water," Father Webb said wearily. "That is why we are here."

Catrin took out her handkerchief and soaked it in the cool water, then applied it to the young man's forehead. "From all I have discovered, the magician is not one of those. He is one of the 'brethren', although I am still trying to discover who and what they are."

"They are reformers," Father Webb said. "They aim to train more preachers, encourage clerical marriage, remove vestments. The more radical among them actively work to secure a Protestant heir to the throne, and groom young men to become reformist clergy."

"Thank you, Father Webb." Catrin let him drink again, her mind full of new possibilities. "That makes a great difference."

The presence chamber was full of people, but there was no music, no laughter, no games or flirting. Everyone seemed to be talking very intently to someone else, with arms waving and feet stomping. Catrin was nearly hit in the head when one gentleman gesticulated wildly, and he did not even notice, let alone apologise.

She slipped into the privy chamber and found it, too, buzzing with conversations. Most of the queen's privy council was there, including Lord Winchester himself. He was wrapped warmly in rugs and sitting on a cushioned chair, but still he participated fully in the arguments happening all around them.

The queen was speaking with the precentor, and glancing uneasily over her shoulder at three more petitioners who were waiting with scrolls in hand. She seemed relieved to see Catrin, using her appearance as an excuse to wave them all off. "Greetings, my talisman. You did well, capturing those messages."

"*You* did well, Your Majesty, allowing me to go. You guessed that Lord Heatherleigh was planning to warn those men, didn't you?"

The queen chuckled. "No, I did not guess. I read the expression on your face and understood what it meant. You are very suspicious sometimes, I have noticed."

Catrin quirked her lip. "So I have been told. But why are so many people here, Your Majesty?"

She gave a weary sigh. "They have all been listening to Ersfield, and now they are demanding immediate action. I called the precentor here to try to reason with them, but even his presence has not calmed them."

"Perhaps the precentor should try to speak with Ersfield himself, Your Majesty. He may be able to make him see the harm that his rantings are causing."

"I thought the same; after all, they are friends. They returned from exile on the continent together, and the precentor has stayed at Ersfield Manor. But alas ... it had the opposite effect. Now even the precentor thinks I should arrest the wise woman."

"Niada? Why?"

"Late last night five fishing boats suddenly caught fire, all at the same time. Three men saw them blaze up, and they are convinced that it is a sign that death is crossing the waters."

Catrin drew her fingernails down her skirt, trying to hold in her irritation. "It is far more likely that one of the fishermen left a candle burning."

"I would agree with you if it had been one boat, but five?" The queen shook her head. "People are convinced it was done by magic."

"There has to be another explanation."

"Lord Robert says that the only thing that could make five boats blaze up at once is Greek fire. Do you know what that is?"

"My stepfather told me about it once. He described it as sheets of flame that fly toward the enemy and set everything alight," Catrin said numbly. "He said it's so fast and causes such complete destruction that it's like sorcery."

"The precentor, among others, is convinced that it *is* sorcery, and the only way to stop it happening again is to arrest Niada."

"But it isn't the only way. It's the wrong way," Catrin said. "The prophecy says 'Halt the death that crosses the waters', does it not? Well, someone recently pointed out to me that 'crosses the waters' could refer to the clergy of the old church. And I have found out that the 'brethren', of which the magician is one, are reformers. They want all remnants of the old church removed from the new."

The queen's eyes narrowed. "And?"

"It seems, then, that the general population is safe. No one is at risk but priests of the old faith."

"There are several of those in the Tower," the queen said. "The former Bishop of Ely, for example. He would not stop his popish preaching."

"Perhaps you should give him additional guards, Your Majesty, at least until I have found out whether any of the brethren on this list could be behind these murders."

"Perhaps," the queen said, and called her privy councillors to join them. "Gentlemen, Lady Catrin may have come up with an explanation for our current dilemma. Please, my talisman, explain it to them."

Catrin repeated her suspicions, and felt her heart sink when the ring of faces stared at her in disbelief.

"It matters not whether the next victim is one person or many," one of them said in ringing tones. "It matters only that we must go to the source to stop these deaths."

"Yes, we need to go to the source — the magician, not the wise woman," Catrin said. "She may have spoken the prophecy, but she did not bring it about."

"She spoke the prophecy, so she must know more about its meaning," another man said, and massaged the Adam's apple bobbing about in his scrawny neck. "We must arrest and interrogate her."

"The people demand justice," a third man said. "Swift justice. They will be appeased only by the wise woman's arrest."

"It is not justice to arrest an innocent woman," Catrin said. "Niada has done nothing wrong. Indeed, she has given us information that led us in the direction of the magician."

"Direction, or misdirection?" the first man said. "There is only one way to know."

"That, at least, is true," the queen said. "We will send Lord Robert to bring the wise woman here, and we will question her ourselves."

Catrin stared at her, aghast. "Your Majesty, she has nothing to do with this! You cannot tear her from her home without reason!"

"There is reason," the scrawny man squawked. "And I myself will not be satisfied until she is safely contained."

"But —"

The queen waved the men away. "Lady Catrin, I have no choice. The magician has knowledge of herbs, just as she does. The magician dislikes the old church, as she does. People are dying all around us, in just the way she predicted they would. All of this is reason enough to put her behind bars."

"But she was helpful — and she did not hide anything. Why would a murderer help us? Why would she be so open about what she did and what she knew?"

"It could be just a clever tactic," the queen said. "Catrin, I tried to distract the crowds long enough to give you time to find the real evildoer. I gave them Father Webb and his men. But it is not enough — they are still baying for blood."

Catrin pressed her fingertips to her temples. "I beg you, Your Majesty, do not do this."

"I'm afraid that I must."

"Then please, release Father Webb and his men. There is no need for them to suffer further."

"Very well." The queen nodded toward one of the guards nearby and he immediately left the room. "They will be released right away."

"Thank you, Your Majesty." Suddenly Catrin felt so tired, so worn out, that her whole body trembled. "May I retire?"

"Yes," the queen said, but her eyes were sharp. "But you may not leave the palace — or send any messages."

Catrin nodded wearily. "I understand, Your Majesty."

CHAPTER TWENTY-FOUR

Catrin went straight to the ladies' chamber and fell into her bed without even removing her gown. She dropped immediately into sleep, and knew nothing more until a tug on her hood brought her back to full wakefulness.

Lucy was sitting next to her, her blue eyes wide with distress. "Oh, woe, I'm so sorry. I thought you would be more comfortable without it, but I didn't mean to wake you."

"All is well, dearling." Catrin sat up and stretched, keenly aware that her heart was still heavy. "Have I slept through the morning meal?"

"Aye, and through the afternoon. The evening meal fast approaches," Lucy said, and bit her lip. "I heard that they would not listen to you, and they have gone to fetch the wise woman."

"Yes, they have," Catrin said, and pushed herself from the bed. "And I fear greatly that they will hurt her, even though she has done nothing wrong."

Lucy sent her a sly look. "I told Lord Pierrick to be watchful. I suspected that you would have a plan for her rescue."

Catrin crossed to a basin of clean washing-water and used a cloth to draw the cool liquid over her face. "Why did you suspect that?"

"Because, as you always say, you prefer to see the executioner's axe land on the right neck," Lucy said. "And hers is not the right neck."

"That is very true, but I am not sure what I can do to save her," Catrin said. "I already advocated for her with the queen, and all that I achieved was an order not to try to contact her."

Lucy knit her brow. "That will make things difficult."

"It certainly will. We may have to use some of the magician's datura seeds to convince the guards that she is still in her cell, and spirit her away."

That made Lucy giggle. "Do we have enough?"

"I am not sure — and the only one who can tell me is the wise woman herself."

"I'm sure we can find someone else who knows about herbs and potions." Her face lit up. "Oh - we can find the person who prepared the balsaminta! Remember? Lady Mary stole it from one of the ladies for her sister. We can find out who Lady Mary stole it from and convince her to tell us where she got it."

Catrin hid a smile. "That lady got it from Niada."

Lucy blinked. "Truly? Was someone here —" She lowered her voice and her eyes widened with horror — "in need of it?"

Catrin chuckled. "No, Niada gave it to *me*. She said that it would help us find the truth … and so it did, after a fashion. I understood when I realized the vial was missing."

Lucy set her hands on her hips. "So all that time you knew what the Grey sisters were hiding and you didn't tell me? You just let me fumble about and did not even give me a hint?"

"I gave you something better than a hint, my dearling," Catrin said, and went over to rest a hand on her friend's shoulder. "I gave you time with your betrothed."

"I could have had time with Lord Pierrick *without* the threat of royal wrath, had you just told me," Lucy pointed out, and her face contorted into a childlike scowl. "Ooh, I'm angry. I have half a mind to run you through with a pin."

"And I would deserve such a punishment," Catrin said solemnly. "I would also deserve to hear every last detail of your courtship."

"It is not a courtship," Lucy said. "We are already betrothed."

"True." Catrin laced her fingers together demurely. "Have you grown to like him?"

Lucy blushed. "Aye, I like him well. But it still isn't a courtship."

A sudden rapid knocking nearly drowned the last word and made them both jump. Catrin went to answer, and Lord Pierrick himself tumbled inside, a riding whip in his hand and his cap knocked sideways. "*Venez — Venez aussi vite que vous pourrez. Ici — il y a des ennuis — venez!*"

"There's trouble — we have to go," Catrin said, although she knew Lucy understood French. Indeed, she was already in motion. They ran out of the room together, and Lord Pierrick managed to find his English again as they flew down the stairs.

"I saw Lord Robert arrive with a woman on his horse, and then I saw Lord Ersfield leave the palace — with his men."

"I thought he was locked up!" Lucy cried.

"He was, but no longer. He crossed the courtyard toward Lord Robert, and then I heard a shriek. A – a scream."

"God save us all," Catrin said, and was the first to burst out of the palace. There, at the edge of the outer courtyard, a circle of men stood like sentinels around a knot of people struggling at their centre. Lord Robert, a cut on his forehead dripping blood into his eye, was fighting to get through, but the sentinels would not move.

Catrin was soon close enough to see Niada at the centre of the knot. She looked tiny in the hands of the two men that held her down, but she fought and screamed with all the strength that was in her. Lord Ersfield hovered beside her, a needle in one hand and a small glass vial in the other. He was stabbing and scratching at her face and arms, drawing beads of blood to the surface which he was trying to collect in the vial.

"Stop!" Catrin cried, and flung herself at the nearest sentinel. Taken off guard, he staggered back, leaving enough room for Catrin to squeeze through and dive on Lord Ersfield. He dropped the needle under the force of her assault, and nearly lost the vial.

He let out a roar and drew his sword, raising it high as if to strike Catrin in the head. Lord Pierrick leaped in front of him and lashed out with the riding-whip. It caught Lord Ersfield's fingers and he dropped the sword with a shout of surprise. Another man drew his sword and slashed at Lord Pierrick, who leapt aside just in time. Lucy ran toward him, crying his name, and he swept his arm wide to keep her away from the man's second stroke.

"Lucy — no — stand back!" he cried and drew his own sword. The two blades clashed and Lucy let out a cry of mingled fury and fear before she ran. Lord Ersfield circled around behind Lord Pierrick, drawing a dagger from his belt. Lord Robert fell on him, and the sound of clashing steel filled the air.

Catrin drew her *stiletto* from its hidden sheath and used it to stab at the men who held Niada down. One let go with an oath and clutched a bleeding hand to his chest; the other fell to a slice across the forehead. Niada fell hard to the ground, and Catrin pulled her out of the fray. "Niada — Niada — have they hurt you?"

Niada's only answer was a moan, and the sound alerted one of the men watching Lord Pierrick fight. "She's free!" he cried. "Grab her, lads!"

Catrin hauled Niada to her feet. "We have to run!"

"I cannot —"

"*Run!*"

Niada gathered her feet under her and they ran, heads down, dodging the sentinels, ducking under blades while Catrin deflected blows with her *stiletto*. She had no time to see where she was going — all was legs and arms and furious faces — and then a wooden door rose up in front of her. She pulled it open and dived through, dragging Niada with her. Her foot caught on something — she couldn't see what — and she tumbled forward, landing hard in water. Deep water. Water with a current that tugged at her feet, pulling her downward.

They were in the Thames. Oh, she was foolish. How could she have forgotten how close the river lay on the other side of the water-door? They had unbalanced in an instant and were now at the mercy of the thick, heavy waters. She was spun around, sucked downward, pushed up and out and tossed aside, only to be sucked down again. It was all she could do to hold fast to Niada's hand and gasp for air at every opportunity.

And then the tumbling current flung her upward and she landed hard against something wooden. She grasped it with her free hand and pulled herself up enough to draw in air, precious air. But Niada did not break the surface; her weight pulled Catrin down, and the current sucked at her heavy gown. She clung desperately to the wood, but knew full well she could not hold on for long.

"What is this? Does the Thames have mermaids now?"

She opened stinging eyes to see a man leaning over the side of a boat — oh, thank God, it was a boat she was holding onto. "Help — please help us."

"Or Triton will smite me, eh?" The lightness of his tone didn't match his grip as he grabbed her around the waist and hauled her upward. Niada's head broke the surface, her grey hair spreading out like seaweed, and the man let out a grunt and an oath. "Can't lift you both — come on, woman, get hold of the side."

"Niada," Catrin said, and squeezed her hand. "Please, wake up."

She stirred, opened her eyes, and her free hand rose up from the water and grasped the side of the boat with surprising strength. "That's it," the man said. "Now kick."

Catrin kicked, and somehow the movement tumbled her forward and into the boat. The man then turned to Niada. She was barely hanging on, and did not have the strength to kick, but she was so thin that he could lift her without aid. He set her down gently but still the boat rocked, and Niada groaned in pain. "Something's broken, I'd say," the man said. "Doesn't look good."

"It looks better than it did a moment ago," Catrin said, and drew in deep grateful breaths of air. "Thank you … thank you so much."

The man looked from Niada's ragged robes to Catrin's court gown, with its jewels still bravely shining on the neckline. "I don't think I want to know who you are," he said. "But since you can't stay here forever, where would you like to go?"

Catrin struggled to sit up, but her sodden gown was a deadweight and every limb was weak from the struggle. "We need somewhere safe. Safe and hidden," she murmured. "There are people who want to harm this lady."

The man's eyes narrowed. "Have you broken the law?"

"No, we haven't — that is why I took her away," Catrin said. "Please — do you know where we could go?"

He grasped hold of the oars and started to row, and the sound of the splashing water made her shudder. "I'll take you to Venours Wharf; if you go into the city from there you'll find inns all about."

It was getting dark, and Catrin was shivering from the cold. Niada lay insensible, and there was no telling whether she could walk. "Goodman, I beg you — could you…?"

"No, I could not. I want no part of this."

Catrin detached a pearl from the limp remains of her hood and held it out. "Please?"

He looked at the gleaming teardrop in her hand. "Very well … I will help."

Lucy curled up in a foetal position on the ground, her hands clasped tight over her head. Sounds of battle raged all around her — feet stomping, voicing shouting, that horrible scrape and clash of steel striking steel. And then, all went quiet. She whimpered as someone tried to take hold of her shoulders, and a kind voice spoke above her. "It's all over, little one, it's all over."

She recognized the voice as Lord Robert's, and that gave her the courage to lift her head and look around. The dim outlines of bodies were scattered all around them in the evening gloom. Some were stirring and moaning, others lying very still. There seemed to be rather a lot of blood.

"What happened?"

Lord Robert helped her to her feet. "Lord Ersfield ran away — with most of his men bleating like sheep behind him. I cannot find Lady Catrin or Niada — have you seen them?"

"No, I —" A horrible thought crossed her mind and she spun from side to side, searching. "Lord Pierrick? Lord Pierrick?"

One of the bodies on the ground stirred, and a hand lifted. Lucy dashed over and dropped to her knees beside him. She heard her skirt rip on the rough cobblestones and did not care. There was blood on his doublet — it covered his left arm and shoulder. Blood, glistening in the rising moon. "Oh, woe! Lord Pierrick — you're hurt!"

"Lady Lucy," he murmured, and let go of the sword he still held in his right hand so he could press his palm to her cheek. "Are you well?"

"Yes, yes — but you — you're bleeding!"

"Do not fret, my lady. Surgeons are on their way," Lord Robert said, and knelt down near Lord Pierrick's other side. "They will help."

"I saw … Lady Catrin," Lord Pierrick mumbled, and moved his chin in the direction of the water-door. "In the Thames."

Lord Robert winced. "With Niada?"

"I think … yes."

Lord Robert rose to his feet. "We will have to start a search at once; we have little time. The river tends to claim those so unlucky as to end up in its depths."

He walked away, and Lucy started to cry. She couldn't help it. Men were dead and bleeding everywhere — Lord Ersfield was free to spread his evil — Catrin might have drowned — Pierrick might die. Oh, woe, Pierrick might die. And even as she faced that thought, she knew that he had become precious to her. He was no longer just her betrothed … he was her beloved. "Please … please … my lord, you must recover. I cannot bear to lose you."

"Be comforted, my lady." Lord Pierrick took her hand in his. "I will fight for you."

CHAPTER TWENTY-FIVE

The dream — the nightmare — had become real. London was the maze of corkscrew lanes and narrow streets, and beneath Catrin's feet were cobblestones — cobblestones coated in mud that smelled of dung and rot. Lanterns offered circles of light, showing the dim outline of windows, rats feeding and cats chasing them, women with hopeless eyes displaying their chests to the dark figure that walked before them.

Niada was the weight at her side, and she had one arm around Catrin's neck. She could not put one foot on the ground, and the other seemed almost as badly swollen and twisted. But she said nothing, even though the pain had blanched her face whiter than bleached linen. She just hopped along, her clear blue eyes fixed on the ground before them.

The water-man moved with purpose, and it took all of Catrin's strength to follow him. Suddenly he ducked down a lane so narrow his shoulders brushed the walls, and paused beneath a wooden sign that creaked in every draught of air. It seemed to have faded blocks of white and black on it, but she couldn't be sure.

A woman came to the door when he knocked, and he murmured with her a moment before he stood back and waved them in. "That's all I can do," he said. "And I'll not tell a soul that I saw you — for my sake as well as yours."

"Thank you," Niada whispered. "And may God bless you."

Catrin nodded her thanks, for she did not have the breath for anything more, and followed the woman inside. The place smelled of lye, as if it had recently been cleaned, but underneath that was the sour smell of damp. Catrin thought briefly of her pomander, but had not the will to lift it to her nose. Nor would it do much good if she had; rose petals soaked in Thames water were not likely to be aromatic.

Without a word, the woman took a lantern from a small shelf and led them deeper into the house. The rush mats on the floor were worn but clean, and the plaster walls were white and free from dust. They passed several rooms where Catrin heard girlish giggling behind the closed door, and it made her wonder whether her reputation would be forever ruined if she was found there.

The woman stopped at the last door, which hung open. Inside was a small bed and large flat chest, with a basin of water and several towels. "I cannot provide food, and if the guards come searching I will tell them where you are at once," she said flatly. "I will not risk my livelihood for you."

"We understand, and we will cause no trouble," Catrin said, and detached another pearl from her hood. "Thank you."

The woman took the pearl and left. Catrin helped Niada to the bed, and she sank down into it and was immediately unconscious. She did not move while Catrin removed her sodden clothes and used a towel to clean her many cuts and scrapes.

Catrin tore a length of linen into strips and wound them tight around Niada's ankles, lifting them up to help the swelling, praying the entire time that there were no bones broken. But even if they were intact, she did not look well. There were huge purple bruises blooming all over her, and she seemed to have lost weight since Catrin had last seen her. She had to find a way to get food, or Niada might fade away before her eyes.

But that was a task for the morning. She used the last of her strength to remove her own clothes and wash, and then wrapped herself in a linen sheet she found in the chest and slid into bed next to Niada. A second later, she was asleep.

You will soon see, Catrin of Aberavon, whether love remains after beauty is taken away.

The hag's voice from her dream echoed in her mind, so loud and insistent that it woke Catrin up. At once she realized that she had a terrible thirst; she got up and poured herself some water from the basin, and sat down on the chest to drink it. The linen sheet fell away, revealing all the cuts and scrapes that scored her legs and arms. The beauty of her skin had certainly been taken away, but she knew it would return.

Not so for Niada. Her injuries were far worse, and her face and arms were covered in tiny scrapes and punctures from Lord Ersfield's needle. It was easy to see that she had been beautiful once, but age and injuries had taken much of her beauty away. Only her eyes still looked young and vibrant … and even they were currently sunken and bruised.

Niada stirred, and Catrin refilled the cup so she could give her some water. Niada tried to refuse it, so Catrin wet a cloth and passed it over her dry, cracked lips instead. She accepted a drink then, but swallowed only a few drops before she lapsed back into unconsciousness.

Time passed. Catrin watched the moonlight grow strong, casting a pearly glow over the tiny room. She rose and bathed Niada's face in cool water, then settled down again. Niada didn't move.

The moonlight faded, and it grew terribly dark. Even the faint yellow of distant lanterns winked out, and still Catrin sat, watching Niada's head toss on the pillow as she murmured insensible disjointed words. "Magic … evil … book… I know,

I know, I will tell... Do I smell fire? ... the queen ... danger..."

Catrin checked the bandages on Niada's feet and saw that the swelling was going down, but wondered if that was a sign of healing or a sign that Niada's body was giving up. But it made no difference to Catrin. Whatever she had to do, she would not give up until the battle was lost ... or, please God, won.

It was very early in the morning when Lady Mary Sidney came to the ladies' chamber and roused Lucy with a shake of her shoulder. Lucy rose listlessly and wrapped her dressing-gown around her, then pushed slippers onto her feet and shuffled after Lady Mary without caring where she was going. After all, Catrin was gone and Lord Pierrick was alone in his chambers, under the care of doctors and surgeons. She had no way of knowing if she would ever see either of them again.

Lady Mary led her down the stairs, through the banquet hall and past the privy dining chamber. They finally emerged by the great staircase, but they went neither up nor down. Instead, Lady Mary crossed to the panelling and pulled some sort of lever.

A hidden door swung open, letting Lucy into a small square room hung with thick tapestries. The queen was there — with Lord Robert. Oh, woe — Lord Robert! If Lucy had known he was there, she would have taken the time to dress. But perhaps it was acceptable to appear as she was; after all, the queen was also wrapped in a dressing gown, though hers was embroidered all over with vines and leaves. Her hair was hidden under a wimple, and her face was marked with the remnants of tears.

Instantly concerned, Lucy moved closer to her and curtsied. "Oh, Your Majesty, is there anything I can do to help you?"

"That remains to be seen," the queen said, and paced around in agitated circles. "All the evening long I was plagued with petitioners demanding that we find Niada and Lady Catrin. They want Niada hanged as a sorceress and Lady Catrin arrested for helping her escape."

"I don't think Lady Catrin meant to help Niada escape, Your Majesty," Lucy said. "She was just trying to get them both away from the men who were attacking her."

"That may be the truth of it, but right now the truth does not matter. Lord Ersfield is running free around the countryside, telling all who will listen that death will soon cross the waters and Niada is to blame." The queen flung her arms in the air. "The city is in a state of terror, and it will quickly spread throughout the realm."

Lucy didn't know what to say to that. "I — I'm sorry, Your Majesty."

The queen abruptly turned to face her. "Do you know of anywhere Lady Catrin might go? Does she have any particular friends who would harbour her at such a time?"

Lucy pressed her fingers to her lips, thinking. "Lady Catrin does not make friends easily, Your Majesty, and as you know she had no family."

"Yes, I am aware."

"She had a favourite inn where she used to stop to rest on the way to Ashbourne … it was called the Rusty Sword. But it burned down last winter."

"So you cannot help us." The queen shunted her a sharp glance. "Is that why you were so willing to answer my questions, Lady Lucy? Because you knew they would not lead us to Lady Catrin?"

"No, Your Majesty. I am loyal to you. I believe that you would do only what is best." Lucy felt her throat close up and had to swallow hard to stop herself from crying. "And I trust that you would not hurt Lady Catrin, who loves you as I do."

The queen's dark gaze shone with new tears. "I do not wish to hurt her or anyone," she said quietly. "But if I must, I must."

"We will do everything we can to prevent that from happening," Lord Robert said. "With your leave, Your Majesty, I will search for her myself. I am sure she will be more likely to come with me than your guards."

"So granted," the queen said. Lord Robert made to leave and she raised a hand. "Hold; there is another task before us," she added, and knocked on the wall. The door opened immediately and none other than Lord Heatherleigh walked in, his hands in shackles and his clothes torn and rumpled. He cast himself onto his knees before the queen and let out a cry of mingled fear and hope.

"Your Majesty — I begged and prayed for a chance to come before you, and pledge my loyalty once again," he said. "Prithee let me explain."

The queen sat down in a cushioned chair and folded her arms. "Speak."

Lord Heatherleigh clasped his hands together. "Second only to my love for you, Your Majesty, is my love for this new church that you have established. I long to see it fully reformed, fully cleansed from all popish dregs, and I have been working with the brethren to that end."

"I am aware," the queen said frostily. "At what point did your religious goals become political?"

Lord Heatherleigh dropped his gaze. "When the king of France died, and it seemed likely that the Catholic Mary,

Queen of Scots, would become your heir. At that time, the brethren and I started working to make Lady Katherine Grey the popular choice. When she refused to advocate for herself, we recruited the Earl of Huntingdon."

"So you have been working to replace me," the queen said rigidly.

"No! No, Your Majesty, not one of us want to lose our queen. We want only to know who will come after you."

"You skirt the edge of treason here, Heatherleigh," Lord Robert said tightly. "If my queen gave the order, I would swipe your head from your shoulders here and now."

"If she ordered my death, I would happily bow to her will," Lord Heatherleigh said, and threw himself flat on the floor. "My sovereign."

The queen wavered, that much was obvious, her rage and her compassion fighting within her. It looked likely that the rage would win, and Lucy started to worry that she would be the one to clean up Lord Heatherleigh's blood. But then the queen rallied. "Rise, miscreant, and take this chance to prove your worth."

Lord Heatherleigh bolted upright. "Thank you — thank you —"

"Heatherleigh, you will go with Lord Robert to find Lady Catrin and Niada."

Lord Robert was not pleased by that decision. "Your Majesty — are you sure it is wise to —"

"He is one of the reformers; Ersfield is more likely to speak to him than anyone." She sent Lord Heatherleigh a look so sternly ferocious that Lucy shivered. "And he is more likely than anyone to work with all his might to bring Catrin and Niada back unharmed. He knows his re-establishment at court depends entirely upon pleasing me in this matter."

"And what if he betrays us?" Lord Robert asked coolly. "What if he takes this chance to re-join this brethren?"

The queen lifted one shoulder and let it fall. "Then he will pay for it with his life. Understood?"

Lord Heatherleigh quaked. "Yes, Your Majesty. Completely."

CHAPTER TWENTY-SIX

Catrin felt sunshine on her face, and it was not a welcome feeling. It meant she had to face the day, and all the danger that lay within it. She forced herself upright, and saw first that Niada was still unconscious. Her whole face was swollen, and her feet, too, had swelled up again so that her toes looked purple. Catrin loosened the bandages and propped her feet up on towels, then turned to the problem of clothing.

Being of thinner fabric, Niada's clothes had dried faster, and it seemed wise not to wear her court clothes in the city, so Catrin chose those instead. She also removed all the jewels from her own clothes and hid them in a cloth bundle in her bodice, just in case her arrival had been noted.

She still had her purse, and there were coins inside, but not as many as she could have wished. So she took her pomander as well; it was made of silver and might fetch a fine price.

It was perhaps fortunate that her court slippers had been so badly damaged by the water and the walk; no one would have thought they had once been beautiful. As she left the inn and took careful note of where it was, she thought herself well disguised.

There were people heading up the street, away from the river, so she fell in with them, keeping her head down. They walked for several minutes and then the road branched into two; she chose the right-side fork and to her surprise emerged onto a street she knew well. She was not far from London Stone, and so it was there that she went, looking for a familiar face.

It did not take long to find it. Finn soon appeared, carrying flowers which he then started selling to hapless ladies who could not resist his engaging grin. She waited until he was running low, then slid in next to him so quietly that he jumped when he saw her there.

"My lady!" he gasped. "Why, ye did give me a turn."

"I am sorry to frighten you."

The boy looked her over, his brow creasing when he saw her bedraggled wimple, uncombed hair and scraped, reddened fingers. "Are ye quite well, my lady?"

"Well enough, and yet not well," Catrin said, and all of a sudden trembled with weariness. "I am in need of food, and a peddlar who can get a good price for this." She held out her pomander, and he took it almost reverently.

"It's beautiful," he said. "Someone will pay well for this. I be sure of that."

"Thank you. I will wait for you here," Catrin said, and found a smile for the boy before he darted away. She shrunk back against the wall, close to the Stone, and pretended to be interested in its solid strength and iron bounds. But in very little time she began to feel oppressed, hemmed in by the surrounding buildings' tiled roofs and massive beams. So she moved toward the cathedral via a wider street lined with vendors.

She bought a shawl from one woman and some hot cooked meat on a stick from another, and devoured it with a hunger more ferocious than she had ever felt before. Only then did she wend her way back, and was hardly there a minute when Finn appeared. He carried a loaf of bread, a lump of cheese and a bottle sealed at the neck, and he was beaming.

"A good price indeed," he said, and pressed a small leather pouch into her hand. It was full of coins, and she dipped in a finger to retrieve two of them.

Finn shook his head when she held them out. "Nay, my lady, I have already taken my share," he said with his roguish grin. "And I used some to buy the food, too. Is it enough?"

"It is indeed. Thank you."

"Your humble servant, my lady." He tipped his hat and sauntered away, and she hid the food and the pouch in the shawl before she set her feet toward the inn. The street was busier now, and she forced herself to hunch her back and shuffle her feet so that she blended in with everyone else. It seemed to work; she got back to the room without anyone so much as glancing at her twice.

Once that lack of recognition would have amused her; now she was just painfully grateful. The queen would be angry with her; she knew that without doubt. Nor was she in any doubt that men were looking for her. If anyone recognized her, the queen would learn of it. At best, she and Niada would be separated, and at worst they would both be executed.

She slipped into the room and found Niada half-awake and shifting restlessly about. "Book … in his room … book of evil…" she murmured, and held out a bruised, swollen hand. "Lady…"

Catrin hurried over and pressed a hand to Niada's forehead. It was burning hot, but she was not sweating. "Niada — what is wrong? What can I do?"

"He prays … prays for the death of the lord…" She opened her eyes and they were bright with fever. "The fairies told me."

"I'm sure they did," Catrin murmured, and hastened to open the bottle Finn had bought. "Here — drink this."

Niada sipped at the bottle and then pushed it away. "Danger … must go."

"You can't go anywhere right now," Catrin said, and wet a towel with the last of the water in the basin so she could pass it over her face. "We must get you well first."

"Lady," she murmured, and lost consciousness.

The morning was over, and Catrin was still gone. Lord Robert and Lord Heatherleigh were still out looking for her. The queen was growing more and more irritated because they had not returned.

Worst of all, the morning was over, and Lucy had heard nothing of Lord Pierrick.

She wandered out of the privy dining chamber, unable to bear hearing people gossip about Catrin and Niada. Rumours were flying about, each one more inaccurate than the last, and no one would listen to reason. So Lucy descended the stairs alone and slipped into the peaceful silence of the chapel. It was cool in there, and the sunlight made the stained glass in the windows glow with ethereal beauty.

She went to the front and knelt down on the stair that separated the nave from the quire. Before her the Holy Table sat solid and unmoving, with the silver cross that the queen had insisted upon placed directly in the centre.

In that reverent, sacred hush, Lucy felt like God was listening. And so she prayed — for Lord Pierrick, for Catrin, for Niada, for peace. Most of all, for peace. That this chaos would stop and people would settle calmly into a new age where no one had to die for what they believed.

Where no one had to die… the phrase brought her mind back to Lord Pierrick. "Oh, God, please let him live," she murmured.

And just then, a figure settled down at her side. "Amen. *Nous te remercions, Seigneur.*"

"Lord Pierrick!" She wanted to throw herself at him, but he looked pale and shaky, and his arm was bound up in a sling. "Oh, Lord Pierrick. You are badly hurt, aren't you?"

He cupped her face in his hand. "Not too bad, *mon amour.* I will be well very soon. Do not be afraid for me."

"I can't help it." She pressed her hand over his. "I just found you … to lose you now would be terrible."

"I feel much the same. And I do not want to leave you with all these worries to bear … *ma pauvre fille,* is it true that your friend Catrin is still missing?"

"Yes, and worse still, the queen might imprison her when she is found." Tears stung her eyes. "She is very angry that Catrin protected the wise woman."

"Why did she?" Lord Pierrick wondered. "I know she considers the woman innocent, but surely she could allow that to be established by law rather than by such a dramatic disappearance."

"She would not take the risk." Lucy bit her lip. "Her father was killed for the sins of another, and Catrin is passionate about ensuring that the right people pay for their crimes."

"A noble sentiment, but still…"

"I agree." He swayed a bit and put a hand to his forehead, and the perils of Niada seemed suddenly much less important. "Have you eaten anything this morning? Let us go to the dining chamber; I don't think the midmorning meal has been cleared away yet."

He pushed himself to his feet. "Yes … perhaps that would be wise."

They walked down the nave together, and it was as they passed the doorway that led to the outer court that something caught Lucy's eye. She squinted until she could see it clearly, and then went still. It was a dark figure, abnormally thin, with a head out of proportion to the body and … horns. Horns rose up from above its forehead. "Lord Pierrick … look."

He went still. "What is that?"

"I don't know." Lucy edged forward, but stayed carefully out of the doorway. "But it is heading toward the gardens."

"I want to go after it, but…" He took a step and swayed once again. "Alas, I cannot."

"I will go."

"No." He took her hand in a tight grip. "I do not want you to chase after anything all alone. Let us go to the dining chamber and find a guard."

Lucy watched as the thing disappeared behind a brick wall. "It might be too late by then."

"Then we will simply tell them to watch for its return." His other hand covered hers, warm and sure. "It is all we can do."

CHAPTER TWENTY-SEVEN

"Lady … Catrin…"

The faint voice roused Catrin from a restless doze on the floor by the bed. She sat up, reaching for the water. "I'm here. What do you need?"

Niada licked dry lips. "It is … growing worse."

Catrin had to force her hands to remain steady as she held a cup for Niada to drink. "That does not mean you will not recover."

"It means I need help." Her hand slid slowly over the woollen blanket and rested on Catrin's. "Take my ring."

It was a cheap brass one, worth little. "I do not need your ring; I have some money."

"It is not for payment." Niada coughed, and winced when the movement jolted her feet. "You must find Zophia. She is the … wise woman who taught me … my trade. If she sees the brass ring, she will come."

Catrin stared doubtfully at the ring, lying loose on Niada's bony finger. "I don't think it wise to leave you."

"You must." She coughed again, and her eyes glazed over. "The fairies tell me … they tell me … so frightened…"

She was fading back into delirium. It was that more than anything else that made Catrin take the ring and rise to her feet. "I will return as soon as I can."

"Be safe … be safe…"

"Yes, I will," Catrin said, and slung the shawl around her shoulders before she left the inn. There she paused for a moment, unsure where to go. Where exactly does one find a wise woman?

She decided to try London Stone first, but Finn was not there, so she wandered down the main streets even though she didn't really know what she was looking for. Eventually she got to the cathedral, and decided that Paul's Walk was as good a place as any to ask for help.

She stepped inside, and cool air swirled around her. The place was full, and people seemed unusually restless. She saw one woman swear at another for bumping her basket, and a man shake a pickpocket for trying to relieve him of his purse. The wine-sellers were doing a brisk business; even the Starlyns were busy. In fact, there was one man there who kept buying cups and downing them, making those behind him wait. He was a big man, round, and he wore a doublet with silver thread that would not have looked out of place at court.

He reached out a hand for his cup to be refilled, and in a flash Catrin recognized his ring. It was Lord Ersfield himself, rapidly becoming drunk and still filled with fury. He snapped at Master Starlyn and rudely shoved the man behind him. Then he started shouting, demanding that the Starlyns tell him where Catrin was.

Catrin faded back into the crowd, trying hard not to show fear, and moved to the far end of the nave as quickly as she could. It was her intention to leave, but then she saw an elderly woman tucked into a small alcove by the doors. She had one basket full of vials and bottles, and another of bandages, and gave Catrin a friendly smile when she approached. "Something for what ails you, mistress?"

"It is not me that ails," Catrin said, and held out the ring. "I am looking for Zophia."

The woman's smile didn't waver. "I do not know that name."

Catrin passed her hand over her eyes, trembling under the weight of her fear. "Do you have anything for a fever, then?"

"There she is! After her, lads! After her!"

The bellow behind her made Catrin leap up in fright. Lord Ersfield was charging toward her, roaring like a bull. "Give up now, for you will never escape us! No matter how long it takes, I will find you! I will catch you, and you will pay for what you have done!"

Catrin darted out the door, flew around the end of the cathedral, and plunged into a crowd of paper-sellers and printers. But even as she fled, she knew that she had little hope of outrunning Lord Ersfield's men. They greatly outnumbered her, and the size of each one meant that they could cover more ground in one stride than she could in three. So where could she go? How could she hide?

She pushed and shoved her way down the lane, earning many a filthy look, and finally arrived at a water conduit. A dozen women were filling buckets there, and chattering with the ease of old friends. Without thinking, Catrin dived into the middle of them. "Please — please help," she gasped. "I've done nothing wrong."

One woman, the fairest and stoutest of them all, peered up the street and understood Catrin's plight in an instant. "Gather in close, all of you, and keep on with your business."

Catrin dropped down and buried her head, and all around her the great wide skirts of the women drew close, hiding her completely. All she could see was the stone of the conduit, and she pressed herself against it as if she could make herself one with the cool, smooth surface — or better yet, one with the running water. Then she could flow along with it to a peaceful place far, far away.

She tensed when she heard a rush of footsteps; they got louder and louder until they blended into the noise all around them and Catrin couldn't tell where they were. And then the women around her let out a collective breath of relief. "They're gone," one of them murmured. "Heading into the market. You had better go down the street in front of us instead, toward St Mary Magdalen Church."

"I will; thank you," Catrin whispered, and rose shakily to her feet.

The women moved away, leaving her feeling terribly alone. But no one shouted at her — no one even looked — and that gave her the courage to move onward. She scurried down the lane, past the cathedral school and several churches, and found herself getting closer to the river. That helped her find her way, through back lanes and alleyways, until she reached the inn. She had failed in her quest, but it was too dangerous to go back. She would have to come up with another way.

Assuming, of course, there was another way.

She pushed open the door with her mind already straining to find it. And there, hovering over the bed where Niada lay unmoving, was the elderly woman she had seen in Paul's Walk. She stood straight and tall, her white hair puffed out around her face and drawn back under a veil. And she was still smiling.

"Good afternoon, Lady Catrin," she said. "I am Zophia."

Zophia worked steadily, quietly, her lips always moving though she did not make a sound. Curled up on a cushion in the corner, Catrin could not help but wonder if she was praying … and if so, to whom.

She wrapped Niada up in several blankets and stoked the fire, making the room stiflingly warm. She cut several rods and burned them one at a time, chanting something in Latin. Then she took a mortar and pestle from her basket and added a handful of dried plants. "Marigold and thistles," she said with a return of that serene smile. "It is but the beginning of the cure; I also need ale and sugar."

Catrin forced herself to her feet. "I will get them."

"No need, my child. Finn will come."

Catrin blinked. "Finn? You know Finn?"

"I know all the waifs of London," Zophia said, and began to grind the plants to powder. "Finn is quite fond of you; he was the first to volunteer." She lifted her head and her eyes flashed with light. "He is here."

A second later, there was a brief knock at the door. Too weary to be astonished, Catrin went to open it and was grateful for the cool air that rushed in. Finn stood there, a bottle under his arm and a folded handkerchief in his hand. "Good evening, mistress," he said cheerfully. "A cure I have, and more."

"Thank you, Finn," Zophia said. "Is that the sugar you're holding?"

"No, though I have that too. This is better." He opened the handkerchief carefully with small grimy fingers, and revealed a small white circle. "'Tis the Host," he said in hushed, reverent tones. "That will cure any fever, that will."

Zophia passed a hand over the boy's hair. "You are a wonder, Master Finn," she murmured. "Go now, and I will meet you later."

"Yes, mistress," he said, and accepted a coin from Catrin with a flash of his engaging grin. "Father Webb is home, my lady, and sends his regards."

Catrin let out a breath of relief. "Thank you, Finn. I send mine in return."

"He'll be pleased to hear it. Goodbye, my lady."

"Farewell." He left, his soft-soled shoes making little noise on the wooden floor, and Zophia laid the handkerchief carefully next to the basin. Catrin shut the door again. "Will that work?"

She chuckled and pulled the cork from the bottle. "God knows."

Catrin wandered over to Niada. All that could be seen was her face, pockmarked from the marks of the needle. "Why did Lord Ersfield do that to her?"

Zophia carefully poured some of the ale into a bowl. "Some believe that the blood from such pinpricks, taken from a magician and collected in a vial, will break the power of their curses."

"So he has hurt her badly for no real purpose," Catrin said, and used a cloth to wipe the sweat from Niada's brow. "I hope he pays dearly for it."

Zophia came over and wrapped her arm around Catrin's shoulders. "As do I."

Lucy and Lord Pierrick were sitting together in the queen's chamber when Lord Robert and Lord Heatherleigh returned. Heatherleigh carried something in his hands — something dark and stiff — and when he laid it at the queen's feet, Lucy immediately knew what it was.

"That is the hawthorn wreath — the crown of the Green Man," she whispered. "The magician was here again."

Lord Heatherleigh abruptly straightened. "Why do you say 'again', my lady?"

The queen nudged the wreath with her foot. "Lord Pierrick and Lady Lucy saw him outside the chapel just yesterday."

"And this morning, Heatherleigh and I chased him through the gardens," Lord Robert said. "He got away from us in Greenwich Park."

"Do you think he is searching for his next victim?" Lord Pierrick asked.

"Perhaps. But there is the possibility that it is not a *new* victim," Lord Robert said. "Perhaps the magician aims to finish what Master Dyer started."

"I think that very likely." The queen picked up the wreath and examined the long red thorns. "We will ensure Lord Winchester is protected, but I would prefer to end the threat in its entirety. Have you any thoughts, my lords?"

Lord Heatherleigh bowed low. "Your Majesty, the next line of the prophecy is 'halt the death that crosses the waters', is it not?"

"It is," the queen said. "Lady Catrin thought it referred to priests of the old faith."

"But it could also refer to a specific person. Perhaps we should consider that." Lord Heatherleigh drew in air through his teeth. "Have any of your courtiers experienced a sort of death by crossing water?"

"Most of them," the queen said dryly. "Many of my courtiers and councillors were exiles during the reign of my sister because of their faith. They left their homes and families and crossed the English Channel to a new life on the continent, and would not have returned had my sister lived."

"Of course; I had forgotten that," Lord Heatherleigh said. "My family did not go. We ... lived quietly in the country during those years."

It was the sort of studied neutrality that many considered cowardly, but the queen merely accepted it. "One does what one must do to survive," she murmured, and set aside the wreath. "Lord Robert, it seems to me that our best option is still to find Niada and Lady Catrin. They are best placed to explain all of this."

"Yes, Your Majesty."

"Lord Heatherleigh will go with you again, but I wish for each of you to work alone, searching different areas," she added. "You will cover more ground."

Lord Robert was less pleased about that. "Yes, Your Majesty."

"And take messengers with you." She rose to her feet. "I wish to hear often about your progress."

CHAPTER TWENTY-EIGHT

The morning sunshine made the room glow deeply yellow, and the warmth from the fire scented the air. Niada lay on the bed, but she no longer tossed and turned about. In fact, she was unnervingly still.

Catrin sat down on the bed next to her and held a cup to her lips. "Wake up now, you need to drink."

Niada's eyes opened, and though they wandered at first she soon focused on Catrin's face. "You found Zophia."

"She found me," Catrin said. "And she left this for you, so you must drink."

Niada tried to lift her head but it soon fell back. "She's gone?"

"Yes, for now. She said she would return later." Catrin tilted the cup and Niada obediently drank. "How do you feel?"

"I am weary … weary…" she murmured, and closed her eyes. A second later she was asleep again, her hands folded over her chest like a corpse in a coffin.

The image frightened Catrin enough to make her leave the bed, but she could not sit. Instead she crossed to the window and stared out at the unfriendly city. It felt like her whole world had contracted down to that stifling little room, but still she knew she would not be there forever. Either Niada would die, or she would recover. If she died … no, she did not want to think about that.

If she lived … somehow they had to convince the queen that she was not responsible for the string of deaths that had so unnerved the populace. They could not do that from there; indeed, for the sake of their reputations they should leave that inn as soon as possible. So where could they go? Was anywhere safe?

Ashbourne. It was far enough away that no one would think to look for them there, and yet close enough that they could get there despite Niada's weakened state. Also, Catrin had weapons and men there, so she could mount a defence against Ersfield and his ilk. From there, she could contact the queen and explain in relative safety.

The question was how to get there. They would definitely have to move in disguise. Perhaps Finn would find her some boy's clothes. And a cart and horse — and firewood. They could stack the wood in a way that would hide Niada, and Catrin could leave the city looking like any other servant fetching goods for his master.

She did not like to retreat, and leave the magician free. He had mutilated that poor child, killed an innocent girl and thrown a boy to the lions, and she wanted to see him torn to pieces on Tower Hill. But as her father had always said, you had to count the cost of winning a battle, because it could easily prove too high a price.

And the loss of Niada — to illness or to Lord Ersfield's madness — was too high a price.

So. To Ashbourne they would go.

Catrin turned away from the window, ready to start planning the journey, and stopped short. Niada was awake. Awake, clear-eyed, and gazing at her with a faint smile.

"'Tis a terrible thing to wake up to bound feet and no clothing," she said. "Do you ever intend to return my gown?"

"Perhaps," Catrin said wryly, and hurried over to the chest. "Zophia said that if you woke, you should try to eat."

She shook her head. "I could not."

"Come now; it's been days since you had anything," Catrin said, and unwrapped a loaf of bread. "How are you feeling?"

"Like I was tossed over a wall by a catapult," she said. "And you?"

"I'm trying not to think about it." Catrin broke the loaf in pieces and gave her one, then settled down to the floor so she could lean against the bed. Niada tore off a small bite and ate it, slowly. Catrin ached with relief. "You do seem better."

"It may not last," she said, and attempted another piece. "Thank you for rescuing me — for taking care of me — for finding Zophia."

Catrin's heart swelled within her. "I could do no less," she said, and knew her voice trembled. Niada looked at her with sudden intensity, her blue eyes burning.

"Why?" she asked quietly. "Why do you feel obliged to me?"

Catrin fell back on her heels, her heart pounding in her chest. "Don't you know? Don't you recognize me as I recognize you?"

Niada covered her face with her hands. "I should not — it would be best if I did not —"

"Prithee, speak plain. I beg you, tell me plain." Catrin buried her face in the sheets to hide her tears. "Mother. My own beloved mother. Have you forgotten me?"

Niada struggled to sit up, thin hands reaching out to gather Catrin close. "No, no, my kitten, of course I have not forgotten you," she said. "I thought *you* did not recognize *me*."

Catrin wrapped her arms around Niada and held on tight. "I knew you from the first moment I saw your eyes. I wanted to reach out to you, but dared not. Oh, Mother, I have been looking for you for so long! Why did you not come to me?"

"I did not want you to look for me, dearling," Niada said. "I did not want to hold you back, and when I saw you — a great lady of the bedchamber! — I thought you had managed to put me aside."

"I thought I had no choice. The queen herself told me you were dead … stabbed, and thrown in the river."

"Stabbed I was," Niada said, her hand going to the scar on her cheek. "The blade sliced my face and hands, as you see, and gave me a great wound in my side. I do not remember being in the river, but I know it was Zophia who pulled me out. She took me to her cottage in the forest — the cottage where I now live — and used all her arts to bring me back to health. To thank her, I helped with her work, and she gradually taught me all I know about healing."

Catrin settled in by her side. "Did she choose the name Niada?"

"Yes; it means 'water nymph'." She smiled when that made Catrin chuckle. "It has been my name now for so long that my old name seems like it belongs to someone else. That whole life seems to belong to someone else."

Catrin stroked her hair, remembering when it was glossy black like her own. "Will you return to it?"

Her shoulders drew in, as if she felt a chill. "I cannot, dearling. Your stepfather —"

"He's dead," Catrin said. "And not a soul on earth mourned him."

Niada pressed her hand to her heart. "I am a widow?" she said, and her breathing turned fast and shallow. "He cannot torment me anymore?"

"He cannot. And no one will torment you again, while I'm living."

Niada glanced at the court gown draped over a nearby chair. "But if he is dead, how are you supporting yourself?"

"The queen made me a countess in my own right. Mother, she gave me Ashbourne."

Niada stared at her in astonishment for a moment, as if not sure whether or not to believe her. "You must be high in her favour."

"At the moment, anyway. And I am learning how to use it well."

"I am so glad, my kitten. I hoped you had the ear of the queen when those words of warning came to me. That is why I spoke them where young Mathilda would hear, and let her write them down. I knew she was returning to court soon, and might repeat them somewhere *you* could hear."

"Words of warning? Do you mean the prophecy?"

"Yes. I don't know where it came from, but I can see its truth, and I know you can see it too. The queen's reign is precarious, and that warning is meant to help her stay in the place her mother wanted her to have." She leaned her head back and her gaze drifted, as if she was seeing into the past. "Anne Boleyn ... Queen Anne ... how well I remember her. Perhaps she sent me those words of warning herself; she was always so concerned with her daughter."

"That prophecy has caused great upset; it is best that you do not mention it again until everything has settled." Catrin took her mother's hands in hers and held on tight. "Tomorrow I will find a way to get us to Ashbourne. You will be safe there."

"To Ashbourne? So soon? Oh, kitten, no ... this is ... this is too much." Her head fell back amongst the pillows. "I'm sorry, but I feel faint. I cannot talk anymore."

"It is time for more of Zophia's potion," Catrin said, and rose up to fetch it. "Then you can sleep, and tomorrow I will find a way to get us to Ashbourne."

"Ashbourne," her mother murmured. "Once a place of terror, now my only refuge."

Catrin held the cup to her lips. "And soon, it will be home."

A tentative knock on the door came not an hour later. Catrin crossed to the door and opened it, expecting Zophia. But it was Finn, his mouth screwed up as if he was unsure whether or not to speak. "Finn! It is good to see you," Catrin said. "Are you hungry?"

He eyed the bread and cheese she offered, but shook his head. "I come with a message."

Her shoulders tensed. "From whom?"

"A court gentleman. He said his name was Lord Heatherleigh."

"What did he look like?"

"Tall and thin." Finn shuffled his feet. "He promised that he would take ye somewhere safe, if ye meet him at the Stone tonight."

"I do not know whether to believe such a promise," Catrin said. "I do not consider him a friend."

"I wasn't sure about him either," Finn said frankly. "But I can tell that ye need help ... more help than a lad like me can give. Perhaps he can."

"You may be right about that, " Catrin said slowly. "Thank you, Finn."

"Yes, my lady," Finn said, and bowed before he retreated down the corridor.

Catrin closed the door and moved over to the window. For a long time she stood silent, watching men come in and out of a long low building that belched smoke and smelled of molten metal.

She heard Zophia's light footsteps, but didn't turn around as the door swung open. "It might be best to stand back, my lady," Zophia said. "You can be seen from there."

A fair point, that. Catrin retreated, but kept watching. "They all seem so busy."

"There's wages to be earned, and families to be fed," Zophia said, and went over to check on the sleeping Niada. "And meanwhile, you're as restless as a woman about to give birth."

"I am trying to solve a dilemma," Catrin said. "A courtier of no small resource and no great sense of justice has offered to help get us out of the city, if I meet him tonight at the Stone."

"And you suspect his motives?"

"I do indeed. He has resisted and resented me since we first met."

"I daresay there are many at court who disagree with your status and how you attained it."

"Aye, there certainly are," Catrin said. "He is only the most recent one."

Zophia soaked a cloth in the basin of water and wrung it out. "Then why would he offer his aid?"

Catrin considered. "The queen knows I have done nothing wrong. Perhaps he thinks that by saving me from those who wish me harm, he will earn her favour."

"Perhaps." Zophia slanted her an amused glance. "But I sense that explanation does not solve the dilemma."

"No. I just can't help but think how easily this could be a trap."

Zophia gently bathed Niada's face. "It is wise to think of that, but this I know: you cannot stay here much longer. It is dangerous for you both, and the foul city air is hindering Niada's recovery."

It decided her in an instant. "Then I will go."

"And may God bless you," Zophia said. "It is a brave thing you are doing."

"Or foolish, and that is why I cannot leave Niada here. If it is a trap, they might force me into a confession I do not wish to make." Catrin wandered from door to window, thinking. "Can Niada walk at all?"

"Short distances, yes, but…"

"Could you take her somewhere safe?" It hurt to say it, but she forced out the words. "Somewhere even I do not know?"

"Oh, child … she does not want to leave you."

"And I do not want to leave her, but needs must." Catrin crossed the room and took Zophia's damp hands in hers. "Please, Zophia — can you keep her safe?"

Zophia squeezed Catrin's fingers and smiled that sweet smile. "I can, and I will. Then you and I shall meet tomorrow for the first walk at St Paul's, and you two shall be reunited."

Catrin closed her eyes, awash in sudden fear. "God willing."

Catrin left the inn before Zophia did, and used some of her precious supply of coins to rent a room in an inn nearby. And there she simply waited, until the day was spent and darkness cloaked the streets.

Then she slipped out of the inn and set out on a cautious journey toward London Stone. She wore her own clothes, so that her *stiletto* lay safe and secure with its hilt along her forearm, but she had unpicked the embroidery and hidden the jewels so that it was no longer fit for a palace but merely a good quality gown, such as any daughter of a wealthy merchant would wear. It was well that she did not favour the garish colours of many court ladies; the oranges and yellows she often saw at the palace would have stood out like a beacon in the evening gloom. As it was, the dark red could blend with the shadows as she moved silently and swiftly through the darkening streets.

She saw the Stone in the distance, a squat pale column crossed with dark bands, and was about to head toward it when something made her stop. Was there movement behind it? Did she see people hiding in the shadows of the proclamation boards? No, it was merely shadows. And another shadow was lengthening beside her, faint in the lantern-light. She whirled, but it was too late. Something struck her on the forehead and she crumpled to the ground.

CHAPTER TWENTY-NINE

Awareness came back gradually. Catrin felt pain in her shoulders first, and a throbbing ache in her head. Then she smelled the foul odour of rot and filth and lifted her head half-expecting to find that she had been captured by the night soil men who collected the contents of outhouses throughout London.

No one was there. She took in a deep breath, trying to calm the hammering of her heart, and looked around carefully. She was in a room where the only furniture was the chair she sat on. The plaster walls were grey with mould and dirt, the floor made of rough planks. There was one window, displaying a square of pale grey that told her the night was past. She must have been unconscious for hours.

Her wrists were tied behind her with a rope so stiff that the knots were loose. They shifted and creaked when she pulled against them, and she was able to twist her hands around so that her fingers could reach the knots.

A squeak on the other side of the door made her freeze. A second later the door swung open, and in strode a tall, thin man dressed in a fine satin doublet. His feathered cap did not match, and the doublet itself did not fit him. It was easy to guess that neither truly belonged to him. "Lord Heatherleigh, I presume."

The man grinned, showing a mouthful of blackened teeth. "Sometimes."

"You were the man who spoke to Finn."

He swept the cap from his head. "The very same."

Catrin lifted her chin. "You must be a very good liar."

"Yes, and that is only one of his talents."

The voice was familiar, but still it was a shock to see its owner stride through the door. "Lord Ersfield," she said. "You were behind this."

Lord Ersfield swung his hand against her face, and the echo of the slap resounded through the room. "I told you I would find you, you pockmarked whore. And now you will tell me everything I want to know."

Catrin spat out blood. "That was not necessary."

"It was just the beginning, I assure you." He leaned so close they were practically nose to nose. "Tell me where the witch is."

Catrin shifted on the chair, and noticed then that her purse was gone. "I am not acquainted with any witches, Lord Ersfield."

"You know the woman who calls herself Niada. The one who spoke the prophecy. You know!" He swung at her again, and this time the slap made her ears ring. "And you will tell me!"

She was suddenly, profoundly grateful that her mother was no longer at the inn. "She died when we fell in the river."

Lord Ersfield stumbled back and his eyes bulged. "That is a lie."

Catrin let her eyes fill with tears, but behind her back she resumed working on the knots that bound her wrists. "It is the truth."

"Then why have you stayed away from court?"

She let the tears fall and leaned backward, as if in remorse. It loosened the ropes. "It is my fault she is dead," she said, and sniffed mournfully. "She was pulling me down — dragging me under — I could not fight her *and* the current…"

Lord Ersfield folded his arms. "Are you saying you killed her?"

"I … I let her go," Catrin wailed, and the sound covered the sound of the loosening ropes hitting the chair. "I let her go and she sunk under … under…"

"I don't believe it," Lord Ersfield snapped. "She is a witch; she would have called on her familiar to save her."

"No one saved her … no one," Catrin sobbed, and caught a loop of rope as it fell from her wrists so it didn't hit the floor and give her away. "She floated away while I swam for the banks."

"You lie. You LIE!"

Catrin broke off her act mid-sob and lifted her face to his so he could see that the tears were false. "Perhaps I do."

The bland admission threw him, she could tell. He took two full steps backwards. "Then she is not dead?"

She took the opportunity to twist her wrists and loosen another knot. "Or perhaps she is not alive."

Lord Ersfield pulled a knife from his belt and she felt a flicker of genuine fear as he brought the blade to her throat. "Do not play the fool with me, woman. Tell me the truth."

"Only if you tell *me* the truth." Her voice shook no matter how hard she tried to steady it, but she pressed on. She had to keep him talking. Freedom was only a few twists of the rope away. "Tell me about Margery Roos."

The name made him stumble backwards. "She has nothing to do with the witch."

"Perhaps not, but I will not tell you about the witch until you tell me what you know about Margery Roos."

He stared down at her in blank confusion. "I am willing to kill you to find Niada. Do you understand that?"

"I certainly do."

"And yet you try to bargain your knowledge. You sit there as if you were a queen on her throne, not a prisoner about to suffer and die."

It was indeed somewhat absurd, but she was so close. Only one small, tight loop held her wrists in place. And she did truly need to know. "If I am about to suffer and die, then there is no harm in telling me."

He raised both hands, palms outward. "I do not wish to speak of it."

"Why not? Were you the father of her child?"

He sputtered in indignation. "Of course not!"

"No, I did not think so." She felt the loop loosen with great relief and clasped her hands to keep him from noticing that she was free. "I thought that Lord Winchester was the father of her child, and that was why she was his one regret. But that was not the case either."

"None of this matters. It was settled years ago." He turned away, walking unsteadily toward the door. "Margery Roos is an old woman now. Half mute and near death."

"And what of her child?"

He swung toward her, eyes bulging with fear and anger. "I know nothing of her child!"

"I don't believe you," Catrin said calmly, and captured his gaze with hers. "I think you know who fathered it. You know who took advantage of that girl."

"No. No, I do not." His flabby lips trembled beneath his wide moustache. "My father told me not to ask."

"Your father." The former Lord Ersfield. A man who was friends with Margery Roos' guardian and powerful enough to force Lord Winchester into a course of action he did not want to take. "Of course. It was your father's child."

"I never said that!"

"No, you didn't," she agreed blandly. "But it is true all the same. I wonder … why was the child a secret? Was it because he feared angering his wife?"

"His wife could not be angry, for he had not yet married. A bastard child did not matter — and now the whole sorry tale matters even less, because my father is dead. Dead … just like Mathilda." The name brought back his rage and he suddenly flew across the room, bringing his knife back to Catrin's throat. "That witch you saved killed Mathilda, and I will kill her. Tell me where she is, or I will slice you to ribbons and then let my men have what's left of you."

"In the river," Catrin said, and didn't have to fake her trembling. But then she brought her knee up and rammed it hard against his privy parts. He fell to the floor gasping, and one of his men gave a shout of mingled surprise and fury. The other simply stood there aghast, staring at his master as he writhed in agony on the floor.

Catrin leapt out of the chair and dived toward the window. They were on the first floor; the ground outside was too far away for comfort but not so far away that the risk was too great. And there was a kitchen midden heap just below her — disgusting, but at the very least a soft landing.

She did not take any more time to consider, but climbed up onto the sill and jumped. Rats scattered as she landed and the smell was far beyond foul. Worse, she felt the knee she had once injured twist under her, and pain shot up her leg. But she did not dare stop; she scrambled out of the heap and ran, limping, into a narrow lane with overhanging buildings that blocked out most of the daylight. A second later she heard the bang of a door and running footsteps, and knew the men had recovered from their shock and were after her.

Where was she? Was this London? She did not know any of those narrow cobbled streets, so she just ran — wildly — as fast as she could. Which was not, she feared, fast enough. Her knee throbbed under her, threatening to buckle with every change of direction. She kept getting hit by waves of dizziness that made the walls and cobbles waver before her. And her shoes were slippery with slime from the rubbish she had landed in, making her stumble.

She had to get to St Paul's. The first walk of the day began at eleven of the clock, and Zophia would be there. Zophia would be able to take care of her, and take her back to her mother. Then they could escape. They could get away from all of it.

Where was the river? If she could find that, she would know which way to go. She forced herself to stop and listen, and heard only the rattle of carts, the chime of church bells, and the great murmur of hundreds of voices. Another wave of dizziness swamped her and she had to lean against the nearest wall. But she couldn't stop — couldn't stay out in the open. The men were coming — she was sure of it. She had to move, but her legs wouldn't obey her. No matter how hard she fought, she could not force herself onward.

"My lady!"

She opened clouded eyes and saw a familiar face bending over her. "Finn? How did you find me?"

"Dumb luck. I've been looking for ye all night." He hauled her upright and put her arm around his neck. "I just kept thinking that there was something wrong with that man. I should never have delivered his message, my lady. I am so sorry."

She leaned on him as another wave of dizziness drew her downward. "It was not your fault, Finn. They deceived you."

"Aye, they did, but they never will again," he said grimly. "Now come, my lady. We have to get somewhere safe."

She concentrated, gathered every bit of strength she had left, and managed one step, then two. "I have to get to St Paul's."

He glanced at her dubiously. "Do you have friends there?"

"Yes, someone is waiting for me."

He shrugged. "Then it's as good a place as any, I suppose. Come; I'll lead the way."

CHAPTER THIRTY

Finn and Catrin wended their way to the cathedral with great caution, staying at the edge of the crowd, moving in short bursts and pausing to hide in the shadows and check that no one was following them. Once there, they circled the cathedral entrances several times before Finn deemed it safe enough to go inside. Then they melted into the crowd, forcing themselves to move at the same steady, measured pace as those who were there mainly to display their rich clothing and full purses. For such people, it allowed time and breath for exchanging gossip, selling goods, and considering their purchases. For Catrin, it was tortuous.

She kept her eyes open for Zophia, and for an entire circle of the nave there was no sign of her. It was only when they were retracing their steps up the northern aisle that Catrin saw her, sitting in the alcove where Sebba the king lay buried. Her snowy hair under its white veil seemed to gather the light, giving the dark alcove a faint glow.

Immensely relieved, Catrin hurried over, with Finn following somewhat reluctantly behind. "Zophia — Zophia, I'm here."

Zophia did not answer. Nor did she move. Finn stopped and looked uneasily around him. "I think we should go, my lady."

Catrin did not have to ask why. Once they drew near, it was easy to see that Zophia's eyes were wide and unseeing. She was stiff and cold, and a band of ugly bruises around her neck told the tale of her death more clearly than words ever could have. "Oh, no. Oh, God, no."

"That lord you told me about got here before us," Finn whispered uneasily. "He might have someone watching. We should go."

"We can't go. She is the only one who knows where Niada is." Catrin heard the rising hysteria in her voice and could not bank it down. "Without her, Niada is lost again. And ill. And, for all I know, locked in a room somewhere unable to get out."

"We'll find her," Finn said, and took her arm. "Please, my lady, we need to go."

"Wait — there is something in her hand." Catrin darted forward and carefully prised it out. It was a small velvet pouch, with something inside that felt both hard and soft at the same time. She tipped the contents into her hand, and the first thing to slide out was small, shrivelled and brown. She thought at first it was a stick, but then Finn's face went white.

It was a thumb. A boy's thumb.

"It wasn't Lord Ersfield who did this," Catrin said. "It was the magician."

"I should have known," Finn said. "He's the only one in the city evil enough to kill Zophia."

Catrin felt in the pouch and drew out a twist of paper. She returned the thumb to the bag and unwrapped it carefully, and her heart rate doubled at the sight of a long lock of grey hair. "He has Niada."

"Why does he want her?"

She tilted the paper toward the light of a candle burning over Sebba's grave. The words were written with heavy strokes of the quill, the ink so thick it had soaked through the paper.

To the false countess

I know who Niada really is. I knew when I first saw her at Ersfield. Her eyes looked at me in judgment, just as they did when we were children and she found my experiments.

All of this has happened because of Lord Winchester. He is guilty. So if you want to see Niada again, you will bring Lord Winchester to Charing Cross by midnight tonight. Otherwise, she will die — as slowly and painfully as possible.

I hold death and rebirth in my hands. Do not doubt that I can do this.

I remain your humble servant,

The Green Man

Catrin pressed her hand to her heart. "Ransom."

"You mean money? He did this for *money*?"

"No. He's doing this so he can finish what he started." The note shook in her trembling fingers. "I have to bring Lord Winchester to him, or Niada will die."

Finn shifted uneasily on his feet. "How can you do that?"

"I can't — and I won't. I will not surrender anyone to this villain. But I have to make him think I will." Catrin did some rapid thinking. "Young Finn, I believe it is time you saw Greenwich Palace."

"I have seen it," Finn said. "My grandmother lives in the village just outside it."

Catrin smiled. "Perfect."

Finn's grandmother had been astonished to find her grandson at the door, but once all was explained she was sweetly hospitable. She set water to heating so Catrin could bathe, and placed the tin bathtub in front of the fire once it was full, so she would not catch a chill.

Catrin folded herself into it with gratitude and scrubbed away the smells of the midden and the dust of London, but she was thinking about something completely different.

For some reason, the prophecy kept coming to her mind. Or the 'words of warning', as her mother had called them. She had spoken as if she had not known what they meant — as if they had come to her from somewhere else — but Catrin was not fooled. Her mother had always loved creating secret messages and giving gifts with hidden meanings. Forsooth, the last letter she had sent before she disappeared had taken Catrin two years to decipher. So Catrin could assume that her mother had sent a message that was designed for Catrin to understand. If she had concentrated on the prophecy from the beginning instead of trying to protect her mother by dismissing it, she might have learned who the magician was long ago.

Catrin climbed out of the bathtub and dried off. A message about the queen and for the queen … that made sense of the first line right away. 'For the green lady to live' — the Tudor colours were green and white. Queen Elizabeth was the green lady, not poor Lady Ingolde.

The sacrifice also made sense; Catrin had always known that the queen could not marry. She had to sacrifice the part of herself that wanted a husband and children, for there would never be a candidate for her hand who would satisfy everyone. Similarly, she had to replace the old religion of the people somehow if the new church was to thrive — she had to create a new altar where they could worship, and find a new Virgin Mary.

Slowly Catrin drew on her clean clothes, which had been retrieved from the palace by Finn with Lucy's help. 'Fell the ancient pillar'. Did that, too, refer to the church? It was the first part of her mother's message that was a command, so it was safe to assume that it was something her mother expected the queen to do, once Catrin told her about it. Fell the ancient pillar … that could mean remove a threat. And the greatest threat to the queen's throne right then was the magician.

A series of images suddenly flashed before Catrin's eyes. A ring — an infant — an ancient ruin. Suddenly she knew who the pillar represented. She knew who the magician was.

All she had to do now was find him.

CHAPTER THIRTY-ONE

Catrin sat down on the step at the edge of the quire in Friars' Church, near enough to the door to escape if necessary, and watched the door at the opposite end, which was closest to the palace. After an age of waiting, three people slipped in: Lord Pierrick, Lord Heatherleigh, and her sweet Lucy.

Lucy saw her there first. "Catrin!" she cried, and ran up the centre aisle. Catrin rose to her feet just in time; her friend threw her arms around her and nearly unbalanced them both. "I was so worried!"

"I'm sorry, dearling," Catrin murmured. "Oh, it is so good to see you."

"Far better to see you! We all thought you drowned." Lucy slid her arms away, her eyes round with remembered fear. "Where have you been?"

"Hiding in the city ... but more of that anon," Catrin said, though she had no intention of telling her any details. Lord Heatherleigh was there, after all, as was Lord Pierrick, and she had a reputation to uphold.

"Where is Finn?" Lucy asked,

"He has returned to the city," Catrin replied. "He said that he wanted to make sure someone was taking care of Zophia's body. He is a good boy, and I hope he manages it. But we have a different task."

"Do we?" Lord Pierrick asked.

"We must find the magician. And I believe I know who he is."

Lucy gave a little jump. "You do? Who?"

"Owain Kyffin."

Lord Pierrick laughed. "The precentor? You must be in jest."

"No, I am not. I saw a ring on his finger — a crystal ring with an inscription. It's the sort of ring that is used to trap the spirits these magicians conjure. I didn't realize what it was at the time, but now…"

"It could be that he inherited the ring, or purchased it purely for aesthetic reasons," Lord Heatherleigh said. "I fear that is not proof."

"Proof is hard to come by in this case." Catrin brushed a hand over her hair. It was not as smooth as usual, and she found that oddly troubling. "But it may be easier to explain if I begin with a confession. There is a reason I tried to protect Niada."

Lord Pierrick nodded. "I thought there must be. A strong reason, at that."

"And I told you what it was, my lord," Lucy said. "Justice."

"That was only part of it, dearling. My reason is stronger still." Catrin folded her hands in front of her, holding on rather more tightly than usual. It was a risk to tell them, but a greater risk to keep it hidden. "I protected Niada because she is family."

Lord Pierrick sucked in his cheeks. "I thought you had no family."

"So did I … until I met Niada." Catrin drew in a deep breath. "Her real name is Angharad Surovell, and she was once the Countess of Ashbourne."

"She is your mother." Lucy sank slowly to the flagstone floor, as if her legs could no longer hold her up. "Catrin, your mother is not dead after all. And you found her. You found your mother."

"Yes. Yes, I did."

"After all this time."

"After all this time." Catrin smiled at her friend, allowing herself a moment to feel the joy of it, but had to return to the problem at hand. "The prophecy. My mother pretended it was 'words of warning' from an unknown source, but it was really a message for me. That was why she said it in front of Mathilda, hoping she would repeat it somewhere I would hear it. And that changes how we must interpret it."

"I can see why it would," Lucy said. "But I don't see how such a change helps us."

"It told me who the ancient pillar represents," Catrin said. "In Denbighshire, near Valle Crucis Abbey, there is an ancient mound, and on the top is an ancient pillar called *Croes Elisedd*. The people of that area are very proud of that pillar, and there is not one among them who does not identify with its fortitude and strength."

Lucy traced her lips with her finger. "The precentor ... didn't he say he was born in that abbey?"

"Yes, and my mother was born nearby. They knew each other as children. I think she recognized him when she saw him at Ersfield, and knew that he was dangerous and needed to be stopped. She also knew that I knew about that ancient pillar, so she included it in the prophecy and expected me to unravel the hint."

Lord Pierrick sucked in his cheeks, making hollows below his cheekbones. "Why did she not just say plainly that the precentor was a threat? If she knew you were at court, she could have sent you a message."

"She didn't want me to know she was alive," Catrin said. "I can explain why — but it is a long story, best suited for another day."

"I still find this difficult to believe," Lord Pierrick said. "The precentor in St Paul's Cathedral? He is a man of status and education. He spends his days praising God and leading in worship. I cannot believe him so evil as to murder and destroy."

"I can," Lord Heatherleigh said heavily. "'Tis my turn to confess, I fear."

Lucy folded her arms and fixed him with a very stern gaze. "Oh, Lord Heatherleigh. What have you done now?"

"'Tis not a new sin, my lady, but the consequences of the old." Lord Heatherleigh tugged sharply on his forked beard. "The precentor is one of the brethren."

Catrin frowned. "But he was not on my list. Why didn't you write him a message?"

"Because I stopped and warned him on my way to Ersfield Manor."

"So he knew what was going on at the palace; he knew the brethren were exposed," Catrin said. "And that was the night the fishing boats burned."

"I'm afraid so," Lord Heatherleigh said. "I considered not warning him; how I wish now that I had followed that instinct."

"Why did you consider it?" Lord Pierrick asked.

"Because I never really thought of him as one of us. His faith was lukewarm at best, and he was always silently, intensely angry whenever we met. He was easily distracted, and seemed more interested in the manor than the cause."

"I think I know why he was so interested in the manor," Catrin said. "His father was Geoffrey, the old Lord Ersfield."

"How do you know this?" Lord Heatherleigh asked.

"Ersfield told me ... after a fashion." Catrin stepped up into the tiny quire; she needed space to move. "But for it to make sense, I must start further back. Lord Winchester said that Margery Roos was his greatest regret, and I feared that it was because he was the father of her child. But she denied it in a letter I received from her son several days ago. She says that Lord Winchester protected her, and I can only think that he did so by hiding the babe."

"In Valle Crucis Abbey, I wager," Lord Pierrick murmured.

"Yes. But the difficulty is that the father, the old Lord Ersfield, was not married when Margery Roos found herself with child. He did not marry and produce an heir until the year after their baby was born. So Lord Winchester could have required him to marry Margery and recognize the baby. He chose not to, and I believe that is why the precentor is now obsessed with the manor."

"Because he thinks it should be his," Lord Heatherleigh murmured.

Lucy covered her mouth with her hands. "Ooh — and that is why the precentor chose Mistress Mathilda as the new virgin. He is angry that Lord Ersfield has the title that he feels he himself should have, and wants him to suffer."

"And that is why he tried to kill Lord Winchester," Lord Pierrick said. "He blames him for taking him away from his mother and denying him his birthright."

"I have learned, to my cost, that he still intends to kill Lord Winchester," Catrin said. "He wants me to bring him to Charing Cross by midnight tonight."

"Why does he think you will help him?" Lucy asked.

Catrin held back a rush of tears. "Because he has my mother."

They all stared at her in horror for a moment, and then Lord Pierrick straightened to his full height. "An evil act, and a heinous purpose. But fear not; we will not allow him to succeed. We will find him long before midnight."

"We shall have to," Lord Heatherleigh said. "But we will need help. More men, fresh horses and supplies — and the queen's blessing would certainly help."

"Perhaps we should talk to Lord Robert," Lucy said. "He has been truly concerned for you, Catrin; I'm sure he will be sympathetic."

"I will go to him," Lord Heatherleigh said. "It is best for you not to be seen in the palace, Lady Catrin."

"I suspected as much," Catin said wryly. "So I will go where we are most likely to find a precentor: the cathedral. Lord Pierrick, Lucy, will you join me?"

"Aye, we shall," Lord Pierrick said cheerfully. "Let the quest begin."

Thunder rumbled across the sky as they boarded the tiny ferry, and the water-man swore under his breath as he pulled out onto the river. The Thames was nearly as black as the sky, and the waves made the boat shift and shimmy as if trying to escape. "Not sure I can get ye all the way to Paul's Wharf, my lord," the ferryman said, and strove to pull his oars through the waves. "Might have to go ashore before then."

"Don't worry, goodman — just get us to the other side," Lord Pierrick said.

"Yes, milord," the man said, and gave a mighty pull of his oars once again. They passed under London Bridge, passed the steelyard that had scented the air around the inn where Catrin and her mother had stayed, passed the broken wharf. The water folded smoothly backwards on either side of the prow, and Catrin found herself staring at it in morbid fascination. Was it really less than a week since she had found herself at the mercy of that dark current?

Lightning flashed and Lucy let out a shriek. Lord Pierrick took her hand and squeezed, just as there was a clap of thunder and the heavens opened. Massive raindrops fell hard and fast, and felt like stones hitting her skin. They were strangely warm, as if the lightning itself had heated them through.

The waves around them swelled and the boat tilted backward in a terrifying slant before it sloshed back into the water again. The water-man swore again and made for the shore, struggling to keep control when the boat rose up on a swell and slammed down again. A gust of wind brought a harsh acidic smell with it, just before lightning flashed again. This time she saw it — a great chain hitting the water with a mighty hiss.

Thunder nearly split the sky as they made it to the shore and scrambled onto the wharf. All of them ran for the protection of the overhanging buildings. "You are mad, my lord and ladies," the water-man gasped. "There's nothing important enough to be out in this weather."

"I beg to differ, my goodman. We shall press onward." Catrin pressed some coins into the man's hand. "You go find somewhere safe until the storm passes."

The ferry man looked up at the boiling clouds. "That might be hours."

Catrin set her sights on the path to the cathedral. "Yes, indeed, it might," she said, and led the way up Paul's Wharf Hill. The storm seemed to be chasing them, thunder growling and the lightning regularly blinding them with hot white light.

"There's something I don't understand," Lucy panted. "If the prophecy was meant for you and it was about the queen, why did it fit what the magician was doing so perfectly?"

"He made it fit," Catrin said. "He simply applied the prophecy to those he wanted to kill."

"If that is so, who will be his last victim — when he 'halts the death that crosses the waters'?"

"Lord Ersfield," Catrin said. "The queen told me that they returned from exile together, crossing the waters on the same ship. With Mathilda dead and no other heir, the title will revert to the Crown. I'm sure he thinks that his friend the queen will grant it to him when he tells her his sad tale."

"He will not have the chance," Lord Pierrick said, and was the first to burst through the cathedral door and enter the nave. The walks were long over for the day, so there was only a single clergyman to see their arrival. Lord Pierrick waved his unbandaged arm to get his attention, and the man moved with an agonizing steadiness of pace to meet them.

"Good evening, my lord."

"Good evening," Lord Pierrick said. "We wish to speak to the precentor."

Irritation flashed across the man's face, nearly as bright as the lightning. "We *all* wish to speak to the precentor," he said. "He has missed all the services today, and with no word of warning."

"Perhaps he is at his home," Lord Pierrick said. "Could you tell us where he lives?"

The man gave him a suspicious glance, one which lingered on the fleur-de-lis stitched into his doublet. "I don't think I should, my lord…"

"But he might be ill," Lucy said with her heartwarming innocence, and blinked big blue eyes. "We mean him no harm, I promise — we just want to help."

The man gave in at once. "He has rooms at Whitehall Palace — a gift from the queen. And he spends a great deal of time at Ersfield Manor … but I doubt he's there now. Lord and Lady

Ersfield are both in the city; I know because Lady Ersfield was here just yesterday."

"Why is she in the city?" Lucy asked. "Does she have somewhere to stay?"

"Oh yes — a house just past Cordwainer's Hall. It's not far."

"Thank you, your reverence," Lucy said, and the man bowed to her with a sentimental smile that vanished when he looked at Lord Pierrick. Then he walked away, at the same maddeningly steady pace, and Catrin drew them back to the doorway.

"I'll go to Whitehall; you two go to Lady Ersfield and see if he is there," she said. Lucy protested and Catrin held up her hand. "There is no time to argue. I cannot go to Lady Ersfield; she could easily report me to the palace — or worse, to her husband. I am less likely to be spotted at Whitehall."

"She's right," Lord Pierrick said, and took Lucy's hand. "Let us meet back here in an hour."

"One hour," Catrin agreed, and plunged into the storm.

CHAPTER THIRTY-TWO

Lucy was wet through. Her sopping stockings rubbed uncomfortably within her shoes, giving her a blister on her heel. And though she told herself it was a small thing, far less important than their quest to find the magician, it seemed to become more and more painful the further they walked, taking up more and more of her consciousness. She feared that she would soon lose perspective and insist that they stop. Stop, retreat, and return to the warm comfort of the palace.

Fresh thunder made her jump, and oh, how she longed to go home. The plea hovered on the tip of her tongue, and to stop it she asked something else. "My lord, is it yet time to tell me about Matthew Dyer?"

Lord Pierrick pushed his wet curls under the brim of his dripping hat. "The secret is out now, my lady. Matthew Dyer is one of a flock of believers who hide a popish priest among them."

"Oh. Why couldn't you tell me that?"

"I could not reveal his allegiance without revealing the existence of others of the same faith."

Lucy avoided a stream of water coming from a pipe above their heads. "I can understand that. But it still doesn't explain how *you* came to know him."

Lord Pierrick sighed. "When I first arrived in England, Matthew Dyer was at my uncle's house being tutored in swordsmanship. We studied and trained together, and I soon considered him a friend. I even considered joining the flock, for they are truly good and kind people. But I soon learned that their resistance to the queen's new church bordered on treason, and that I could not accept." He glanced up as lightning forked above them, making the air sizzle. "I severed ties with them, which greatly upset Master Matthew. He vowed never to speak to me again."

"But he changed his mind when you came to court."

"Yes, and by then his faith seemed darker still. There was little of the Christian in it, and far too much of the pagan. I did not realize then that he was working with an evil magician, but I could certainly see the darkness in him."

Lucy shivered at the thought, and shivered again when they passed out of the shelter of a house and the rain fell full on them. She looked up without thinking, received a face full of water, and noticed something when she had wiped her vision clear. "Lord Pierrick — that looks like a lady sitting in that window. Could it be Lady Ersfield?"

"Let us hope so," Lord Pierrick said grimly, and strode over to knock on the door. Two peals of thunder rang out ere the door opened, but it seemed they had found their quarry. The woman was tall and large, with a heavy oval face. And she wore black, with a sprig of rosemary pinned to her bodice for remembrance. "Lady Ersfield?"

She drew back a bit, her hand on the door ready to slam it shut. "Yes?"

"We have come from the palace, and we need to speak to you."

She ushered them in reluctantly. "Stay on the tiles, there. I don't want you dripping all over my rush matting; I just had it replaced."

Lucy looked longingly across the room at the fire roaring in the grate, but did not protest. "We are looking for Owain Kyffin. Have you seen him today?"

"I have not seen him for weeks."

"Since he stopped coming to the manor for meetings of the brethren, I would guess," Lord Pierrick said.

"Since he went into a rage about London Stone," Lady Ersfield said. "Someone killed himself there, and he was furious. He said that the Stone's sanctity was destroyed by that act, and he could no longer bear to go there."

"Why did he go there in the first place?" Lucy wondered.

Thunder grumbled above their heads, but Lady Ersfield paid no attention. "He found people to help him there, he said. With what, I do not know, and nor do I care. Is that all?"

"For now," Lord Pierrick said. "If you do see him, prithee send word to the palace. It's important."

"I will, I will, but I doubt he will come anywhere near here. Unlike you — and unlike my husband — he has the sense to stay in out of the rain."

Lucy bit her lip. "Lord Ersfield isn't here anymore?"

"Someone came to the door with a note about an hour ago. He read it and ran out, shouting that he knew where the sorceress was. I tried to stop him but he pushed me away. Knocked me down, he did." She pressed a hand to the back of her head and tears briefly shone in her eyes. "After that, I let him go. I don't care if he catches his death in this weather."

"Nor would I," Lucy said honestly, and Lord Pierrick hid a smile.

"We will try to find him for you," he said. "And perhaps we will take him back to the palace instead of here."

"Take him wherever you want," she said, and chivvied them back toward the door. "Now go, and let me clean up this mess."

They went, and Lucy for one barely noticed the fresh onslaught of the storm against them. Her mind was wildly busy. "Are we truly going to look for Lord Ersfield?"

"I suspect that we will find him when we find the precentor," Lord Pierrick said.

Lucy winced. "Because he is the last victim, and the precentor himself sent that note."

"Yes, exactly." He started down the street, bending forward against the wind that whipped around them. "We need to return to the cathedral at once and tell Lady Catrin that Lord Ersfield is free."

Lucy followed him, raising her voice as thunder rolled once again. "We must tell her about Thomas Starlyn, too."

"What about him?"

"Thomas Starlyn chose to hang himself by the Stone to stop the precentor going there," she said. "He knew the precentor thought it was sacred."

Lord Pierrick glanced down at her in puzzlement for a second, but light dawned just as lightning flashed. "Sacred, and useful. He found his assistants there, and if he could not go there because it was no longer sacred, he might not find another."

"Yes." Lucy's heart ached. "In a way, Thomas Starlyn died to stop the magician's murders before they started. It was a noble act."

"It was." Lord Pierrick put his arm around her. "I'm glad he never knew about Matthew Dyer."

She leaned her head on his shoulder. "So am I."

The vicars' houses lined the river at Whitehall, connected by a river-walk made of boards that extended out over the water. Catrin ran along it, lashed by wind and rain and soaked by waves that hissed up over the boards and pulled at her feet. She had no way of knowing which house belonged to the precentor, and was just about to knock on a door and ask when she noticed a sprig of hawthorn lying on a windowsill.

The door was unlocked. She slipped inside and shut it tight behind her, blocking out the noise and fury of the storm. Water streamed down over her body and pooled on the floor, but she didn't notice. Her attention was completely absorbed by the paper pinned to the plaster wall before her.

Owain Kyffin had written out the prophecy in large, flowing script, leaving a large margin all around the words so that he could add his own notes. And there it was, all laid out. Mistress Mathilda's name was written in red ink next to the line about the new virgin and crossed off. Matthew Dyer's name was scratched in so heavily it had torn the paper, and crossed out with an angry slash.

Lord Winchester's name was next to a sketch of a pillar, crossed off and then rewritten. A line connected it to Lord Ersfield's name, which was written next to the last line about death crossing the waters. So it was as she suspected: Lord Ersfield was the last victim. And there was something scribbled above his name — notes perhaps? It took her a few minutes to decipher them.

He must die in a sacred space, the spirits have decreed it so
Not the Stone — it has been violated
An ancient sacred space
Ripe for fresh contemplation

Contemplation? Where did one go to contemplate in London? The Tower, perhaps — one had a lot of time to contemplate when imprisoned. Some found Westminster Abbey a good spot to pray, but she had always found it too busy.

So where? The cathedral? It seemed the most likely, but this was no time to guess, so Catrin looked around the space for further clues. Thunder rumbled as she looked through the papers on the table below the prophecy, which contained mostly complicated formulas and strange symbols. It looked like the precentor had been practicing alchemy as well as conjuring spirits; she found one set of notes that claimed that urine from a young boy mixed with mercury might turn metal into gold. That made her glance at the wooden barrels that sat in the corner of the room, wondering if that poor child had been forced to give even more than his thumb for the magician's spells.

"Who are you? What are you doing here?"

The sudden voice startled her. She spun around to find a young man in the doorway, with two giants behind him. "I could ask the same thing, sirrah," she said coolly. "This is no more your home than mine."

"I am here on the behest of the great magician," the boy said proudly. "He has charged me to bring him those barrels."

Catrin winced. "You're his new assistant, then," she said, and started edging toward the window. "Have you heard what happened to his last one?"

"He played the magician false," the boy said, and his eyes burned with determination. "I will not do so. Samuel! John! Make sure she doesn't try to stop us."

The men pushed their way through the small door, and a flash of lightning threw their faces into sharp relief. Angry, determined faces. "If you harm me, the queen will learn of it," Catrin said. "I am one of her ladies."

"Wait," the boy said. "The magician knows the queen; he doesn't want to anger her."

"She's probably lying," one of the men growled. "Everyone says they know the queen when they are trying not to die."

The boy hesitated. "I daren't risk it; killing is something that can't be undone. Tie her up instead; if the magician approves, we can return to finish her off."

The men grunted in reluctant assent, and one turned away to retrieve some rope from a heap in the corner.

Catrin took the opportunity to dive for the window, but she was not fast enough. Arms wrapped around her waist and she was dragged backward, knocking her head on the frame. It made her woozy, the whole world dissolving into mist. She was only vaguely aware of her wrists and ankles being tied together, but little darts of pain shot through her as they drew each knot tight.

She saw them taking the barrels from the corner as if from a great distance, and then the door shut behind them and she was left alone. She tried to fight against the ropes, but it was no use. A wave of dizziness swamped her and she lost her grip on consciousness.

Lucy and Lord Pierrick arrived back at the cathedral and found it deserted. No amount of pounding on the doors roused anyone, so they were forced to crouch under the inadequate shelter at the entrance to wait and wonder.

"Is Whitehall further away than Lady Ersfield's house?" Lucy asked.

"Yes, and Lady Catrin may have had difficulty securing a ferry," Lord Pierrick said, and tried to hold his cloak over her head. It was a fine gesture, but the cloak itself was so wet that water dripped down onto Lucy's head in a steady rhythm. Soon enough he gave up, and as the cloth fell from around her she caught a flicker of movement out of the corner of her eye.

Lucy set her hand on Lord Pierrick's chest. "Do you see that?"

He wiped his eyes clear and squinted. "Men — with barrels. I think they're going into the cloisters."

"The cloisters haven't been used since the monks were sent away — why would anyone take barrels in there?" Lucy asked. "It can't be for storage: the centre of the cloisters is open to the elements. It's really just a giant covered walkway."

"And it's raining," Lord Pierrick said, and a roll of thunder accompanied his fine example of understatement. "I cannot think what could be important enough to move in this weather."

Lucy bit her lip. "What do we do?"

"I'll go into the cloisters for a closer look; you wait here for Lady Catrin."

"Oh, no, my lord —"

She was too late. He had already moved off, merging into the thick mist that arose from the steaming pavement. Lucy bit her lip, not at all sure this was happening the way it should. Once again, she was alone. Catrin was missing, Lord Pierrick was missing.

What was that? A rhythm like trotting hooves. Was it the pounding rain, or was she actually hearing horses? To her astonishment, it was actually horses. Even as she watched, Lord Robert and Lord Heatherleigh loomed into view, riding up Paul's Wharf Hill and already soaked to the skin. "My lords! I am so glad to see you!"

Lord Heatherleigh hunched his shoulders against a fresh onslaught of rain. "I did my best to convince the queen that the precentor is our magician, but she remains doubtful. She charged us to bring you back to the palace."

"We can't go!" Lucy cried. "Lady Catrin hasn't returned, and Lord Pierrick has gone into the cloisters."

"Where did Lady Catrin go?" Lord Robert asked.

"Whitehall — the vicars' houses."

"Come up, then. We'll go find her," he said, and hauled Lucy onto his horse. "Heatherleigh, find Lord Pierrick and meet me at the barge. This storm is growing worse; there will be no devilment tonight by anyone, including the magician."

"Yes, my lord," Lord Heatherleigh said, and swung down off his horse as Lord Robert turned his around. He set the stallion at a fast pace, so Lucy had to hold on tight to the pommel to avoid being shaken off. She was very glad when they arrived at the river and one of the royal barges was waiting there. It was large enough to stay steady in the rough waters, and had no fewer than four oarsmen steering it. They were able to ride right onto it before they dismounted, and then two of the men pushed off. In such a storm and with such a tide they moved quickly, and only such skilled men could have safely tied up at the docks by the vicars' houses.

Lord Robert lifted Lucy out onto the docks, and they hurried along the row, searching for any sign of Catrin. The water rose up through the boards of the river-walk with a sound like all of Medusa's snakes hissing at once.

"There!" Lucy said, and pointed at the hawthorn twig in the window. It still had its sharp red thorns, as if daring anyone to pick it up.

"Well done, my lady," Lord Robert said, and opened the door with a single well-aimed kick. They rushed in and the wind caught a dozen papers and threw them up in the air. They swung and flapped like agitated birds, and one came to rest on the prone figure of Catrin.

"Oh no!" Lucy cried. "Is she dead?"

"No, merely unconscious," Lord Robert said, and hastily removed the ropes that bound her. "Bathe her face with your sleeve; the water will revive her."

Lucy hastened to do so, and a second later Catrin moaned and her eyes flicked open. "Lucy? Lord Robert? What are you doing here?"

"Chasing after you, once again," Lucy said, and relief made her voice sharper than intended. "Come; we must return to the palace. The storm is too bad for anyone to be out."

"No — no. We have to go back to the cathedral." Catrin struggled upright and pointed to a barrel in the corner. The wood had cracked so that some of the liquid inside was coming out … a thick syrupy liquid that smelled of pine and rotten eggs. "The magician intends to kill tonight — with that."

Lord Robert leaned close and sniffed. "God's heart. It's Greek fire. The same thing that set the fishing boats alight."

"Yes, and the magician's new assistant just took at least six barrels of it to the cloister."

Lucy shivered. Lord Pierrick was in the cloister. "Why there?"

"It was once a place of contemplation." Catrin pushed herself upright and headed for the door. "I'll explain on the way."

CHAPTER THIRTY-THREE

Three of them could not ride on one horse, so they left the stallion on the barge and ran up the hill. The air was thick with the smell of sulphur and lightning constantly forked overhead, and Catrin found herself wondering whether they had all somehow crossed over into hell.

They reached the cathedral and saw the south entrance standing empty. "Lord Pierrick and Lord Heatherleigh haven't returned," Lucy cried. "They must be lost — or — or hurt —"

"We will find them," Catrin said. "We will find them, and Niada, and get them to safety."

"And then we will grind the magician into dust," Lord Robert said, and led the way to the cloister. A door swung open in a gust of wind and he grabbed the handle just before it hit him. "As good a place as any to start, I suppose," he said, and pushed his way inside.

Catrin and Lucy followed, and the sudden change from ferocious wind and rain to a gentle, secret hush made Catrin shiver. Doors lined the wall on their right side, weathered to grey and somewhat unsteady on their hinges. On their left, a black void that Catrin knew was the courtyard and the chapter house. No light showed — not a candle, not a single beam from a lantern.

They walked together along the walkway, picking their way around fallen stones and avoiding hanging cobwebs, and came to another open door. A torch burned in a wall-sconce, nearly down to the embers so that it provided only a dim orange light. But they went in, climbing the worn stone stairs and emerging into another open walkway. On the wall in front of them was the remnants of a wall-painting, so faded and cracked that it was hard to see the scene. Only one image remained clear: a group of sheep on their hind legs, with bunting and bonfires all around them.

"Big sheep dancing at a fair," Catrin murmured. "The boy wasn't dreaming after all."

A large pile of fallen plasterwork blocked the path to the left, so they moved to the right. Slowly, carefully, they crept along the walkway and turned left into the flat part of the 'u' shape, the part closest to the cathedral. And there, Catrin went still. "Look at that door," she whispered.

Lord Robert squinted at it. "No dust," he announced, and strode forward, flinging the door open and filling the space with his sword in hand. "Empty ... so to speak," he said, and pressed his sleeve against his nose as the smell of urine hit them all. It was so strong that Catrin actually choked.

"This must be the place," she said, and wished she still had her pomander. "The boy told me the magician's chamber smelled like this."

"I fear it is merely a jakes," Lord Robert said. "It certainly smells like one."

"We shall see," Catrin said, and walked in.

The room was dim, with only small slits in the wall for light, and a fire that was nearly out. She took a torch from the wall and held it to the embers, and when the flames flared up they could see the entirety of the small room.

There was a table along one wall, with items scattered on it. She saw half-shaped faces carved onto naked wax figures, crystals gleaming as if with inner light, and strips of parchment bearing Hebrew symbols. A black book bound with leather straps sat in the centre of it, reminding Catrin of her mother's fevered mutterings about a book of evil. Hawthorn petals fluttered underfoot, gathering around the base of several wooden barrels.

"There is our proof. He *is* the dark magician," Lord Robert said, and pointed a shaky finger at a circle drawn in chalk on the floor. In its centre lay a silver sceptre and a collection of half-burned candles. "These are the tools they use to cast spells."

Catrin spied something in the corner and felt a rush of relief. "It is my mother's veil," she said, and snatched it up. "He does have her — he did bring her here."

"So where is he now?" Lord Robert wondered. "Do you think he heard us coming?"

She had no time to answer. There was a great flash of light and a roar so loud the ground shook, followed by a crash and a sound like meat sizzling in a pan. Catrin dropped the torch, and Lord Robert snatched it up. "We need to get out of here before the building comes down on us," he said grimly, and led the way out of the room. They emerged into a world where dark had turned to day — orange light was pouring into the courtyard from above and smoke was mingling with the mist and rain.

Lucy shrieked. "Lord Pierrick!"

Below them, Lord Pierrick and Lord Heatherleigh were struggling against bonds that held them to a wooden stake. "Fire!" Lord Heatherleigh shouted. "The cathedral has been hit! Fire!"

They ran down the stairs and burst out of the same door where they had entered. The acrid smell of burning hit them as soon as they stepped outside, and over the roof of the cloisters they could see a plume of black smoke rising up from the spire to meet the clouds. Red flames were already licking at the lead roof, which was turning silver as it melted, and the weathervane was engulfed.

The three of them ran out into the rain and across to the wooden platform surrounded by barrels. Lord Robert cut the ropes with a few slices of his dagger and then dragged the two men free of the barrels. "We have to retreat. If the fire reaches this far, these barrels will explode."

"I cannot go," Catrin said. "The magician still has my ... has Niada, and I won't abandon her."

"God save us all," Lord Robert said, and rubbed both hands over his face. "I don't know what we can do to save her now, Lady Catrin. We do not even know where to find her."

Lord Pierrick pointed upwards, his eyes wide and terrified. "Yes, we do."

Catrin looked up just as a maniacal laugh cut through the hissing rain and roaring flames. "You found me! I should have known that you would find me!"

The precentor himself was standing on the flat side of the cloister, one floor above the room they had found. He held the struggling form of Niada in one hand, and the sight made Catrin furious. "Let her go!" she screamed. "You have no reason to harm her — no reason to take her!"

He laughed again. "Have you brought the bastard Paulet?"

"Yes," Catrin said. "He is waiting for us in —"

"YOU LIE!" he screamed, and shook Niada so violently she cried out in pain. "And for that, this woman will burn!"

"No!" Catrin cried, and started to run toward the door. Lord Heatherleigh caught her arm.

"Wait — look," he said in awe. "He just ... vanished."

It was true. Owain Kyffin was gone as suddenly as he had appeared, and taken her mother once again. But at least this time she knew where to find him. "He is going into the cathedral. He wants them both to burn," Catrin said through gritted teeth. "And I will not let that happen."

"What do you think you can do?" Lord Heatherleigh said, and pointed way above their heads at the glowing red spire. "Battle against the flame?"

"If I have to," Catrin said, and ran. Her heart pounded with determination, but her legs would not obey her. The closer she got to the cathedral, the slower she moved. It felt like she was trying to run through the Thames.

You will soon see, Catrin of Aberavon, whether love remains after beauty is taken away.

The cackling howl of the hag from her dream rang in her head. She stopped in the very doorway of the cathedral, breathing hard. What if she was maimed in her attempt to save her mother? What if she was burned — disfigured? Could she live that way?

She pushed the thought aside. Far better to suffer for her mother than to lose her once again. And the magician had to be stopped. She could not let him harm another soul.

She pushed the door of the south transept and forced herself in, expecting a raging inferno and hellish heat. But no ... it was strangely peaceful, with the vast empty nave to her left and the glossy wooden pews of the quire to her right. If it were not for the smoke, growing thicker every second, and the faint creaks and pops coming from the dome, she would not have known that a fire raged above her head.

She took a deep breath that immediately burned her lungs. "Owain Kyffin!" she shouted. "If you are not a coward and a scoundrel, come out and face me!"

A faint laugh to her right. She moved in that direction, stumbling over the step that led up to the quire. "I know that you killed Mathilda, and Matthew Dyer, and poor Zophia! And all for nothing!"

"It was not for nothing!" The voice was right ahead of her, and she moved hastily toward it, one hand out so that she did not run into anything in the smoke. "It was revenge — beautiful revenge! The spirit I conjured told me that the prophecy was the pathway to all I desired. I could kill, kill and kill again, and no one could stop me."

"You sent innocent people to their deaths! Why do you think you would gain anything from that but death and hell?" She nearly choked on the words, so she pressed her mother's veil against her mouth. It was damp from the rain and seemed to make it easier to breathe.

"You don't understand. No one ever understands. But I do — I saw it. I saw the truth of what had been done to me. In the polished thumbnail of a small boy, a true magician can see the face of the one who has wronged him," Owain Kyffin said. His voice was off to her right now, and seemed closer, so she quickened her pace. "I saw the face of Geoffrey Ersfield."

"Geoffrey Ersfield is dead!" Catrin made herself laugh scornfully. "You cannot hurt him, no matter how many people you kill."

"But I can hurt his son, and I have! I drove him to madness and killed him with water!"

So Ersfield was dead ... and she could not quite find it in herself to mourn him. "And what of his daughter? She was innocent — she was a child."

He roared with fury. "She was the heir! That stupid slip of a girl was going to take everything that belonged to me and I was not going to allow it. This time the white dragon will not flee! This time, I am the falcon who will rise and soar!"

There was a great crash that sounded like metal. Catrin instantly thought of the communion vessels on the high altar, and knew where he was going. There were places to hide behind that altar, including a small chapel with many corners and cupboards.

Catrin hurried forward, stumbling over a footstool that stood too far out from its pew, and the great wooden communion table rose up in front of her. The precentor stood on the far side, one hand around Niada's throat and the other holding a knife. With his wild eyes streaming and red from the smoke, he looked like an ancient pagan priest about to perform a human sacrifice.

Without thinking, Catrin launched herself at him.

CHAPTER THIRTY-FOUR

Lord Pierrick grabbed Lucy's hand and pulled her into the cloister. "We need rope," he said. "A lot of rope."

"No, we need water," she said, but his urgency was such that she started opening doors and searching hidden corners for rope, even though she didn't know why. "If we don't douse the fire, they will die in there."

"Do you hear that?" Lord Pierrick said, and that was when she first noticed the shouts and cries from outside. "People are already trying to douse the fire. I need to get Catrin out of there."

"How?" Lucy asked, and then gave a cry of triumph when she found a coil of rope hanging from a disused bracket.

"*Parfait.*" Pierrick snatched it and led the way back. "Go back to the palace, *mon amour.* You are not safe here."

"Neither of us are safe here!" Lucy grabbed his sleeve as he pushed back out into the noise and chaos of the storm. "And I am going nowhere without you!"

"I must go into the cathedral if I am to find them," he said, and nodded toward the building. The flames on the spire were visible now, and liquid lead poured from the roof to the ground in great glowing pools. "And I cannot in good conscience take you in there."

"I am going," she said, and to prove it she took the rope and darted around the building. There was a crowd there, jostling, shouting, passing buckets of water along a long, long line of people and throwing it as high as they could reach. Some brave men had balanced ladders along the roof and were climbing up, buckets in hand.

Lucy wove between them all and tied the rope to the iron ring of the door to the south transept. Pierrick caught up with her then, and did not try again to dissuade her. "We must move quickly, before the spire comes down."

"Onward, then," Lucy said, and plunged into the smoke.

Catrin landed on top of the precentor and felt his knife enter her side, slick and strangely cool. Her attack knocked the wind out of him, and Catrin lifted herself away while he was busy catching his breath.

Blood immediately started seeping through her kirtle, but she did not have time to think about it. She kicked the knife out of his hand and turned to her mother, who was still caught in the man's grip. Her lips were turning blue, so Catrin drew her *stiletto* and stabbed Owain Kyffin's forearm several times, short quick blows that bled but did not break any bones. Finally he let out a cry and his fingers went slack, and Niada fell to the floor, gasping.

Catrin pressed the damp veil to her mother's mouth. "Breathe, breathe," she said. "Then we will —" The rest of the words were lost when her foot was pulled out from under her and she crashed to the floor.

"Heinous salt-bitch whore," Owain Kyffin said through gritted teeth. "I will end you here and now."

Catrin lifted her knife, ready to bury it in his chest, and he knocked it out of her hand with a sweep of his arm. It infuriated her, and she grabbed his bleeding arm with both hands, digging in with her fingernails until he howled.

Then he drove his free fist into her side with such force that blood spurted out and stars burst before her eyes. She screamed with the pain of it and fell backwards, and saw the precentor rise up before her. He had recovered his knife, and she could see in his eyes that he was determined to use it.

She was about to die.

She tried to rise up, tried to push herself away out of his reach, but the pain had sapped the strength from her limbs. She was completely helpless, and what's more the loss of the veil over her mouth meant she was drawing in more smoke than air. Her lungs were burning — her vision was blurring — she could do nothing to save them.

Niada rose from the floor and the smoke swirled around her head and shoulders like a hooded cloak. She held Catrin's *stiletto* in one hand, and even as Owain Kyffin turned to face this new threat she buried it deep in his chest. He fell without making a sound.

Niada knelt beside Catrin. "Come, my kitten," she said. "We must go."

"I — I can't." Catrin tried again to rise and pain radiated outward, weakening every limb. "Mother — I can't move."

Niada looked at Catrin's side and tears filled her reddened eyes. "Then we will stay here together."

"No — you can go. You can still get out."

"The smoke is too thick; I would get lost," Niada said, and bent to kiss her cheek. "And I will not leave you again."

"You must," Catrin said. "Please, Mother —"

"Tush — do you hear that?"

All Catrin could hear was the roar above their heads, but Niada rose and squinted into the smoke. A second later a smile broke over her face just as two figures emerged, their faces covered with wet cloth. "Lord Pierrick and Lady Lucy, I presume."

Catrin let out a cry. "Why are you here? Run — get out — it's not safe."

"Oh, tush," Lucy said, and tied a wet cloth over Catrin's mouth. "You knew we could not let you make this attempt alone."

"Of course not," Lord Pierrick said, and tied the rope to the nearest pew. "Now follow this out, both of you, while I carry Catrin."

Lucy grinned. "Yes, my lord."

Lucy stumbled out of the cathedral, her arm wrapped tight around Niada, with her beloved behind her carrying poor Catrin. The queue of people leading away from the cathedral was thicker now, with everyone in it passing full water-buckets forward and empty ones back in a regular relentless rhythm. More men carrying buckets soaked the walls nearest the flaming building, while others pulled down any thatch. Children rescued horses from stables and chickens from coops. Women emptied houses of precious goods, carrying them quickly away and returning to gather more.

Everyone worked with fiercely silent determination. The only sounds were the roaring flames, the hiss of the rain and the rolling thunder. There was no sign of Lord Heatherleigh or Lord Robert.

"The Greek fire," Catrin said. "They must be trying to get the barrels."

"They cannot move them alone," Lord Pierrick said. "I will go help; you three should return to the palace."

"We cannot go while the cathedral burns," Lucy said. "We have to stay and help."

"But if the flames reach the Greek fire, this whole place will be destroyed," Lord Pierrick said. "I cannot bear to lose you to such a death, my lady."

"Fear not; I know how to stop the Greek fire," Niada said. "Catrin, rest here in the shelter of the doorway for a moment. The rest of you, follow me."

Catrin sunk down at once, her hand pressed tight to her side. Lucy and Lord Pierrick followed Niada into the cloister, and they soon found Lord Robert and Lord Heatherleigh by the platform underneath the precentor's secret room. They were straining to turn over one of the barrels, probably with the intention of rolling it away.

Niada hurried over to them. "Do not try to move them. Break them open instead — all of them."

"I'm not sure that's a good idea," Lord Heatherleigh said.

"Trust me, it is. Lady Lucy, Lord Pierrick, Lord Robert — follow me."

They followed, and Lord Heatherleigh reluctantly started to do as she asked. Once they emerged from the staircase into the open walkway, they could hear the sound of his dagger over the splash and rush of the rain and wind. Lucy had a single glimpse of a slick, oily pool spreading around his feet before Niada led them to the precentor's room, where the smell of urine was all the stronger. She went over to one of the barrels and started to push. "Help me take them out to the balcony — quickly."

They obeyed, but it was very difficult. It took all three of them to move each barrel, and the urgency pounding in their hearts made it harder still. Lucy could not help but think of the fire — of Catrin, waiting outside all alone — of the storm that still raged above their heads — of that spire burning above them, ready at every minute to fall and kill them all.

All three barrels were finally on the balcony. Niada leaned down and looked at Lord Heatherleigh, who was standing at the edge of the oily slick, breathing hard. "Stand back, my lord; this will not be pleasant."

He moved back immediately, and Niada took Lord Pierrick's dagger from its sheath at his waist. She stabbed at all the barrels, hacking each one until the liquid inside poured out. A yellowish brown liquid that smelled all too familiar. Lord Pierrick made a face. "Are we really fighting Greek fire with … that?"

"We are." Niada watched with satisfaction as the stinking liquid splashed down over the floor, covering the slick. "Only three things can stop Greek fire: vinegar, sand … and urine."

CHAPTER THIRTY-FIVE

The fire burned for four hours, destroying the roof of the nave. Then the great spire collapsed with a roar, amidst a whirlwind that smelled like brimstone. The eagle that had spent centuries hovering four hundred feet above the city landed in the southern cross aisle, blackened nearly beyond recognition.

Lucy and Niada did not see the spire fall; by then, they were back at the palace binding up Catrin's wounds and treating their own. Lord Pierrick told them the next day, when they brought him a treatment for his damaged lungs. Then Lord Robert told them that the buildings around the cathedral had been saved, but for some water damage. And Lord Heatherleigh, from his bed where he lay with a cool cloth over his eyes, assured them that the Greek fire had never burned.

Three days later, Lucy reluctantly returned to her duties. She found the queen in the privy chamber, standing in the window staring out over the river. "Welcome, little Lucy," she said with a faint smile. "Are you well?"

"Yes, Your Majesty. And you?"

"I cannot decide." The queen turned back to the window. "They found Lord Ersfield's body in the Chapterhouse yesterday. He had been drowned in a water trough."

Lucy shuddered. "As Catrin predicted."

"Yes." The queen wrapped her arms around herself, holding on tight. "Was it terrible? The fire, I mean ... was it terrible?"

Once again Lucy smelled the smoke, heard the horrible crackle of the flames. "I'm afraid so, Your Majesty."

The queen reached out and took Lucy's hand, but did not respond right away. "All talk of magic and curses has stopped," she murmured. "People speak only of St Paul's now. Methinks the horror of it has unmanned us all."

"It is truly a great tragedy."

"Yes. And I feel I must see it," the queen said abruptly. "You and Lord Robert will accompany me."

"As you wish," Lucy murmured.

The queen hesitated for a moment, then lifted her chin and went out to the water-steps, where the royal barge was waiting. Yeomen of the Guard were already on board, as was the queen's litter and four strong men to carry it.

Lord Robert arrived just as they boarded, and the queen invited him to sit next to her with a strange sort of smile that showed more sorrow than pleasure. Lucy pondered the meaning of that smile as the barge cast off and moved with elegant grace upriver to the city, but then she saw faint trails of black smoke on the horizon and forgot all about it.

The queen caught her breath. "The horizon looks so empty without the spire," she whispered. "It's like a missing jewel in a necklace."

"It is a great loss," Lord Robert said. "I went to see it yesterday and the damage made me see just how much the whole building needs repair."

They drew up at Paul's Wharf, and the queen hastened into her litter. Lord Robert and Lucy took their places beside her as the guards got into position around them, and then they all marched at a stately pace up the hill.

People gathered to watch them pass. They all looked exhausted, but their chins were up and their eyes glittered with a sense of purpose that touched Lucy's heart. Signs of restoration were everywhere — roofs were under repair, smoke-damaged goods were being cleaned, water-soaked items were drying in the summer sun.

Then the blackened building loomed into view. They could see inside because the entrance on the south side was nothing but an open arch; the door itself had burned away. The nave was open to the skies, and no one was walking there anymore. Charred timber, chunks of plaster and piles of grey, flaky ash covered the floor. The Communion table had been taken away for repair, and any vessels that had not melted were also gone. Huge puddles of lead were still there, but only because they were still too hot to carry. Lucy had no doubt that the valuable material would soon disappear.

The queen stifled a sob with her hand. "Oh, how terrible. How terrible," she whispered. "What are we to do?"

For Lucy, it all fell into place then, as if Catrin and Niada were speaking in her ear. "Let the lions roar and the fires burn."

Lord Robert gave her a sharp glance. "An odd time to mention that."

"Not as odd as it may seem," Lucy said. "That prophecy was meant for you, Your Majesty. Niada told Catrin so. You are the green lady who must live."

"I thank you, but..." The queen wiped a tear from her cheek. "I am more concerned with the life of my people right now, little Lucy."

"One cannot survive without the other." Lucy turned to face her. "Do you know how they saved the rest of the cathedral? Lord Pierrick told me that a group of men scaled the roof and chopped away some of the wood, so that the fire could not bridge the gap."

"That is true; I saw them. They were remarkable men," Lord Robert murmured.

"Yes; remarkable men who knew what to do. The people here, like your advisors at the palace, know what to do. Your task, Your Majesty, is to balance their skills and enable them to succeed."

A light of understanding dawned in her eyes. "They are both the lions and the fire."

"Yes, exactly."

The queen sat up straight and tall. "Then we will start with our own gift of money — one thousand, in gold," she said, and seemed not to notice that she had slipped into using the royal 'we'. "And in addition, we will provide timber from our royal estates. Then we shall ask other churches to give what they can, and let the people themselves restore this building."

"That is an excellent plan, Your Majesty," Lord Robert said.

"Yes. The nave will return to its former glory ere the new year." She indicated that she wanted to return to the barge with a wave of her hand. "Come. Let us begin."

Catrin opened her eyes, vaguely aware of a certain tightness in her side. She was on a bed that had thick luxurious hangings, drawn back with silken tassels. There was a large window to her right, and light pouring in over a table filled with bottles and vials.

"Hello, my kitten."

Catrin turned her head and saw her mother, wearing a simple grey gown and a veil. The lines of pain and worry were gone from her face, and her frame was no longer painfully thin and frail. It made tears rise to Catrin's eyes. "Mother. You look well."

"So do you, my sweeting. Do you feel better?"

She considered. There was no pain in her chest or head, and the pinch in her stomach was merely hunger. "I believe so."

"That is good news, for you have a visitor who is most anxious to see you."

"I do?" Catrin immediately tried to smooth her hair. "Who is it?"

Her mother pointed, and to Catrin's astonishment Finn walked into the room, wearing a page boy's livery and carrying a long leather case in his hand. He was grinning from ear to ear. "My lady," he said, his bright blue eyes sparkling. "I am so glad to see that you are recovering."

"Thank you, Finn. I'm glad to see you here."

"Not nearly as glad as my mother," Finn said wryly. "I fear she will soon be guilty of the sin of pride."

Catrin chuckled, and even that slight movement made a sharp pain burrow into her side. "I'm sure your grandmother will keep her from it."

"She will do her best, I'm sure. But I am here for another purpose." He held out the case. "I was entrusted with this when I was given my place at court, my lady, and I am pleased to return it to you."

"Thank you." Catrin opened it up, and found inside her precious *stiletto*. "Oh — how lovely. I thought it was lost forever."

"Lord Robert found it, after the fire was out," Finn said. "It was … easy to retrieve it by then."

She chose not to ask for further details. "Thank you," Catrin said, and set the knife on the table by her bed. It made her feel safer, having it nearby.

Finn smiled and backed out of the room with cheerful goodbyes, and Lucy came in as he left. Her eyes lit up when she saw that Catrin was awake, and she ran to Catrin's side. "I would hug you if I was not worried that I would hurt you," she said with a laugh, and took Catrin's hand instead. "Oh, my dearling, we were so worried."

"So was I," Catrin said. "How long has it been since the fire?"

"Nearly two weeks."

"Was anyone else hurt?"

"We were all just exhausted for the most part, and had some difficulty breathing for a few days," Lucy said, and waved the thought away. "But we are all as well as can be now … and Lord Pierrick is much better."

Catrin eyed her pink cheeks. "You blush when you say his name. Have you gotten married without telling anyone?"

"Catrin! Of course not," Lucy said primly, and blushed all the more. "But we have set a date. We will be man and wife ere the queen goes on progress this summer."

"Lovely," Catrin said, and meant it with all her heart. "I wish all the best for you."

"And I for you," Lucy said, and giggled. "But beware: the best may include Lord Heatherleigh. There are rumours that he intends to ask for your hand."

"He will be disappointed," Catrin said dryly. "Prithee forget him. Tell me all that has happened since the storm instead."

Lucy lowered her voice. "They have discovered that Lord Hertford is the father of Lady Katherine Grey's baby."

"Isn't he on the continent?"

"He is now. He wasn't … at the time."

"It would have been quite the feat if he had been. Has the queen taken action?"

"No, not yet. She still waits and watches."

"Has the magician's assistant been found?"

Lucy lowered her gaze. "A boy's body was found in the quire. It seems he went in looking for the magician and was overwhelmed by the smoke."

"It would have been all too easy," Catrin murmured. "Is the queen still determined to marry Lord Robert?"

"There are hopeful signs that her ardour may be cooling," Lucy said. "But I doubt he will ever stop being her favourite."

"Nor should he; he is a strong, honest man." Catrin's heart ached. "I am sorry to see her hope die, even though I know it must. How it must hurt her, to set her love aside."

"Yes, but she will do it for her people," Lucy said. "As my mother says, we do the impossible for those we love."

Another week passed before Catrin felt well enough to go to the queen. Her mother helped her dress, then let Catrin lean on her arm during the walk down the gallery and into the royal lodgings. They found the queen in the privy chamber, listening to Lord Pierrick playing the lute.

"My talisman. No, do not kneel; I do not wish to cause you any discomfort," the queen said, and extended her hand instead. "Calm is restored in my court and my city, and I know it is in large part due to your efforts."

Catrin set her hand on her mother's shoulder. "And those of this lady, Your Majesty," she said. "It is she who stopped the Greek fire."

"So I have heard, and I am grateful. You averted a terrible evil." The queen tilted her head. "You are Niada?"

Catrin's mother sank into a curtsy as naturally as if she had never left court. "Yes, that is my chosen name, Your Majesty. I left the former one behind when I was saved from drowning."

"And what was the former one?"

Catrin answered, for her heart swelled within her and she could no longer hold it in. "Angharad Surovell. Your Majesty, this is my mother."

The queen fell back in her chair, astonished. "I was told you were dead."

"I wanted people to believe that, Your Majesty. My husband … Lord Roger … he was not kind." Niada ducked her head. "I could not return to being his wife."

"I understand," the queen said gently. "But it must have been a great sacrifice to leave the life you knew — and the daughter who loves you."

"It was, but I thought it best for her," Niada said. "Would she have been able to achieve as much as she has, with a poor scarred wise woman for a mother?"

"I fear you underestimate the value of wisdom … and mothers," the queen said, and looked away when sudden tears filled her eyes. "You served my mother as a lady-in-waiting, did you not?"

"I did." Niada clasped her hands together. "I was present when you were born, and a fairer babe I never saw."

"Then you will always be welcome in my court," the queen said. "And I hereby restore you to your status and title, as Dowager Countess of Ashbourne."

"You are very kind, Your Majesty," Niada said. "But I would rather be restored to my first title: Baroness Aberavon. Catrin's father was my true husband, and I wish to honour him."

"So granted," the queen said with a smile. "And will you lodge at court?"

"With Your Majesty's permission, I will take a place in the city," Niada said. "The people there have lost their wise woman, Zophia. I would like to help them."

"That is very generous of you," the queen said. "Will you offer them words of warning, as you have offered me?"

"I will, if the words are given to me to say."

"And will you explain those words?"

"As best I can."

"Begin with me, then. I have pondered the words you sent to me for many hours, and cannot fathom the last admonition: 'halt the death that crosses the waters'. What does it mean?"

Niada lifted her chin and closed her eyes, as if listening. "That is an admonition for the future, Your Majesty. Someday, a threat will loom from foreign shores, and you must stop it before it causes death among your people."

The queen stared at her through wide dark eyes. "A formidable task."

Niada smiled. "Fear not, Your Majesty."

"Aye, fear not. You are the falcon that will rise and soar." Catrin sunk into a curtsy and pressed her hand to her heart. "And you will always have help."

A NOTE TO THE READER

In 1550, a London merchant started doing something that very few people did at the time. He wrote down what was happening around him, including his own life events, the great happenings of the age, and some oddly random tidbits and tales. He kept doing this until his death in 1563, and the result was a wealth of information about the mid-Tudor period which has been published as *The Diary of Henry Machyn*.

Some of the entries are delightfully mysterious, for they offer facts without explanation or context. These entries inspired some of the events of this book, such as the simple statement: 'was unladen a[t the water] ... serten vessselles with (blank) and carried to the Tower'. Other entries provide poignant details about conflicts and tragedies, including the devastating fire at St Paul's Cathedral that took place in June 1561.

I hope you enjoyed reading this novel, and thank you for choosing it. If you enjoyed it, please tell all your friends, and post a review on **Amazon** and **Goodreads**. Reviews are really important for authors, so it would be much appreciated.

Readers can connect with me **on Facebook (Angela Ranson Author)** and through **my website (Angela Ranson)**, which includes not only updates on the Catrin Surovell series but humorous thoughts on writing, reading and Tudor history.

Angela Ranson

Sapere Books is an exciting new publisher of brilliant fiction and popular history.

To find out more about our latest releases and our monthly bargain books visit our website:
saperebooks.com

Printed in Great Britain
by Amazon

42520450R00175